"He has commanded us to wed this day!

"He demands that I marry a—"

"A what?"

"A Highland savage," she retorted, shaking a finger under his nose. "*Mais oui,* I can tell by your speech that is what you are, despite that fine mail you wear! And ignorant, as well, by your own admission!"

"Unlettered, Lady. 'Tis not the same as ignorant. And devil take ye with all yer plaguey French airs! Ye're still a Scot yourself!"

"Praise God, only *half!*" she shouted.

"Then I wish to God 'twas the upper half with the mouth!"

She gaped. "Why would my late husband do this to me?" she demanded.

"Well, how d'ye think I feel?" Alan countered. "Trapped, is what! Bound by a stout chain of friendship reaching inta the very grave. I'd as lief fall on my dirk as surrender my freedom, but my word's my word, by God!"

Dear Reader,

If you've never read a Harlequin Historical novel, you're in for a treat. We offer compelling, richly developed stories that let you escape to the past—written by some of the best writers in the field!

Author Lyn Stone is one of those writers. Since her debut in March 1997 with *The Wicked Truth,* Lyn has sold five more romances. Her warm and entertaining writing style has captured the attention of many critics, including *Publishers Weekly,* which has reviewed all of her previous Harlequin Historical® novels, and claims that she "creates characters with a refreshing naturalness." This month's *The Knight's Bride* is about a very *true* knight who puts his honorable reputation on the line when he's forced to marry the beautiful widow of his best friend. It's great!

Be sure to look for *Burke's Rules* by the talented Pat Tracy. This is an adorable story about a Denver schoolmistress who falls for the "protective" banker who helps fund her school. *Pride of Lions* is the latest in Suzanne Barclay's highly acclaimed SUTHERLAND SERIES. Two lovers are on opposite sides of a feud in this tale of danger and passion set in medieval Scotland.

Rounding out the month is *The Heart of a Hero* by Judith Stacy. Here, a bad boy turned rancher has thirty days to prove he'll be a good father to his niece and nephew, and enlists the help of the new schoolmarm. Don't miss it!

Whatever your tastes in reading, you'll be sure to find a romantic journey back to the past between the covers of a Harlequin Historical® novel.

Sincerely,
Tracy Farrell, Senior Editor

Please address questions and book requests to:
Harlequin Reader Service
U.S.: 3010 Walden Ave., P.O. Box 1325, Buffalo, NY 14269
Canadian: P.O. Box 609, Fort Erie, Ont. L2A 5X3

THE KNIGHT'S BRIDE

LYN STONE

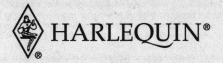

TORONTO • NEW YORK • LONDON
AMSTERDAM • PARIS • SYDNEY • HAMBURG
STOCKHOLM • ATHENS • TOKYO • MILAN • MADRID
PRAGUE • WARSAW • BUDAPEST • AUCKLAND

ISBN 0-373-29045-4

THE KNIGHT'S BRIDE

Books by Lyn Stone

Harlequin Historicals

The Wicked Truth #358
The Arrangement #389
The Wilder Wedding #413
The Knight's Bride #445

LYN STONE

A painter of historical events, Lyn decided to write about them. A canvas, however detailed, limits characters to only one moment in time. "If a picture's worth a thousand words, the other ninety thousand have to show up somewhere!"

An avid reader, she admits, "At thirteen, I fell in love with Brontë's Heathcliff and became Catherine. Next year I fell for Rhett and became Scarlett. Then I fell for the hero I'd known most of my life and finally became myself."

After living four years in Europe, Lyn and her husband, Allen, settled into a log house in north Alabama that is crammed to the rafters with antiques, artifacts and the stuff of future tales.

This book is for my Allen the True.
Thank you for all the promises kept
and for the happily ever after we share.

Prologue

Near Stirling, Scotland
June, 1314

Alan of Strode grimaced at the sickly sweet smell of impending death. Putrefaction. The fever raged now. Tavish would be damned lucky to see the morrow dawn. Alan's own wound, superficial by comparison, ached with empathy.

"Four days," Alan said, forcing the smile into his voice, "Five at most, and your lady can tend ye. We'll make it, Tav."

Carefully ignoring the groans Tavish struggled to suppress, Alan busied himself raking through one of the many English packs he had captured as spoils. He unfolded a crimson silk surcoat embellished with a yellow griffin. Rich stuff, he thought, rubbing the fabric between his fingers.

Another foray yielded an ornate silver cup, which he filled from his own humble flask of good Scots spirits. "See how much more of this ye can hold, Tav. Ye'll still hurt, but ye won't care."

Tavish pushed it away. "Only numbs me from the chin up. Have you a quill in there?" he asked, his voice choked with pain.

Alan poked deeper into the hidebound pouch. "Aye," he answered as cheerfully as he could manage, "parch and ink as well. Ye've a mind to write, then?"

Tavish nodded slightly and exhaled the words, "To Honor. Help me sit."

A half hour later, Tavish Ellerby made a final, stronger scribble and let the feather fall from his hand. "Done." His weary eyes rested a moment under their grime-crusted lids before he met Alan's steady gaze. "See if you...agree."

"To this?" Alan asked, biting his bottom lip. He touched the page of slanting marks that meant nothing to him.

"Orders for my lady," Tavish explained through gritted teeth. His white-knuckled hands clutched the moth-chewed blanket as his breathing grew labored and irregular. "Good plan, eh?"

Alan followed the wavering lines of lampblack ink and came to rest on the larger, ornate loops at the bottom. "Well writ, Tav." He tapped the parchment with the back of his fingers and smiled. "'Tis braw advice. She'll be minding ye, too, if I've aught to say to it." His friend's peace of mind justified Alan's small pretense. And the Lady Honor would take comfort in her husband's last thoughts and wishes, no matter what they were.

Though he could see Saint Ninian's roof from here, Alan knew that moving Tavish would only hasten death. He hated to tell Lady Honor that her husband breathed his last neath a gnarled old oak at the edge of the battlefield. But no lie would make it finer. Dead was dead. And if ever a soul made heaven without benefit of a final blessing, it would be that of Tavish Ellerby.

Everything south of Stirling lay in ashes. He prayed Tavish's keep, nestled in the Cheviot Hills, lay out of both armies' paths. What the English had not laid waste to in the last few weeks, Robert Bruce had, in order to keep his enemies shelterless and hungry. Now many Scots would suffer the same, even though they had won the battle.

Tavish reached out, fingers weak and trembling as they grasped Alan's forearm. "You will take me on home? Lay me under a cairn by the Tweed? Do not…let Honor see me first. Not like this. Promise?"

"Aye, I will. Got yer leg, by God, and I'll take that, too."

Weak laughter trickled out like the dregs from a wineskin. "Put me back together, will you?" The eyes closed again and Tavish shuddered. "Alan, tell her. Tell my Honor…that 'tis for the best, my dying. Say how much I…cared."

"She'll be knowing that, Tav. I'll sing it like a bard, I swear. Sweet things she'll be weeping over long after she's grown old and…Tav? *Tavish?*"

Alan drew in a deep, ragged breath and expelled it. Stinging wetness seeped down his cheeks. "Ah, Tav, lad. Would that yer Honor coulda seen ye smile just so."

He looked long into the blank, blue eyes before he closed the lids at last.

Chapter One

"I saw murder in his eye, my lady. Lord Hume will never let the marriage stand if he finds you. God alone can help you if the comte de Trouville becomes involved."

Lady Honor Ellerby fought her rush of alarm at the messenger's words. She must remain calm, think what next to do.

Could her father possibly find her here in this little-known border keep? Would he remember her friendliness toward Tavish Ellerby when they had met at the French court? If so, he would guess where she had flown. Since nearly a year had passed, Honor had begun to hope he would have given up the search. She should have known better, since she was his only heir.

He could force her to return home with him unless Tavish could hold out against Hume's forces. Her marriage was very probably invalid. After all, she had stolen and altered the documents her father had prepared, which named the comte de Trouville as her intended bridegroom.

The very thought of that man caused her to shiver, even now.

Trouville had come to her father's house in Paris, not three days after the death of his second wife, and demanded Honor's hand. After spending nigh to a week locked away with no food and little water, Honor had reluctantly signed the contracts her father provided. In her mind, that certainly constituted force and was not legal. But since when must relatives of the king adhere to law? If the comte had gotten away with murder, what penalty need he fear for a mere marriage by force? Since wit was her only weapon of defense, Honor had devised a way out of the match.

Tavish would never have married her unless he believed her father approved, so she had brought her father's copies of the signed contracts with her, minus, of course, the comte de Trouville's name. A careful scraping of the parchment had eliminated that, as well as the listed property her father was to receive from the comte in the exchange for her. Honor had inserted some nonsense about her own happiness being sufficient to satisfy her sire. Then she had sold her jewels to provide the mentioned dowry.

Neatly done, if she did say so, but a dangerous ruse for all that. Consequences could be deadly if her father and the powerful comte regained control of her life.

She should have confessed her misdeed to Tavish once he had come to care for her, but she had needed to wait until she was absolutely certain he would fight to keep her. Then he had left so suddenly to join Bruce's forces near Stirling. Hopefully, there would be time to make amends for her deception and soothe Tavish's anger on his return. She must do so before her father arrived. And he would likely be here, sooner or later, if Melior had the right of things.

"His lordship is truly furious, Lady Honor. They do say at first he thought you had been stolen. Your lady mother tried to foster that belief, and for a while, succeeded. Then he finally discovered the betrothal and marriage contracts were missing, and that your jewels and clothing were gone."

Melior continued, "Not long after I returned from showing you the way here, he began to question the prolonged absence of Father Dennis. When he decided that you had run away, his rage knew no bounds."

The musician continued, "Even had I not promised to come and warn you did he guess what happened, I could not have remained there a moment longer. He strikes out at everything and everyone in his path, even after all this time!" Melior declared with a shudder.

"When has he not?" Honor asked wryly, though she could recall such a time when she was very young. Her father had once been a fair, if not doting, parent. Some unaccountable and violent madness had overtaken him once she reached an age to wed.

Seven long years she had matched her will to his in selling her off. She meant to have a kind and loving husband, and he had chosen only irksome court toadies. A good dozen suitors Honor had sent running, employing every device possible from outrageous insults to feigning madness. But the comte de Trouville would not be put off by her. And her father had starved her into submission that time. Temporarily.

"How long before Father finds me, by your reckoning?" she asked Melior.

"He has already surmised whom you wed, but he dares not abandon his place at court until he has completed his business there. Once that is accomplished, who can say how long his search will take? Not long, I should think. You know his resources as well as I.''

"You do not believe he has informed the comte de Trouville?''

''Not as yet, unless he did so after I left. He has stalled your betrothed with some tale of a prolonged illness you had contracted. Said he had sent you to the countryside to recover. Afterward, he vowed to your mother he would have you in hand for the wedding come autumn, and that is nearly upon us, my lady.''

Honor sighed and shrugged. "Not many know the location of Byelough Keep. Please God, Father cannot find one who does know it until my husband returns from the war.''

''At least that should happen soon enough,'' Melior assured her, imparting the first good news she had heard in many a day. "I did hear upon landing on this coast that there has been some great victory for the Scots at a place called Bannockburn close by Stirling. The English fled like frightened rabbits. Most of the Scots are following into England, giving chase. Some are not, however. I met many on the road, bound for their homes.''

''Thank God for it. No doubt my lord will rush back with all speed since he seemed so loath to be away.'' Honor felt she had seen to that with her parting kisses. Tavish swore he would leave her not an hour longer than he must.

''I only hope your husband is warrior enough to withstand the wrath when Lord Hume does come,'' Melior added with a grimace.

''As do I!'' Honor quaked with apprehension at the very thought of the gentle Tavish facing either her tyrannical sire or the vicious brute who had been her betrothed.

Unfortunately, she had not had the time to search out a

man who was strong as well as kind. At the moment, *kind* had seemed infinitely more important. "Go and make yourself comfortable, Melior. Will you stay here?"

"Would you mind, my lady? My journey was no dance around the Maypole. I spent many a year singing keep to keep here before crossing to France, however, and I like Scotland. Have you need of a troubadour?"

She smiled and reached for his slender hand. "I have need of a friend, which you have certainly proved yourself to be. I owe you much and this will be your home for as long as you like, Melior. You are well come. We have sorely missed your music."

Relief flooded his foxlike features as he bowed over her fingers. His thin lips brushed her knuckles in a manner that seemed a bit too familiar, but she knew it was only gratitude mixed with a bit of flattery. The well-traveled minstrel possessed a sly nature and kept an eye out for the main chance, but he knew his place well enough. Entertainers who reached above themselves, especially with a lady, did not survive two score years as this one had done.

Honor understood Melior's needs well enough to keep him faithful to her cause. So long as she paid him generously, both in coin and praise for his music, he would serve her without fail. If only she could judge every man as neatly as she did this one, she would not need to fear.

Her husband presented no challenge at all, though he believed himself cannier than most. Tavish desired her body and the wealth she had brought him. Honor thought those a fair trade for his name and protection.

He swore he loved her, and she was inclined to believe that he did. She tried as best she could to return the feeling. Once she had even said the words to him and made them sound real. Though Tavish had been overjoyed by it, Honor felt a bit guilty. She had never employed a pretense of affection with any man. It seemed unfair now that she must pretend. She wanted to love him.

Tavish's devotion, real or otherwise, certainly sweetened the fact that she had followed him here from France and placed herself at his mercy apurpose.

She had chosen Tavish Ellerby because he showed himself to be the exact opposite of her father and, not least, for the fact that he owned a secluded keep in the wild borderland of Scotland. To Honor's relief, she had come to care for her husband in the two short months they had shared. She looked forward to his return from the war so that they might know each other better. Though quite new to this marriage business, Honor felt she could become an excellent wife, given time. Her words of love to him would be true soon enough, for Tavish was a lovable sort.

For the first time ever, a man with the power to alter her life, willingly gave her some say in her future. He considered her as a real person with desires of her own. However, Tavish's placid nature might not serve her so well once her father found them.

Would her husband give her up without a fight once he realized she had deceived him about her father's consent? Would he even have the choice? Of a sudden, Honor experienced another sharp stab of the guilt she tried to hold at bay. Had she stated her reasons truthfully at the outset, would Tavish have wed her anyway? Somehow, she did not believe so.

"Ah, well, hindsight serves nothing," she muttered to herself. Under no circumstances would she surrender to her father's keeping. To escape him and his onerous plans for her, she had lied, stolen and wed under false pretense. She felt no satisfaction at all in that. Only relief, and even that now proved temporary, considering Melior's news. However, wrongly as she had behaved, Honor admitted that whatever else it took to maintain her sanctuary here, she would do without hesitation.

More than her own life lay at risk now.

Alan had brought Tavish home. The huge stone settled into place as though it had formed there. Alan released the ropes lashed to it from his captured warhorse and tethered the fractious beast to a nearby tree.

Blood trickled down from beneath his crudely wrapped right shoulder. *Damn!* The wound had broken open yet again. He cursed the mess even though he realized the fresh bleeding might likely save him from Tavish's fate. Hopefully any poison would leak out with the blood and sweat. He swiped his arm clean with the tail of his plaid and hoped he had not lost his needle.

After a longing glance toward the cool, rushing water of the nearby burn, he sat down beside the smooth, rounded rock and began to chisel on it. Plying a fist-size rock and a sharp jag on his old, broken broadsword, Alan pounded out the design.

Poor Tav, he thought as he worked, had everything in life a man could ask. Snug home, bonny wife, a bit of coin put by. Alan supposed he would never know suchlike himself. Considering that, mayhaps Tavish had been the luckier one after all. For two months, at least, Tav had lived every man's dream. "Leastways, *most* men dream of it. Not me, o' course," Alan muttered, chipping away at the stone. "Aye, ye had it all, old son," he grunted. "And 'tis sorry, I am, ye lost it too soon."

When Alan finished, the outline of a shield listed slightly to one side and the wolf's head he had intended resembled a bitten apple with two leaves. Well, the Lady Honor could replace this if she wished. For now it would serve to mark the place. Frowning at his clumsy effort, he piled up a pyramid of small stones in front to form the cairn. Then he rose, straightened his muddy breacan and shook the kinks out of his legs.

Drawing himself up to his full height, Alan held the hilt of the broken sword high above the marker he had made to cast the shadow of the cross over it. "God keep ye, Tavish Mac Ellerby."

He thought to say more of a farewell, but the sudden thunder of hooves shook the ground beneath his bare feet. Facing the approaching riders, Alan drew Tavish's undamaged sword from its sling on the horse and assumed a battle stance. Just then, the wind unfurled the colors held by the advance man.

Lion D'or on a red field. The Bruce.

The party of horsemen surrounded him in a flurry of jingling harnesses and stamping hooves. Alan dropped to one knee and grinned up at the rider on the prancing gray.

"We might have been Edward's men, Strode. Did it never occur to you to run and hide?" Bruce asked.

Alan threw back his head and laughed. "If there's an Englisher this side o' London, I'll kiss yer beastie's arse and call him sweeting!"

Bruce dismounted and stretched out his arm for a clasp of greeting. He winced when he noticed Alan's wound. "We're collecting Douglas's men just south of here, and then on to York. My brother told me he gave you leave after our victory, and now I ken why!" Bruce wrinkled his nose at the sluggish red trail still working its way down Alan's bare arm. "See to that hurt or we'll be burying you. You're like to lose that arm."

Alan nodded once and looked away, over the hills that separated him from Rowicsburg castle. "It will heal. Mayhaps I'll join ye later."

"You would see your father first, then?" Bruce asked, more than a hint of warning in his voice.

"I'll never go to Rowicsburg," Alan answered with a lift of his chin. "Neither will I go north. I have done with Uncle Angus as well. Neil Broglan is his tanist now, and a good laird he'll be. I've no business wi' either side of my family." He cocked his head toward the new grave. "I am here because Tavish Ellerby sent me with orders for his widow. And the news of his death."

He had nowhere to go after this mission for Tavish. His English father had packed him off to the Highlands, to his mother's people when he was but a lad. The uncle who raised him there had chosen another nephew, a full Scot, as the next MacGill chieftain. That was as it should be, Alan supposed.

Life as a soldier suited him well enough. However, stubbornness and one strong arm were all he had to offer any cause at the moment. This king of his clearly had no use for either.

"Aye well, I believe you then. 'Tis well known, your love of the truth." Bruce glanced over at his men. "Some do say you take it to extremes." Several of Bruce's retinue nodded sagely and exchanged wry looks.

Alan knew why. He never said what he thought a man—or a woman, for that matter—wanted to hear, unless it was true. Not even when a falsehood would serve him better than a fact. 'Twas a thing all the Bruces depended upon. As had his uncle. Alan took tremendous pride in the one inarguable attribute he possessed and held so dear. He was an honest man.

Only Alan knew the reason behind his one constant and unwavering virtue, and why holding to it had become a near obsession over the years. His father had lied, saying that he would bring Alan home soon. His mother had lied, promising to write to him regularly and come for him when the border troubles eased. His uncle had lied, vowing to the mother that her son would be groomed as the next laird. None of it came to pass. Disgusted with the lot, Alan vowed to himself that he would never visit a lie on anyone, regardless of the price. So, he was known as *Alan the True*. His reputation had followed like a faithful hound when he left the Highlands. Sometimes it bit him, but for the most part, served him well. As it did now.

The Bruce glanced at the crudely carved device on the stone marker and back to Alan. "Give Ellerby's lady my condolence. I heard that he fought well. He made plans for the lady and his property, did he?"

"Writ and sealed, sire. Betwixt him and her, I'm thinking."

"I'd see it, Alan."

"I think not. 'Tis private word from the deathbed to his beloved."

Bruce turned away and paced for a moment, then came face-to-face with Alan, looking up, since he was a head shorter. "Give me the letter, Strode. I command it."

Alan tensed, his left hand closing over his sword hilt.

"Give me the goddamned letter, man, or we'll take it from you!" Bruce thundered.

"Och, but ye've less than a score o' lads wi' ye, sire!" Alan remarked.

Bruce tightened his lips. His eyes bugged out for a full second before his crack of laughter shattered the tense silence.

Alan waited, wearing a beatific smile. He knew well the image he presented, even enhanced it whenever he could. The irreverent, overgrown jester. Opponents usually underestimated him because of his demeanor, but not Robert Bruce. The king knew well what lay under the cloak of humour. And would brook no insubordinance concealed by it. Much as he hated to do it, Alan prepared for surrender.

Bruce sobered after a bit and raised an arm, draping it casually around Alan's shoulders. "Now listen to me, Strode, and listen well. Byelough Keep is important because of its protected location. The hidden caves near it could hide an army. Or a wealth of supplies to keep one victualed. I'll not have it fall into unsympathetic hands by some whim of a dead man.

"Now then," Bruce continued, "we could kill you and take the letter. I suspect we would have to. Even should you overpower my *wee* troop here and escape, I would simply follow you to Byelough and demand it of the widow. You choose."

Alan considered. Tavish's lady would be upset enough as it was. Devastated, most likely. A visit from Bruce would hardly provide any consolation, especially given the king's current mood.

"Verra well, have it then." Alan reached beneath his wide leather belt and drew out the folded packet, slapping it into Bruce's outstretched hand. "But I mislike this."

Bruce frowned as his long fingers broke the amber glob of crude candle wax sealing the letter. "And I *mislike* you at times, Strode. I ought to kill you for insolence, you know. Might do so yet."

Silence reigned as Bruce read the words Tavish had written at the hour of his death. A calculating smile stretched his noble face as he finished and refolded the parchment. Then the smile swiftly died. "Kneel!" he ordered in a sharp voice.

Alan knelt, bracing himself as the Bruce raised his steel to the level of Alan's neck. It hovered just above his left shoulder. He did not want to believe Bruce meant to kill him, but neither could he disregard the fact that he was on his knees with the man's blade at his throat. A protest seemed cowardly under the circumstances, as well as futile, if the Bruce meant business.

"Could I have a priest?" Alan asked conversationally, holding Bruce's gaze.

"You'd shock one out of his frock, and I am in trouble enough with the church as it is," Bruce declared.

"Ah, well, then. Proceed wi' what ye were about to do." He hoped Robert only meant to make a point, frighten him a bit. God knew the rascal had a wicked twist to his mind. Then Alan recalled the blow Rob had dealt the English deBohun just before the battle when they rode out one to one. The man's head had bounced along the ground like a sheep's bladder ball while the rest of him rode a ways on down the field. Laugh, the man might, but Bruce never wasted time with idle threats.

Alan closed his eyes and gritted his teeth, trying to recall the prayer of contrition, the first bead of the rosary, his mother's face. Nothing came to mind.

Death held no appeal for him in the best of circumstances, but he had always faced it without fear. Determined to brazen it out to the very end, he looked up at the king and smiled. "I expect ye'll be sorry for this."

"No doubt." Bruce chuckled. Hardly a royal sound, but then he was new to the post, Alan thought.

The sharp edge of steel pressed threateningly against Alan's jugular for a long, nerve-racking moment. Then Bruce's voice rang out, "I dub thee Sir Alan of Strode." The flat of the blade bounced on his left shoulder and gently touched the damaged right. "Serve God, king, protect the weak and strive for right." He turned the sword, holding the jeweled hilt for Alan to kiss.

Alan tasted the metal-and-emerald surface against his lips, cool and faintly salty with sweat. He welcomed it like a lover's lips, smacking of honeyed mead. Kiss of life, he mused, barely restraining a shudder of relief. He even prolonged the gesture, bidding for time, since his legs felt too weak to support him just now.

It was not that he had feared dying, he told himself, for had faced death often enough in battle. But dying like this, on his knees, and for no good reason, would have troubled him a bit.

"Ready for the buffet?" Bruce asked, clenching and unclenching his gloved right hand, grinning with new merriment. Alan could just imagine the strength waiting behind that blow. The cuff supposed to help him remember his new charge of knighthood might well render him unable to recall his own name.

"Aye, ready." He rolled his eyes and puffed out his cheeks. The king's fist connected with a solid thunk that knocked Alan backward to the ground in an ungainly sprawl.

"Rise, Sir, and do glory to Scotland!" Bruce let out a bark of laughter. "And right that plaidie, mon. Yer own glory's naked to th' breeze!"

Alan scrambled to his feet and made a sketchy bow. *He was a Sir!* He wished to high heaven Tav could have witnessed this farce. He glanced at the cairn under which he'd laid his friend, and then up at the clouds. A unexpected breeze fluttered through the leaves of a rowan tree. Mayhaps he had.

"Do I do homage or some such?" he asked Bruce, uncertain of the protocol. The whole event bore no structure at all and damned little ceremony. He had witnessed a knighting only once. There was a good deal more to it than this if he remembered rightly.

"I took your oath last year, if you recall. Knowing your penchant for truth, I don't doubt me that will last your lifetime. Plus, you've killed at least a score of English in the past fortnight. We'll let that do.''

Bruce picked a wad of grass off Alan's muddy elbow. "Clean yourself up a bit before you call on the lady, eh? You look as if you've been dragged through a bloody bog. Have you soap? And proper clothing?''

Alan drew himself up, ignoring the noisy mirth of Bruce's men. "Aye, I do. Ye needn't worry I'll disgrace ye, sire. 'Tis just that war dulls a mon's polish.'' He followed the king's gaze as it traveled downward to Alan's bare legs and feet.

"It does that.'' Bruce slapped him on his good shoulder and turned to mount up. "Oh, by the way, tell Lady Ellerby that I second her husband's behest. Nay, wait. Say that I *command* she follow his directions to the letter. Immediately, as he instructs.''

With a hoot of laughter, the king kicked his horse and galloped away.

Alan shrugged and grinned. King Rob was a daftie. Always had been.

Chapter Two

Byelough Keep blended well into the landscape, nearly invisible. Had Tavish not given such clear directions, Alan knew he might never have found it. The cottages bore the same gray-green color as the surrounding hills of mottled stone and bracken. 'Twas just as Tavish had described a hundred times in the hours he had spent longing for the place. If not for the wisps of smoke from the evening home fires, Alan might have missed seeing it altogether.

He urged the English warhorse onward toward the gates of Byelough, towing his own highland pony and the two wain drays loaded down with booty from the battle.

"Who goes?" came a steely voice from the lichen-covered watchtower. That tower looked nothing more than a massive tree from a distance, rising from a wall that appeared a naturally formed cliff. Ingenious. And difficult to breach, he reckoned, despite the lack of drawbridge and moat.

"Sir Alan of Strode," he announced gravely. "I bear word from Lord Tavish Ellerby for his lady wife. Open and bid me enter." Alan marked the two archers poised on the battlements.

A long silence ensued before the heavy gates swung

open. Alan rode through. He noted immediately the cleanness of the small bailey. There were well-kept outbuildings and neatly clipped grass, what little there was of it. Even the bare ground looked raked and free of clutter and mud holes.

The few people he could see appeared scrubbed to a shine and well fed. A silent stable lad took the reins as Alan dismounted, and a young, dark-haired priest met him at the steps leading into the keep itself.

"Welcome, my son. I am Father Dennis," the priest intoned in a voice that sounded three times as old as its owner. Alan suppressed his laughter. *Son*, indeed. He likely had a good five years on the holy lad. The lanky priest smiled serenely as though he divined Alan's thoughts. "Our lady awaits within."

Alan nodded and followed the cleric inside, uncertain whether he should have kissed the laddie's ring. Priests were as uncommon as clean linen where he had spent his last nineteen years. They trod the fresh, fragrant rushes toward a door at the back of the hall.

Several servants arranging trestle tables paused to study him. He threw them a smile of approval for the looks of the place. Colorful tapestries softened the stone walls and the few tables already set up bore pristine cloths without any obvious holes or spots. A brightly painted depiction of the Ellerby device crowned a large fire hole built into the wall near the head table. And where, he wondered, were the hall's dogs? Banished or being laundered? He chuckled inwardly at the image of hounds spitting maws full of soapwort. Dead easy, this ranked as the cleanest place he had ever been. No wonder Tav had loved it.

Alan silently thanked the Bruce for suggesting the bath and change of clothes. Of course, given a moment or so, he surely would have thought of it himself. After scouring himself raw with the grainy soap and drying in the sun, he had prepared his knightly regalia with care. He had ripped the yellow gryphon device off the red silk surcoat and donned the garment over the confiscated English mail hauberk and chausses.

Chain mail had necessitated the wearing of a padded gambeson and a heavy loincloth, as well. Both of which he despised. Even his hair felt too confined, its dark auburn hank bound at the back of his neck by a remnant of the torn yellow silk. Altogether discomforting, was this grand chivalric posturing. But necessary.

As soon as he established the fact that he was a knight to these people of Byelough Keep, he would change back into his breacan and be damned to them all if they thought him common.

Being a baron's son had never counted for much in his life, but he did feel pride in his newly earned title of *Sir.* The least he could do was make a good first impression.

"This way," the priest said, beckoning Alan toward the sturdy oak portal at the back of the hall. "Milady's solar," he explained.

"Sir Alan of Strode, the lady Honor," Father Dennis announced in his low-pitched voice. "He comes from your lord husband, milady."

Alan's stomach clenched with apprehension as the lady raised her gaze from her needlework. Eyes the color of a dove's breast regarded him with bright curiosity. Her dark brows rose like graceful wings. The small, straight nose quivered slightly as her rose petal mouth stretched into a blinding, white smile. He stood entranced, just as he had expected to. Tavish was ever an apt one for description, and Lady Honor proved no exaggeration. Alan thought her the most beautiful woman he had ever seen. Perfect.

"You are well come, good sir. Pray, how fares my hus-

band?'' She rose from behind the large embroidery frame
and came to meet him, holding out her hands.

Her heavy, voluminous overgown hid her form. It
caused her to appear a wee bit stout despite the daintiness
of her face, neck and hands. Nonetheless, her movements
proved graceful as a doe's. Alan released a sigh of pure
pleasure in the mere seeing of her.

''My lord husband has been detained?'' she asked, her
soft speech as welcoming as her smile. He supposed the
speaking of French most of her life had mellowed it so,
though she spoke the more gutteral English with hardly
any accent. He recalled her father was a Scot, a baron and
a highly educated man. Living at the French court a goodly
part of her life would have exposed her to many languages.
Tavish had boasted of her accomplishments. A woman of
vast charm and keen wits, he had said.

Alan cradled her soft palms, raising her fingers to his
lips. He closed his eyes and drew in a deep breath, reluctant to release her. She smelled as heaven must, of rose
water and absolute cleanliness. The woman radiated gentleness and contentment; a contentment he must now destroy. God's own truth, how he hated this task.

Placing her palms together, he encased them in his own
and shook his head sadly. ''Because I stood his friend and
comrade-at-arms, Tavish bade me bring ye all his love,
Lady Honor. His last thoughts were of ye.''

''No!'' she cried, snatching her hands from his. A fiery
epithet scorched the air between them. A French word, if
memory served him, and one that ought not be uttered in
the presence of a priest. Surely he had misheard, but that
and others like it were the only French he knew.

He watched her, in awe of the change. She paced fran-
tically, kicking her heavy skirts forward. Her palms
slammed against the needlework frame, scattering skeins

of silk thread the length of the room. Then she marched smartly back to where he stood and cracked her palm against his newly shaved cheek.

Alan stood fast, hurting for her as he saw her fury dissolve into grief.

The young priest hovered uncertainly as Alan took the lady in his arms, cradling her lightly against him, muttering softly in Gaelic. He held her loosely as she repeatedly pounded one small fist against his silk-covered mail. By the rood, how he had dreaded doing this, and 'twas worse even than he had expected.

He shot the priest a look of helplessness over the top of her head. "Father Dennis, a posset to soothe?" he suggested, hoping to stir the befuddled young fool into action. Some priest, this one. Unmoving as a standing stone and about as much use. "Th' lass is overset! Bestir yerself!"

"No! No posset!" she said, shoving away. "I'll hear this now. All of it." Savagely, she wiped her face with the edge of her linen undersleeve and sniffed loudly. Within seconds, she had composed herself and raised her brave wee chin. Large, luminous eyes brimmed with more tears, which she refused to let fall. Her braw courage near cracked his heart in twain.

"Come you," she ordered briskly. She grasped Alan's wrist with both hands, guided him to the padded window seat and pushed him onto it. She remained standing so they were near eye to eye. "Now you will tell me. Father Dennis, would you see to—" She paused to draw a deep breath. "See to my lord's remains?"

Alan shook his head, looking from her to the priest. "I did that already. He bides little more than a league away, 'twixt the Tweed and a wee burn. That's what he wished."

The winged brows drew together in a scowl. "Not home to Byelough? Why?"

"He didna want ye seeing him as he was. I promised."

She gulped, touching her chin to her chest. "How…how was he, then?"

"Met death as he met life, head up and leanin' forward. 'Tis all ye need know."

"Devil curse you, sir! I would know it all. Everything. I must!" she demanded, biting her lips and wringing her hands together. A visible shudder ran through her, but then she braced up like a soldier.

Alan drew her to the wide seat and pulled her down beside him. Looking directly into her tear-brimmed eyes, he gave exactly what she asked for. "Toward the end of the fight, an English blade took Tav's leg 'twixt knee and hip. I tied it off and put fire to seal it soon as I could strike one up. Then I found an English baggage wain to cart him home. He died four days ago. I gave him what solace I could, my lady. Ye gave him more, I'm thinking, if 'tis any comfort at all. He loved ye well and worried for ye."

She absorbed the words in silence, her fingernails biting his palms, her eyes searching his. Suddenly she nodded, released his hands, and stood, dismissing him. "Stay to sup and sleep in the hall. Tomorrow you may take me to him."

"Aye, and glad to," Alan agreed. Then he reached into the lining of the English surcoat and pulled out the folded message from Tavish. "He sent ye this."

She thumbed the broken seal and frowned. "You have read it?"

"Nay, I swear not. The Bruce did so agin my wishes, but he strongly approved the words. Made them his own command and bade me tell ye to obey. Immediately, he said."

The lady seemed not to hear as her gaze flew over the

message. Disbelief dawned on her face, then contorted the fair features into something approaching horror.

The troubled gray eyes flew to his and narrowed with suspicion. "You wrote this! Oh, it bears Tavish's name and is signed by his hand, but you made the rest. Foul! And you call yourself his friend? Shame on you to use a dying man for your own gain!"

"Lady, I did not...could not," Alan protested, looking to the priest for help. "I swear!"

"You did! See how the lines waver, not his fine, steady letters at all!" Her forefinger punched viciously at the crinkled parchment.

"Pain and fever racked him as he made the marks," Alan explained. "On my soul and all that's holy, Lady, I canna write! I canna even read! God's truth, I dinna lie. I *never* lie!"

Lady Honor turned away from him, dropping the letter as though it were filth. The priest picked it up and read. Alan heard him gasp. "You are to marry!" Father Dennis exclaimed.

So that was all. Ah well, Alan understood now. The poor lass hated being dished out like a treat to whomever Tavish wanted to hold his lands. He could not blame her in the least.

Marry, indeed! Why, she needed time to accept Tav's death. He would see she got her time, and no mistake. All the time she wanted. The hell with Bruce.

He laid a hand on her back and patted gently. "I'll bide and protect ye, my lady. I'm certain Tav only wanted to—"

She rounded on him with her hands on her hips, leaning forward with her chin up. "What about what *I* want? I have no wish to wed anyone. Especially not *you!*"

"*Me?*" Alan heard the word croak out of his mouth,

leaving a bad taste behind. Then another followed, more in the nature of a groan. "Marry?" He backed up and dropped to the window seat, his knees too weak to hold him. "Oh, shite!"

"Just so!" Lady Honor snatched the letter from the priest's hand and, crumpling it under Alan's nose, assaulted him in rapid French. Still shocked by Tav's orders and unable to grasp more than the occasional word, he simply stared at her until she switched to English.

"Saints! He has commanded us to wed this day! This very day! He swore that he loved me and now he demands that I marry a—"

"A what?"

"A highland savage," she retorted, shaking a finger under his nose. "*Mais oui,* I can tell by your speech that is what you are in spite of that fine mail you wear! And ignorant, as well, by your own admission!"

"Unlettered, Lady. 'Tis not the same as ignorant. And de'il take ye wi' all yer plaguey French airs! Ye're still a Scot yersel'!"

"Praise God, only *half!*" she shouted.

"Then I wish to God 'twas th' upper half wi' th' mouth!"

She gaped. Her chest heaved up and down like a bellows. Alan wrestled with his anger until he had a firm grip on it. Surely 'twas only her grief speaking here. Shock had undone her, and him carrying on as if she were to blame for it all.

"Why would my husband do this to me?" she demanded, turning to the priest.

"Well, how d'ye think I feel, eh?" Alan countered. "Trapped, is what! Bound by a stout chain of friendship reachin' inta th' verra grave. Hist, I'd as lief fall on my dirk as surrender my freedom, but my word's my word, by God!'' He slapped his forehead and groaned toward the ceiling. "Och, Tav, what've ye wrought us here? What have ye done?''

He fumed. She paced. He could hear the scuffing of her feet through the rushes, the rustle of skirts about her legs. The sounds were near as loud as the thudding of his heart.

Alan realized Tavish had no way of knowing the words he had written to his wife had gone unread that night. And just who bore the fault for that misunderstanding? Alan himself, none other. Tav had asked whether Alan agreed to the missive and got a ready answer for his trouble. *Aye, braw advice.* Ha!

That had been as near to a lie as Alan ever uttered, and it troubled him sorely. Everyone he knew remarked on his word and how he could be trusted to speak nothing but the truth in all matters, never mind the consequences he must suffer for it. That was a thing of great pride for a man who had little else in the world to recommend him. His departure from honesty—even in such a small way— had brought on disaster.

Lady Honor spoke truer than she knew just now, he thought. He had acted as ignorant as the barmiest village idiot in this. How stupid to agree to a thing when he had no idea what it was. Just proved what he had always known. A lie, even a near lie, led to one sort of perdition or another. This one had cost him his freedom. And the poor lady, her peace of mind.

Oh, he admitted he might have imagined himself lolling about a castle with a well-born woman now and again, especially when Tavish had waxed poetic about his own, but Alan knew very well such a life did not suit him. He had been thrust out of that sort of existence and into a rugged bachelor household too early on. But not so early that he did not know what he had lost by the move. To be perfectly honest—and he strove always to be honest, if nothing else—Alan simply was not equipped to deal with marriage and family life. Even if he wanted to, he did not know how. Now, due to this *almost lie* of his, he knew he must learn.

Father Dennis cleared his throat. ''Pardon, sir, my lady, but the hour grows late. If there is to be a wedding—''

''No!'' she shouted, throwing up her hands.

''Aye!'' Alan declared, rising again on steadier legs. ''Go, Father, and gather all who will come to yer chapel.''

''We have no chapel, sir. The hall must do.''

''There will *be* no wedding!'' the lady said heatedly, her arms crossed over her chest.

''Leave us, Father, and make ready,'' Alan repeated. When the door had closed, he turned to his new intended. She looked ready to scratch out his eyes and he could hardly blame her.

He forced himself to speak calmly, reasonably. ''If ye loved yer husband, Lady Honor, ye must mind his last wishes.''

''That fever you spoke of baked his brain! Right-minded, Tavish would never have wished this on me. Or on you,'' she added belatedly, obviously hoping now to enlist him in her rebellion.

Alan wondered if she had the right of it. Had the fever affected Tav's mind? No matter. ''Even were that true, my lady, Bruce made Tav's wish a command. We dare not go agin' the king.''

She laughed, a mirthless sound if he had ever heard one. ''La! King, indeed!''

''Aye, well, he is that and owns Scotland now. Ye might flee to France and yer father if ye wish to escape the royal wrath. Where am I to go, then?''

In truth, he had no fear left of Robert Bruce. The man

would either kill him or not, and everyone died sooner or later. He only thought to stir a bit of guilt in the lass. She had hurt his feelings, calling him ignorant. Even if it was true, she had no call to treat him as pig droppings on her foot.

Her fury seemed to die out on the instant and leave her sad. The tears were back, trailing one after another down those petal soft cheeks. "You don't want this any more than I," she said softly.

"Ye have the right of that. But 'tis a matter of duty now, yer own as well as mine. Tavish asked it of us."

He cocked a brow and gave her a half smile for her forlorn little nod of agreement. "I know ye grieve for him, sweet lady, as do I. But come now and we'll make the best of it, eh? 'Tis all we can do for him."

"Wait!" she cried as he grasped her hand more firmly and headed for the door. "Hold a moment, sir. We must speak further before we do this thing."

Alan capitulated with a weary sigh. "Look ye, we have years in which to know each other. As yer priest said, the hour grows late and I'm fit to drop to the nearest pallet."

She colored to a bright rose hue and glanced guiltily at the curtained bed in the corner. "Well, that is the problem, you see. I cannot…that is, we must not—"

"Lie together?" he said and laughed at the thought. "Lady, I've ridden four long days wi' no rest or aught to eat but dry oats, dug Tav's grave one-handed wi' a broken sword, faced down the king and near lost my head to the bargain. All that, after herdin' a hoard of lowland pikers through the bloodiest battle of the century. 'Tis not bed sport on my mind this night, so dinna worry on it."

She shook her head and wrung her hands. "I must tell you, I am *enceinte*," she blurted.

Alan frowned. *Enceinte? Enchanting? In sin? What?*

"Verra well, then," he said agreeably, hoping she would elaborate so he wouldn't need to admit to further ignorance.

She looked vastly relieved. "God bless you for your understanding, sir. This babe is all I have left of Tavish."

"Babe?" The news hit him harder than Bruce's fist had done earlier. "God's truth, ye carry Tav's bairn?"

Alan had not grasped until that moment how the thought of bedding her had wormed its way into his mind. He had not intended to do it this night because of the reasons he had just given her, but he certainly meant to do it soon. Guilt washed over him like a cold wave. Taking Tavish's woman to bed ought not have occurred to him at all. Even with Tav's blessing—and king's orders—it seemed devilish wrong even to consider it, let alone do it.

"You will wait until after the birth?" Her fingers worried her lips as though she were frightened he would change his mind.

"Aye, of course I'll wait," he said gently, nodding, even as the import of his promise sank in. He had been celibate for nigh on a year, since just before he had joined Bruce's army. Now he must needs delay until Lady Honor delivered of her child and recovered from the birth.

Easing himself with another woman after wedding Honor would be unthinkable. Even were she not breeding, Alan wondered if he could really allow himself to bed his best friend's widow. But he would have to bed somebody. Eventually.

Ah well, his own discomfort was not the lass's fault, and she looked nigh to collapsing from fretting over it. He smiled and reached for her hands. When she allowed him to clasp them, he squeezed her fingers with gentle reassurance. "Ease yer mind, my lady. We'll share yer chamber for the looks of the thing, but ye need no' worry I'll risk Tav's heir. 'Tis precious to me, too.''

A single tear broke over her lashes and trailed down one cheek. With a callused thumb, he brushed it away. "There now, dinna greet. Come, let's go and give yer wee'un a foster da, eh?''

Honor sniffed and nodded. ''We will need protection.''

''Just so,'' he agreed as he placed one of her hands on his mailed arm and led her to the hall.

Three women surrounded her as they entered, the skinny one gabbling excitedly in French and shooting him wary looks. He kept an eye on Lady Honor as they led her away from him, noting the quiet reserve in her manner now that she had accepted her lot.

A pang of longing pierced him like a crossbow quarrel. What must it be like to win the heart of a woman like herself? Fairer than dawn, she was, so cool and clean, and sweetness itself until she thought something threatened her babe.

He blamed her in no way for her recent defiance. She did not know him at all, and had only sought to protect the child. Honorable as her name, she was. So brave, for a lass.

Tavish had known and appreciated her well. He had loved her dearly despite their short acquaintance and brief union. Two months of heaven, Alan did not doubt. Tav had declared as much, more than once. How proud he would have been of his wife's courage, and to know of the coming child.

Alan knew Honor had led a sheltered life until now; born and reared in her mother's castle in Loire Valley in France, a frequent visitor to the court. No doubt shamelessly indulged by her father, a Scots baron embroiled in the tangle of French politics. Coming to Scotland with naught but her women and one lone priest must have been a shock for one born into cultured splendor.

She had weathered it well, Tav said. The hall Alan stood in shone as proof of that. She had made this keep a home, a comfortable refuge and delight to the eyes. Tavish often had boasted of it and rightly so.

Now, newly widowed and pregnant, hardly more than a child herself, wee Honor risked the wrath of a rough warrior husband by denying Alan his marital rights even before they said the vows. All to protect Tav's bairn. Her loyalty and courage stirred something inside Alan that pushed aside his dread of a loveless union. It would not be completely loveless, after all, if he loved her. For all he knew of the woman now, he believed what he felt might be more akin to worship.

"Ah, Tav, I see now. I ken why ye sent me here. She'll be needing a strong arm and I'll try to do ye proud," Alan whispered. "Lady Honor has, and so shall yer son. I'll see to it."

Chapter Three

Honor only half listened as her women exclaimed over the news of Tavish's death and this eve's rushed nuptials. She barely noticed their comments on the hard-muscled warrior who stood alone in the midst of the hall. She just watched him.

He waited at his ease, as though he had nothing better to do. She supposed he did not. He just stood there, weight resting on one foot, arms crossed, and green eyes lively as they surveyed the gathering of castle folk.

"You should send him away, madame," said Nanette, her trusted maid. The woman spoke in French so the others would not understand. "Even smiling, that one looks fiercer than your lord father ever did on his worst of days. You mark me well, he means you no good! No good at all. How can you marry such as he, especially now?"

Nanette's dainty hands fluttered like crazed butterflies when she got excited and this Scottish knight certainly provided excitement if nothing else.

Honor ignored Nan then and stole another long look at Sir Alan. In a strange way, he appealed to her senses. However, handsome did not exactly describe him if one judged by court standards. No doubt many women swooned over him with a combination of terror and wild fantasy. Or simple lust. Not sensible women, of course. Not her.

His hair, a wild dark chestnut and probably combed with his fingers, escaped bit by bit from its tenuous tethering at his nape. A soft waving strand drifted over his high, wide brow and just missed covering one dark-lashed eye. Thick brows, a darker auburn than his hair, rose and fell, changing his expression from curiosity to satisfaction when Father Dennis approached him, Book of Prayers in hand. She liked the fact that he did not make the least attempt to conceal his feelings.

The knight's full, mobile lips broke into an amazingly open smile, revealing two rows of even, unspotted teeth. He had good strong teeth, Honor noted, exasperated with herself for giving attention to that. One did not judge men as one did horses, after all. If so, Tavish might have been a fine, sleek Arabian, while this fellow looked a hell-in-battle destrier. But the teeth were fine, nonetheless.

Why had God seen fit to take her gentle Tavish and leave this warlike specimen to live? She could not help but question, though she knew it impious. Well, piety had gotten her nowhere.

Nanette pulled on her arm. "Listen to me! This man will be your undoing, madame. He will! Send him away and forget this nonsense."

Honor tore her gaze from the knight and settled it on the old maid. "And then what, Nan? You know as well as I, someone would take his place. If not tomorrow, then the next day or the next, another will come. I cannot hope to hold this place alone. At least this chevalier knew my husband and cared enough to bring the body home. He promises to foster my child and protect us. Tavish knew I would need someone and he sent me this man. The king commands that we marry, so he surely trusts him. What would you have me do, forfeit everything I have to the Bruce and flee to France?''

''*Oui!*'' Nanette said with an emphatic nod. ''Just so! Let us go home.''

''Never!'' Honor declared. ''I would wed the devil himself before the comte de Trouville.''

''God help you, my lady,'' Nanette whimpered. ''This man may qualify! Look at those arms and fists. He might very well kill you should you raise his ire. And with your temper,'' she said with a bob of her head, ''I do not doubt me you will.''

Honor heaved a loud sigh and shook off Nan's clutching hands. Her maid could be right, but life with her father held absolutely no hope at all. Honor felt reasonably certain she could handle this knight. He responded gently to her tears. She sensed an underlying compassion, concealed by that rugged warrior's exterior. And surely there would be benefits in all that strength.

Chances were good that she might control the man and make him do her bidding. She had found a way with Tavish Ellerby and she would find a way with this one, though the two were different as a pigeon and a hawk. La! First comparing them to horses, then to birds. Consigning men to the level of animals stirred a bitter smile. Not so farfetched as all that.

''Go on, Nan, and order the women to prepare the solar. Take in some of the best wine and see to a tub for his bath. Father Dennis beckons me, so it must be time.''

She quit the group of women and approached the priest and the knight. This might prove the greatest mistake of her life, but thus far, her instincts had led her aright. She sensed Alan of Strode would wax tame enough if she kept her wits about her.

The father of her child lay dead now, unable to keep her past at bay, unable to secure their little one's future. But perhaps he had, in his last moments, seen to it that someone else would. She thanked Tavish for that, for thinking of her, and for loving her as he had. Her husband had been a noble and admirable man and she would miss him greatly.

Despite her first stunned reaction and her grief at hearing that Tavish had died, Honor realized now that Alan of Strode offered her the only chance she had to hold what belonged to her and to Tavish's child.

Unlike her first, this marriage would be real and binding for certain. Properly documented and witnessed. Tavish had arranged this union for her and wished her happy in it. She would comply with his plans, for his sake, her own and especially for their child's.

"Sir Alan, Father Dennis, shall we proceed?" she asked, chin lifted and eyes bright. If the man respected bravery, she would pretend it. She certainly had enough practice in pretending.

"Well, ah, there are certain procedures," said the priest. "There is the confession. You made your own just this morn, my lady, but—" He eyed the knight warily. "Sir Alan, if you would step into the alcove yonder, I would hear yours."

Strode shook his head, his hands resting on his narrow hips. "Nay, I canna think of any reason to hide what I've to say. The lass should know what she's gettin'."

Honor perked up at that. A public confession? Unheard of.

"B-but, sir, 'tis always done in private!" Father Dennis gnawed his thin lips, glancing from one to the other several times. A titter of nervous laughter rippled among those listening to the exchange.

The knight stared them down with an arrogant look. When they fell silent again, he looked directly into the priest's eyes. "Let her hear it. I'll not lie."

His brows drew together, this time in a thoughtful frown, as though searching his mind. Then he snapped his fingers and grinned. "Och, now I remember it! *Forgi' me, Father, for I have sinned!*"

Father Dennis cleared his throat and folded his hands in front of him, clutching his rosary and prayer book between them. "How long has it been since your last confession, my son?"

Strode flashed another frown, the tip of his tongue worrying the corner of his mouth as he rocked heel to toe to heel. Mental calculation apparently completed, he steadied. "Nineteen years, give or take a six-month. Aye, that's right," he said with a firm nod. "I was goin' on seven."

Nineteen years! There were murmurs of horror and a few giggles, quickly squelched with another piercing green glare.

"And what have you done since that requires forgiveness?"

Honor wondered just how long they would be standing here if he decided to list everything.

Strode seemed at a loss. He started to speak, snapped his mouth shut, then began again. "Well, what is it that matters here?"

"Do you believe in the One God, keep the Sabbath holy, honor your father and mother?"

"Aye for th' most part, though I dinna *like* 'em all that much. The father and mother, that is. But I do give 'em proper respect. 'Tis only right." He looked triumphant. "Is that all, then?"

"Not all, but a beginning," the priest said, looking askance at the penitent. "Have you killed anyone?"

"Oh, aye to that as well! Twenty or so, all English, mostly. Mayhaps one Welshmon. Before that, I recall only three. One, a thieving Cameron, and two nameless reivers what tried to steal my horse. All good, clean, righteous kills. Should be clear on that score!" His proud smile was blinding and totally guilt free.

A shocked silence ensued while the priest drew in a long breath and expelled it slowly. "And have you stolen?" he asked.

"Aye, all the cattle I could trod up for my uncle Angus. A few sheep here and there, but the buggers are devilish hard to herd!" He paused thoughtfully. "Did my part, but I'm thinking I coulda done a bit more had I put my mind to it. Aye, all right, then, I admit to a wee touch of sloth a few years back. Is there a penance for sloth, Father?"

Honor bit her lips together. Small wonder Tavish had liked him. The man was amusing, she had to give him that, though it seemed to be inadvertent.

She could hear Father Dennis's teeth grind before he spoke. When he did so, he adopted a slow cadence, as though speaking to a half-wit. "These things—the killing, the stealing—are sins, Sir Alan. *Sins!* Not things you should do, but things you should *not*. Now then, have you lied?"

Strode clasped his hands behind him and hung his head, peering from under thick, dark lashes like a guilty child. There was something endearing about it, Honor thought. As though one could always depend on that very look every time he sinned. "I let Tavish Ellerby believe I could read, when I could not." Then he went on the defensive. "But, mind ye, I ne'er *said* I could."

"A lie of omission, the same thing," the cleric declared in a stern voice. "Now, have you committed adultery?"

The answer accompanied a vehement shake of the head.

"Nay, I would not! I never took another's wife or betrothed." A quick shadow of worry darkened his open features. "Unless...unless some of the lassies lied. Then that would be their own sin, eh?"

"Fornication!" the priest gasped. "You've had sexual congress with many women!" Father Dennis did not phrase that as a question.

Sir Alan grinned and combed a hand through his long waves, dislodging the frayed silk tie altogether. Honor never thought to see embarrassment and pride combined with such equality. "I'm hoping ye'll not be asking for a head count there, Father. Guilty, wi' damned little regret!"

The hall erupted into raucous laughter. Even Honor could not keep her face composed. She hid her mouth behind one hand and turned away. She was appalled, but God help her, wanting to giggle. What an outrageous scoundrel he was. Then her silent laughter faded to nothing. Tavish meant for her to marry this scoundrel. A killer, a thief and a womanizer. An unrepentant womanizer!

The priest waited until the hall quieted and then resumed. "Have you ever coveted another man's wife or possessions?" he asked in a hushed monotone.

Alan of Strode answered in kind, looking directly at Honor with a troubled expression. "Aye, I have that."

The admission and the man's distress over it bothered Honor. He looked as though he meant he had coveted her. But the knight had never met her or, as far as she knew, seen Tavish's lands or keep.

Father Dennis cleared his throat again and broke the spell. "Well, I should need a tally stick, mayhaps several of them, to tote up your penances. Will you repent for your sins?"

"Aye, certainly," Strode answered. "Could we settle up later, d'ye think? I'm good for it."

Father Dennis blew out an exasperated breath and shook his head. "Fine. Consider yourself absolved for the nonce. Go and sin no more." Then he threw a surreptitious glance at the waiting tables. "Shall we get on with the ceremony?"

Honor stepped forward. She could see little point in postponing the inevitable—and what she now believed necessary—event. The more she thought on it, the more she appreciated Tavish's idea. He could not have known the trouble she would encounter, but somehow had managed to send her a solution of sorts. She hoped.

While the priest's words droned on, she let her gaze rest on Sir Alan's hand, which supported her own. Rough calluses and broken blisters covered his broad, square palm. His nails looked recently pared, the fingertips scrubbed almost raw. He did not tremble as she did, Honor noticed. Strong, steadfast, supportive.

Hands told much about a person. She thought of Tavish's hands, slender, well-groomed, agile, like the man himself. By comparison, this knight standing beside her looked a rough-and-tumble piece of work, the kind of man she dreaded. And needed.

"I will," she responded when Father Dennis prompted her.

"You are man and wife together. Tate, the marriage lines, please," the priest called to the tall young crofter he had selected to assist him. Spreading his brief document flat on the nearest table, he motioned Sir Alan forward and placed a slender finger on the bottom of the parchment. "Make your mark here, sir."

Alan dipped the quill Tate provided and laboriously scrawled his name. Honor noted the pride with which he did so in spite of the awkward, all but illegible results. He then handed her the plume and she signed with a scratchy flourish.

"So, it is done. Felicitations, sir, my lady. May God bless and keep you both. The kiss of peace, if you please?"

Honor turned her face up to the knight, who blushed dark red. His wide-eyed gaze darted everywhere but at her. She smiled. Good lord, the man was shy? After all those women he had bragged of bedding? This seemed too much to hope for.

Honor reached for his face and pulled it down to hers, planting her closed lips squarely on his as was customary. Just as she relaxed her hold, she heard it; a soft, almost inaudible sound of yearning mixed with denial.

Their eyes locked at close quarter and she felt trapped in a green sea of anguish. Slowly, the lashes dropped over the emerald orbs and his lips descended again, this time open and probing. Here was a kiss, not of peace, but of raging need and dark promise. Her insides melted like butter on a hot scone.

Honor stumbled back, breathless, when he released her. At least he was not gloating. In fact, he looked as astonished as she felt. Her mouth throbbed, tingling with the taste of mint and something wild and uniquely him. Unsettling did not begin to describe how she felt.

Thoroughly disconcerted, Honor looked away, unable to face him longer. The crowd around them seemed stunned, or scared to death for her.

She was frightened for herself. What in the name of heaven had she done, wedding this wild Scotsman? She could as soon control the tides, or a tempest force wind as to order this knight about.

Honor jerked back instinctively as he lowered his mouth near her ear. He only meant to speak, she chided herself, gathering false calm like a cloak around her. "What is it, sir?" she whispered.

"Could we eat now, do ye think? I'm fair starved."

She laughed a little, as much with relief as at his earnest inquiry. His kiss had shocked her, but perhaps he meant no harm by it.

Upon reflection, she realized Alan of Strode had done nothing underhanded, nothing sly at all since the moment he had arrived. So far as she could tell, he said what he thought, made clear his needs, and did what he felt was right even when it went against his own wishes. Could any man be that simple, she wondered?

Only time would reveal his true nature. At least she grasped a fighting chance to keep what Tavish had left her. More of a chance than she'd had yesterday.

Pushing aside her worries, Honor nodded toward the dais. "Our feast, such as may be, awaits. You must understand, rations are shortened with winter coming, and we had not expected a wedding. Roast hare is the best we can offer this night."

"Tomorrow I'll hunt," he promised with a grin. "Have ye neeps?"

She rested her hand on his as they stepped up to the dais and took their seats in the carved chairs. "Turnips? We do, and in great supply. Also mutton for slaughter when the weather cools more. Our location was protected from the armies, thank God." But not from the neighbors, she thought. Time enough later for him to realize that burden. Pray God he proved as fierce to her enemies as he had first looked to her.

The meal revealed that what few knightly virtues she had credited to Sir Alan of Strode did not extend to his eating habits. Honor fair lost her appetite watching him devour everything within reach.

His pleasure in the meal seemed almost wicked in its intensity. Little groaning noises of pleasure escaped his throat as it worked to swallow with gulps the steamed turnips. She looked away to hide her reaction.

Honor heard the slurping of ale go on as though he never meant to stop. The tankard thumped down on the table accompanied with a tremendous belch. "God, 'tis good brew, that!" he exclaimed.

She ventured a sidewise look and saw him rubbing his flat stomach with both hands. "Just how long since you last ate, sir?"

He grinned and pushed away from the table. "Like this? Oh, nigh on a year. Not since I left Malaig. Afore that, I canna say. On the march, we made do wi' oats, most times dry when we couldna light fires to heat water. Some small game, half-cooked and wi' no salt. Grubbed up wild tatties when we found 'em. Picked a few greens here and there. Fish when we could tickle 'em out.

"Ahh," he crooned, stretching one arm full length above his head. "Nothing like a full belly! I'm for bed an it please ye, lass. Sore tired, I am."

He rose and held out a grease-filmed hand.

Honor took it gingerly. "Your bath awaits, husband."

He threw his head back, affronted. "I had a bath this day!"

"You need another!" Honor retorted, risking his wrath. "You reek like ⹁—"

"Soldier?" he offered with a wry twist of his lips. He plucked at the surcoat. "Aye, 'tis this garb here. English. The gambeson was a bit gamey when I donned it, I will admit."

Honor snapped her mouth shut and appraised what he wore with a careful eye. "English?"

He nodded, wrinkling his nose. "Took at Bannockburn.

'Twas this,'' he ran a hand down the front of his chest, ''or m' breacan. That's still wet from th' wash I gave it in the burn.''

''Come,'' she ordered, feeling much like a mother with an errant child in tow. ''We'll see you to rights.''

Aside to Nanette who stood waiting, she instructed, ''Unload his packs and have all the clothing cleaned.'' Then she called to Tate, the priest's assistant. ''You, come and help Sir Alan off with his hauberk. Sand scrub it and dry it well so it does not rust.'' To Father Dennis, she bade good-night and tugged her new husband into the solar.

So far, so good, Honor thought with satisfaction. He followed her suggestions like an overgrown lamb. Would he always be so docile? Dare she push him further? Not tonight, she decided. Tomorrow would prove the true test. When he had rested and realized that he, by law, ruled where he roosted, she would know the full extent of her folly.

For safety's sake, Honor allowed Tate to complete the knight's disrobing and get him settled in the tub of steaming water. Meanwhile, she retired behind her dressing screen to ready herself for bed. When the splashing stopped, she reappeared wearing her long woolen robe. He was asleep in the tub, his knees drawn up to his chin and his wet head lolling forward.

She ventured a soft prod to one heavily muscled shoulder. ''Sir? Sir Alan? Wake up. You cannot sleep in the bath. The water cools. Come now!'' She poked again, this time harder.

''Hmmph,'' he grunted, sitting bolt upright and sloshing water over the edge. ''Och, sorry, lass! Stand away.'' Hefting himself to his feet, he stepped out and fumbled for the toweling draped over the stool.

Her breath caught in her throat. She tried to force her

eyes away from the massive body that looked twice as large unclothed. Smooth sun-browned skin reached to just below his waist. Resuming downward at knee level to include his huge, well-shaped feet. His nether cheeks gleamed almost white, as did the muscled thighs, which were dusted with golden hair.

Honor thanked God he was turned away from her. If he proved anywhere near as generously proportioned in front, she was not ready for a glimpse of *that!* A shiver of apprehension rippled through her middle.

With an industry to make any housewife proud, Honor busied herself turning back the coverlet and shaping the pillows. Anything to keep her eyes from straying near the bath.

"I'll take th' floor," he said, so near her shoulder, she jumped with fright.

"No, do not!" she shrieked before she could stop herself. The words were meant to stop his advance, but he obviously misconstrued.

"All right, then," he said. "If ye insist. I only thought 'twould make ye a mite shivery to sleep beside me."

Still not daring to look at him, Honor heard the rustle of the mattress stuffing as he climbed into bed. She finally ventured a peek and saw about a third of the wide bed vacant and waiting. His strong back glistened with droplets of bathwater.

What should she do? Take to the floor herself? Were she more spritely and not heavy with child, she might. But there was nothing to sleep upon unless she rolled up in her robe and lay on the hard wooden boards. The cold window seat boasted only a few thin cushions. Where would she rest?

Soft, intermittent snores drifted up from the pillow, drawing her attention to the man in her bed. Honor quirked a brow. He appeared harmless enough for now. All she had to do was lie down and then wake before he did. He would never even know she was there, fatigued as he was. Gingerly, Honor stretched out beside him, carefully not touching.

After a few tense moments, she relaxed. What an exhausting day. But sleep eluded her as she reviewed the happenings. First Ian Gray had ridden up to her walls and offered—insisted, rather—on giving her his protection. His unruly gaggle of reivers frightened half the occupants of the keep into hiding and the rest to gathering makeshift weapons.

Honor had paid no mind when Gray loudly expressed his desire to wed her. She had called down that she already had a husband. Her men issued a shower of arrows over the visitors and cut short his next exchange. No marksmen, her small troop of defenders, but their hail of missiles pricked some few. Thusly treated, and probably given the lateness of the afternoon, Gray rode off, laughing and shouting promises to return anon. His keep, Dunniegray, lay nearby. She knew that from questioning her men.

Honor had to wonder now whether Ian Gray came because he had known she was already a widow. It stood to reason he did know it, else why would he have come here offering marriage?

Honor had barely seen the last of his men disappear into the wood when this rackety knight rode in with the shocking orders from Tavish and the king.

As wedding days went, this one left a lot to be desired. But it could have been worse, she admitted. Much worse. Ian Gray probably would not have been so kind as Alan of Strode in announcing her loss of Tavish. Or in waiting on a consummation.

She balked at the very thought of a marriage to the

deranged Ian Gray. The man laughed and thumbed his nose at everything, even the threat of death! Sir Alan might not be the deepest of thinkers, given his rather amusing confession tonight. But at the very least, he did seem capable of an occasional serious thought.

Honor stole a glance at the broad back not half an arm's length from her face. Light from the single bedside candle threw dancing shadows across the tanned expanse left uncovered by the sheet. The muscles, even in repose, appeared formidable. His skin, still damp, gleamed bronze like a statue after a soft rain.

An absurd longing to touch it proved almost irresistible. She closed her eyes against the impulse. What a foolish thought, prodding a sleeping giant. Still, against her will, her hand stole out and the pads of her fingertips pressed lightly against his shoulder blade.

Warmth suffused her as she allowed her palm to rest flat against the indentation of his spine. How different he was from Tavish, the only other man whose body she had ever willingly touched. The skin felt smoother, more finely grained, not downed and lightly freckled as Tavish's had been. The padding over these bones felt solid, dense, in no way soft. Honor flexed her hand.

Huge muscles quivered, tensed, and then moved like flash lightning.

...

Chapter Four

Honor shrieked and snatched her hand away as the huge knight turned, almost rolling on her as he shifted to his back. Dark green eyes, heavy-lidded with fatigue, regarded her with a sleepy, unspoken question.

"Pardon," she muttered, nearly nose to nose. "I did not mean to wake you. You are wet. I worry for your health."

He gave a little grunt of a chuckle. "Lady, I've slept wet on th' ground for nigh on a year now. This be my first night in a real bed since I turned seven years. Should I sicken, 'twould be from too much comfort, not lack of it."

"You jest!" she exclaimed, subtly inching away from him to the very edge of the bed.

"Aye, betimes, but not about this. Dinna look afeared. I recall my promise and the bairn ye carry. 'Tis grateful I am ye let me share this much."

He arched his back and sighed, wriggling out a comfortable niche in the soft, feather mattress. "Sheets," he crooned. "I forgot how sleek they be."

Honor inhaled sharply, her trepidation increasing with every shift of his overly large frame. His chest fairly commanded her attention. She could not seem to pull her gaze away from it. Mounds of muscle, crowned by small, flat nipples, heaved with every sensuous breath he took. An intriguing mat of springy curls lay in between, beckoning her hand. Tavish's chest had been pale, flat and almost hairless. She clenched her curious hands into fists.

He moved again. Then Honor saw that what she had first thought a large patch of dirt he missed washing was a huge bruise surrounding an ugly, poorly stitched cut on his shoulder. "Sir! You've taken a wound! Why said you naught of it? Let me see!" She scrambled to her knees and leaned over him, touching the skin near the injury to see whether it felt feverish.

Sir Alan glanced down at it and winced. "I tended to it again today. Mayhaps my sewing's not so dainty as yer own would be, but 'twill hold this time. 'Tis on the mend."

"I have herbs to aid that," she offered, gently probing the area around the awkward stitching. How could a man sew his own flesh together? It did not bear thought. "It looks reddened."

He cocked a brow, grinned, and looked straight at her nipples, which were beaded and quite visible through her bedgown. "So will yer face if ye don't get off me."

Honor flung herself back to her side of the bed and groaned with embarrassment.

"Are ye ill, lass?" he asked with what sounded like real concern. He rose up on one elbow and peered down at her. "Ye look a bit fashed. Does the child make ye sick?"

"No," she replied quickly, forcing a smile. "I am past the time for that."

"Ah well, I know naught of such things," he admitted in a conversational tone, turning to his side and resting his head on his left hand. "But I should learn now, should I not?"

Honor shot him a wary glance and tried to scoot farther

away. The very idea of his touching her made her shake with need. He would surely misunderstand her if she allowed his nearness. A plea dammed in her throat, but she feared what she might plead for if she let it out. She badly needed holding this night, but simply for comfort.

He looked quite willing to do that, but Honor knew he might insist on more. Saints, but she felt ridiculous! Looked ridiculous, as well, she supposed, this far gone with child.

"Will the babe come soon?" he asked as though he read her thoughts.

Honor let out the breath she was holding. "Next month."

"Ye seem verra small to be so far gone," he remarked, frowning at her mounded middle, which the covers hardly concealed.

In truth, she was. Nan had told her the babe would be a mite of a thing, given Honor's own tiny size and Tavish's slender build and lack of height. "I am fortunate there. Some women become quite unwieldy and have trouble getting about the last few months of confinement. Everything goes well, however. He is quite active, you see."

"He? Who?" Strode asked, his brow wrinkling as though he had missed some part of their conversation.

"The child," Honor said, laughing in spite of herself. The man must never have known a pregnant female. "The babe turns and kicks in the womb. Did you not know this?"

The look of surprised wonder on his face almost undid her. He caught his bottom lip between his teeth and his eyes widened in delight. Then he laughed. "Truly? Do you tweak me?"

"No, it is true!" Honor declared, feeling quite superior and not at all afraid of him now. A gentle giant, she thought, smug in her newly confirmed assessment of him. Harmless.

He laughed again, softly this time. "I wonder what that must feel like to ye. Passing strange, I'd think."

Without aforethought, Honor reached for his right hand, recalling its comfortable strength from the wedding ceremony and even earlier when he had delivered the awful news about Tavish. "Would you like to know?"

"To know what?" he asked, again a quizzical frown marred his brow.

"How it feels," she explained as she dragged down the covers and placed his palm on top of her abdomen.

He uttered an exclamation of absolute awe when a tiny limb rolled against his hand. He shifted his palm. "There! Again! This is wondrous!" His ready laughter rang out around the chamber and he rolled closer to her, warming to the event as though it were a fascinating game.

Strong fingers undulated gently against the soft fabric that separated his touch from her tightly stretched skin. "Ah, Honor, how do ye bear such sweetness all the day and night? Can ye no' wait to hold him in yer arms?"

His excitement like that of a small boy, the big knight's features grew animated. "I cradled a babe once! The mother had a case in the laird's court—stolen pig or some such—and she thrust the bairn at me to hold when she was called up." A wistful expression softened his features even more. "I ne'er forgot the trust in those wee lights. The smile. No fear or worry atall," he said, recalling the incident with a faraway look. Then he pulled himself back to the present and beseeched her, "Could I hold yers when 'tis small, do ye think? Would ye mind?"

Honor felt tears rise at his question. How could she ever have feared a man who wore his feelings so near the surface, who felt such wonder at tending a peasant's babe?

She touched his face with her fingertips. "Tavish was wise to trust you, I think."

Surprisingly, he retreated from her then, his smile dying as he withdrew his hand and lay back with a sigh. "Mayhaps not so wise."

"You had other plans for yourself, did you not?" Honor guessed.

He smirked. "Oh aye, I did. Planned to chase the English right out of England and inta the sea, soon as we finished routin' them from Scotland. There's a right ambition, eh?"

Honor toyed with the edge of the coverlet, feeling even more at ease now that the conversation turned to politics. "You hate the English so much?"

"Nay, not all of them. My father's English. I dinna hate him, though I feel no great liking for him, either."

"What!" This one, half-English? Nothing he could have said would have surprised her more. She would have sworn Strode was a woven-in-the-wool highlandman.

He elaborated with a negligent wave of one large hand. "When my father was a young mon, a minor baron with a prosperous estate in Gloucester, he swore to King Edward. He rode under Gloucester's banner in the war against de Montfort. Longshanks rewarded him with the post of sheriff at Rowicsburg and had him wed a MacGill lass for her dower lands. An Englishmon wi' property in Scotland is apt to fight the harder to keep it under English rule, y' see? Da's land in Gloucester would be forfeit if he did not. So there he was then, a foot in both camps."

"Your mother left him and took you north?" Honor guessed, since Alan was obviously reared in the Highlands and Rowicsburg a border castle. What other explanation could there be?

"Da sent her to her old home and me with her. What

with our barons, Wallace, and Old Edward all scrambling for power, Da said we'd be safer well away from the border. King Edward was not above taking hostages to insure loyalty.''

Honor sensed his anger. "How old were you then?"

"Seven," Alan replied.

"You hated leaving him, did you not?" She knew she ought to leave well enough alone, but he seemed to need to speak of it.

Alan smiled sadly, his profile clear, even in the near darkness. "Aye, I missed him, missed the family I took for granted, missed my friends. Especially Tav."

"You knew Tavish even then? I assumed you just met on this last campaign."

"He fostered a while at Rowicsburg before I left. Did he not tell ye? His mother married an English knight when she was widowed of Tav's father. Old Beauchamp sent Tav to Da for training up in the English way. We were like brothers, though Tav was four years older than I." A moment of silence hung between them. "When I had to leave, Tav stayed on. I hated him for it then, not knowing that he left as well soon after. We only just met up again when he came to fight fer th' Bruce."

Honor wanted to comfort that young lad torn from his home and friends. "At least you had your mother with you when you went away."

He laced his fingers through his hair and sighed. "Aye, for a whole fortnight. Then she returned to Da."

"*Mon Dieu!* She left you there?" Honor could not imagine a mother abandoning her child. "How could she!"

Alan smiled at her, apparently amused at her belated defense. "I was seven, after all. 'Tis the usual age to send out for fostering. Mam told me her brother Angus would treat me as the son he never had.''

''And did he?'' Honor found herself caught up in his story, worried for the boy he had been.

''Aye, he did that. Beat me every day thereafter!''

Honor moved closer without a thought but to comfort. She cupped his face with one hand. ''Beat you? Oh—'' Tears streaked down her cheeks, but she made no effort to stop them. Her memories of swinging slaps and harsh accusations rose up and broke free.

A huge arm encircled her and drew her close. ''Well, dinna greet over it!'' She felt his laughter as much as heard it since her head rested against his bare chest. ''Ah, Honor, ye have too tender a heart. I'd ne'er have told ye had I known ye'd weep.'' He drew away a little and caught her tears on one rough finger. ''Here now, 'twas not so bad as all that.''

Honor knew how bad it was. She found it near impossible to stop crying long enough to speak. He made light of what had happened, his only defense against it. His pride would not allow him to admit the true horror of it to her, but she knew. God, how she remembered. ''Only a base, mean coward raises his hand to his child! I hope you killed him when you grew old enough!''

''Killed him? What a thing to say! He's my uncle, Honor.''

''He beat you! Called you foul names! Locked you away in the dark!'' she accused. ''You should *kill* him!''

''Nay, sweeting,'' he soothed. ''He didna do all that, I swear. He only strapped me when I cursed him and tried to run away. My own hardheadedness caused it. I acted the hellion on every waking hour for nigh a year. I earned every blow and more, believe me.''

Honor grasped his arm and drew him close, frantic to

let him know she understood in spite of his denial. Better than anyone in the world, she understood. "You lie to soothe me, husband, but I know what you feel inside. You hurt still, but it's over now. He cannot hurt you now. I will never let him beat you more!"

"Stop this!" he ordered, his voice brisk. "I tell ye 'twas naught more than my uncle's caring to make me behave as a mon and not some snot-nosed weakling. Ye make yerself ill wi' all this weeping. Now cease!" He shook her gently.

Honor caught herself in midsob, aghast at her mistake. Her body lay flush against him, her heart thundered with grief for a much abused child. But Alan of Strode was not the child she wept for, she realized suddenly.

"I would sleep now," she whispered, horribly embarrassed and at a loss as to how she might explain away her foolishness. Surely he would guess why she had taken on so.

"Aye," he agreed, tenderness softening his voice to velvet as he smoothed her hair with his hand. "Sleep, *mo cridhe.*"

She almost missed his vow, hushed as it was. "No mon shall ever raise a hand to ye again. Not whilst I draw breath. I swear it on my life."

Exhaustion stole over her as she lay within his arms. Did she dare believe he would keep such a promise? She feared she had already revealed too much of herself, far more than she had ever let Tavish see. Great danger lay in admitting one's fear and vulnerability. No, because of all she knew to be true of men, Honor dared not take him at his word. She could not possibly give this knight her full trust after only a few short hours' acquaintance.

For all his seeming straightforwardness and honorable promises, Sir Alan of Strode would bear watching. And her subtle direction, as well, in order to keep the upper hand in this alliance. This new husband of hers seemed entirely too good to be true. And if she had not learned anything else in her twenty-one years, Honor knew that what seemed too good to be true, was. Always.

Alan feigned sleep until he heard the slow, steady breathing that marked Honor's slumber. Poor angel, he thought with a frustrated sigh. Her defense of him against his uncle told a clear enough tale of her own poor treatment. How long had that rogue father of hers tormented her?

Alan's blood boiled with an eagerness to kill the man. Slowly. Painfully. Muscles tensed and trembled with the need of it. Red bursts of fury clouded his reason. He fought the tremendous urge to leap from the bed and head for France. Sorely tempting, but impossible, of course. Alan sucked in a steadying breath.

Hatred proved an unfamiliar and unsettling emotion for Alan. Even the opposing forces at Bannockburn had not engendered this feeling. That had been war, an impersonal conflict in which he understood the enemy's motives. Greed and lust for power, he could fathom well enough in a man. He could not hate his uncle Angus just for being what he was, or his parents for their neglect. They were his blood and he loved them despite what they had done. But for a parent to attack a defenseless girl-child? Hatred might be new to Alan, but it had a name now. *Lord Dairmid Hume.*

Tavish had told him of the man, wondering why Hume laughed in his face and threw him out that summer in Paris when he had asked for Honor's hand. Then, before the snows came, Honor had arrived in Scotland with the marriage contract in hand and her priest in tow. Perhaps Hume ran mad on occasion. Still, that did not excuse cruelty to one's own get. The man sorely needed to die. God help the wretch if he ever set foot on Scots soil again and Alan heard tell of it.

He turned his head and examined Honor's sleeping profile. A draft in the candlelight sent shadows dancing across her perfect features. God's own jest, this faultless lady was his wife.

She had been right about one thing. Tav must have been caught up in the devil's own fever to have wished her such a fate. Alan knew if he lived to be one hundred, performed all manner of charity, gave up all his sinful ways and prayed every hour on the hour, he would never deserve her. Not that he was likely to do all that. He was what he was. But even Tavish had not been good enough for Honor and had been quick to admit it.

Sadly, Alan closed his eyes and denied himself the pleasure of regarding her tranquil beauty. He would not impose himself on her, he decided firmly. Not ever. Such a gentle one as she must not be sullied by his rough touch.

He would husband her in his own way, then. With his life would he protect her. With all the wits he possessed he would try to amuse her and keep her content. He could guide her through life's trials and train up her son to be an honorable man. All this he would do and gladly, he vowed fervently to himself. "But I will not touch her wi' lust," he whispered vehemently. "I will not!"

Next he knew, it was morning. Alan woke without the usual need to assess where he was. Long months of lying on a different spot each night engendered that in a man. This day he opened his eyes to a place that must be home. Alan had felt a peace creep through his very bones the moment he set foot inside Byelough Keep. So Tavish must have felt, he thought with a twinge of the guilt that had made itself a part of him the moment he set eyes on the lady Honor.

His heart had opened and enfolded the woman and this place immediately, before he ever heard the words Tavish had written to Honor. Even had his friend not bequeathed him the right to claim both, Alan knew he would have stayed on in some capacity. Mayhaps steward, guard, or crofter. Anything. He seriously doubted he could have made himself leave had the lady ordered it so.

For a long moment, he lay there, eyes closed, savoring the warmth of the small body curled next to his. Behind his lids, pictures of her teased him, Honor angry, Honor surprised, Honor smiling as she laid his hand against her middle, so generously offering to share her joy in the child.

Her sweet scent clung to the pillows, comforting his weary soul even as the down-stuffed linen cradled his head. The cadence of her soft breathing barely broke the silence of the dawn. A man should not ask for more than this, he thought. This perfect golden moment would he keep and hold forever.

She stirred and stretched, uttering a small groan. Alan lay still, watching her beneath his lashes. In the weak light from the window, he could see little more than the outline of her form. Still he did not move when she carefully rolled to her edge of the bed and stood with some effort. Without her usual grace, one hand pressed against her back, she moved behind the screen that partially blocked his view of the bathing tub.

He counted the sounds, most of which he identified. Intimate sounds he felt no right to as yet. Sounds a husband would hear as his wife readied herself for her day. There now, the soft splash of water poured from pitcher to bowl. The squeezing of a soaked cloth into it. A louder breath, just short of a sigh. Rustling fabric as she dressed herself. Alan smiled. Here was home.

Patiently he waited, feigning sleep so as not to betray his fascination, until she emerged to locate her comb. It lay on the table near the bed. Only when she took it up and began to draw it through her long, dark tresses, did he pretend to wake.

"Good morn," he muttered. She only jumped a little. "You rise early," he commented as he sat up and ran his hand over his face, stopping at his mouth to stifle a yawn.

"There's much to be done," she said a little breathlessly. When she began to fight a stubborn snarl in her hair, he reached out and stilled her hand.

"Allow me," he said, taking the comb from her. "Come closer, then," he ordered. When she did, he took over the grooming of the silky mass, loving the way it slid through his fingers and trailed over his wrists. "Bonny hair."

"My thanks," she murmured, and drew away. She twisted the length into a coil and secured it with combs. To his disappointment, she then covered most of it with a simple linen headrail and secured that with a silver circlet.

"Will you take me to Tavish's grave now?" she asked, all formal. Her lady of the keep voice, he supposed.

"When there's light enough," he agreed. "'Tis not far."

She avoided his gaze. "I shall await you below. We will break our fast first, of course. By the time we finish, the day will be on us."

"Of course," he agreed, smiling at her. "Have someone hitch a cart."

"I shall ride," she said as she started for the door.

"Is that wise, my lady?" he asked, concerned that she

seemed to move more awkwardly than she had done the eve before.

She nodded. "If we are set upon along the way, I would rather be on a mount than dragged behind one in a chase."

"No one would dare," Alan assured her. "I will go well armed."

"All the same, sir, I shall ride!" she declared firmly and did not stay to argue the matter.

For all her soft sweetness, Alan suspected the woman he had wed possessed a strong will of her own and was not above exercising it.

Her behavior on learning of Tavish's death proved she was no weakling. He could still feel the slap on his cheek and envision her railing about angrily. But wasn't that all to the good? She had spirit, his Honor. His. Well, she was, he argued with his conscience. By law, she was his now, even if Tavish did still hold her heart.

Even that spoke well of her, that loyalty, that ability to love even past the grave. Alan longed for someone to love him that way. He even dared hope that Honor might do so, should he somehow become worthy of her. She was a treasure, that woman.

Most women faced with news of a husband's death would have taken to their beds and become inconsolable. If not for loss of their beloved, then for loss of a strong arm to protect them. That reaction might yet happen once Honor realized the full impact of Tavish's death. Mayhaps this very day.

But thank God, she had borne her grief with such strength thus far. At least her courageous forbearance, however temporary, had allowed them to get on with what must be, the business of their necessary marriage and the change of command at Byelough.

When shock wore away and Honor finally allowed the

mourning to take hold of her, Alan would be in a position to give solace. No longer would he be the stranger bearing wretched tidings of her true love's death. He would be her friend, and foster father to her child.

That assuaged his guilt over wanting her heart for himself. At least a little.

Chapter Five

"Fitting weather for this," Honor murmured as Alan lifted her to the rain-wet saddle. She centered her weight as best she could and suppressed a tired sigh. Sharing her bed with this stranger last night had done nothing to aid her ability to sleep. Now she must ride the short way to the gravesite and say her prayers over the husband who had left her. The husband who had loved her. Honor shifted forward, her back aching like a sore tooth.

Sir Alan handed up the reins, pinning her with a worried look. "We needna do this today," he reminded her. "Riding cannot be comfortable for ye even should the day be fair. Ye even excused yer priest from this."

She forced a smile. "Father Dennis is on his knees this very moment."

"Well, at least he offers prayers. That's something."

Honor shook her head. "He's shoeing his mule. He will say a mass for Tavish later today. This is a thing I must do and I thank you for coming with me. You are kind to bear with my groans. Truth told, embroidery wrings the same sounds as riding in a deluge would do. No comfort to be found anywhere, I fear. I want to go."

"'Twill soon end,'' he remarked as he swung up on his mount.

"This drizzling wet? It rarely stops, as you of all souls should know.''

"Nay, not that. I meant your…uh…'' He gestured vaguely toward her lower body.

"Condition,'' she finished for him. "Yes, I suppose it will end, though some days I do wonder.''

They sauntered out the gates and along the road through the village. Sir Alan's huge roan frisked and tugged at the bit when they reached the open expanse of the valley. Honor could see mount and master quiver with eagerness for a wild run across the moor. Their barely suppressed energy roused her envy, irritated her. The long silence wore on her nerves. She wished she could gallop away some of the dreadful unease that stifled her breathing. Her backbone felt rigid, imprisoned by muscles drawn tight as fitted bowstrings.

This knight of hers, so at home in his saddle, appeared no knight at all this morning. He had forgone his silk and mail and donned the garment she had ordered her woman to dry for him last evening. Honor wondered how he had managed to pleat the long woven fabric so deftly with no stitches to hold it. A wide leathern belt with a tarnished buckle kept it in place over his well-worn saffron shirt. Several ells of the wool, secured with a huge round silver pin, draped his left shoulder and covered most of his back. Her gaze wandered down to muscular thighs, half-bared as he straddled his mount. Boots of brown hide encased his feet and legs to the knee. He had cross-gartered them with strips of thick sinew. So strange he looked. Almost savage.

Honor marveled at his donning of a purse. Attached to the wide belt by copper chains, the pouch hung to one side now, but had rested directly over his netherparts when he stood. Altogether, he presented a primitive picture. A high-land savage, Father would have called him, a terrifying animal feared by all and sundry.

She hoped to God Sir Alan could live up to that image. They both might have need of that fearsome wildness one day. The broadsword slung from his saddle offered reassurance.

Honor rode on, enduring the discomfort, impatient to be done with this necessary farewell yet determined to carry it out. They traversed an almost nonexistent path betwixt the barren hills leading out of her valley and into the next.

"Ye're angry," Alan finally stated in a flat voice.

Stunned, Honor issued a short huff of denial.

"Aye, ye are. I know why. Tav left ye, didn't he? Left ye alone when ye've need of him. 'Tis natural to feel so. I felt it myself right after he died."

When she did not answer, he turned to rake her with those knowing green eyes. "'Twill pass." He returned his gaze toward their destination and nodded toward the burn. "He lies just there."

Honor watched Alan dismount when they neared the stream and allowed him to assist her off the palfrey. She stumbled once and felt the strength of his arm grasp her shoulders to right her. Neither said another word until they stood staring down at the poorly etched stone marking Tav's grave.

Then Alan moved away several strides, bent down and gathered two stones. He walked back and handed one of them to her. She watched him close his eyes and kneel to place the rock next to the large one with the device chipped into it.

The crude rendering of the wolf's head touched her somehow. Sir Alan could not make the letters to identify his friend. Neither could he make the design, but he had tried. "Tavish would laugh," she whispered, voicing the thought. "He...he would have laughed.... Damn him! Damn!" She choked on sudden tears and threw the stone at the grave. At Tavish.

"I know," Alan breathed against her ear. "Ah, Honor, I grieve for ye. I grieve for him. And for th' child never knowin' his da. I tried to make Tav live. I tried!"

She pummeled his chest with her fists as she had done before. Great sobs shook her body as he drew her closer and held her. Soft Gaelic phrases soothed her, as comforting to her as they were meaningless.

If this man only knew her heart, she thought with a deep shudder. He would shove her from him in disgust. Guilt racked her anew for the way she had used poor Tavish. The man had loved her, truly loved her, and she had encouraged that so shamelessly. She had tricked him into marriage, a marriage that probably was not even legal if anyone troubled to examine it. And her father *would* trouble to do just that if he ever found her. Tavish's child might bear the shame of bastardy because of her foolishness. Because of her cursed fear.

Honor pushed away and dropped to her knees beside the cairn. "Forgive me," she whispered repeatedly, a litany as futile as prayers for her soul. Her womb squeezed painfully as though the child sought retribution for the father. She gasped and leaned against the large stone, grasping it, feeling the cold, rough wetness against her cheek.

Strong hands tried to lift her but she moaned a plea for solitude. She deserved it, the soul-wringing misery. The grip on her shoulders lessened, but the warmth of his palms seeped right through her woolen cloak. She wept the tears of the damned and welcomed the keen knifing that twisted through her midsection. Her due. Her lot.

Something warm and liquid gushed from her, jerking

her out of her self-absorbed guilt. "Nooo," she moaned. Honor curled forward and surrounded the unborn babe with her hands. Another hand joined hers, exploring the tightness of her belly.

"Nay! 'Tis too soon!" he declared.

"Too late," she groaned through her teeth, fresh grief already immobilizing her. "Oh God help me, too late." She felt all the reason she had left slip away as she embraced the agony.

Alan hefted her into his arms, wincing at the pain in his damaged shoulder as he carried her to the waiting mounts. He lifted her up and swung up behind her before she could slide from the saddle. Lord, what was he to do now? Could she make it back to the keep? A good hour's ride if he kept a pace that wouldn't bounce her about.

He recalled passing a scorched bothy a half league back, but it would offer scant protection. A rough-made shepherd's dwelling was certainly no place to pass a gentlewoman's first confinement.

Jesu, his hands were shaking. He knew precious little of babes to begin with. He had taken lambs from the ewes, a troubling colt from its dam once, seen pups aborning. Was it the same? "Nay, nothing like that," he mumbled to himself. He knew it was not the same at all. Human females needed more help, a great deal more than he knew how to give.

She stiffened in his arms and moaned again. The sound wrenched his heart. He dared not tell her how inept he was or he would scare her to death. With a deep breath to shore up his courage, he tried to foster hers. "Dinna fash, Honor. I may know naught of 'em inside th' womb or after they come inta th' world, but I can bring a babe. Dinna fear, sweeting, for that I can do." *Please, God.*

Alan set the beast to a slow walk toward the heap of

scorched stone and wattle. He asked more of heaven during that half league's ride than he had done in all his twenty-six years.

Vines surrounded the crude hut, making it all but invisible. Alan blessed his keen eyes and thanked God he had noticed the place, such as it was. The low walls were scorched, but someone had piled leafy branches over the burned out section of the roof to ward out rain.

He slid off the mount and reached up for Honor. She had bent nearly double and maintained the position for the whole of the trip. Aside from an occasional catching of her breath, she had hardly voiced her misery. Braw in the face of her pain, he thought proudly. A woman of courage, his Honor. Her body felt rigid in his arms as he carried her to the humble bothy.

He bent his head and shoulders to fit through the low doorway. The rasp of metal jerked his attention to the far corner of the one-room hovel as he straightened. His eyes adjusted quickly to the darkness. A thin form reclined on the packed earth floor in one corner, its scrawny arms holding aloft what appeared to be a short sword.

"Put that blade down and help me here," Alan ordered, "else I'll take the damned thing and spit you where you lie."

The ragged apparition did not move.

Alan spoke in Gaelic. "My lady's time has come on us unaware. Get you to Byelough Keep and bring a woman to help."

"Nay," came the answer. "I canna."

"Do it or die," Alan ordered quietly.

"My leg's broke," the raspy voice declared. "Put her down there." The tip of the sword waved toward the darkened fire hole and a lumpy nest of furs beside it. From the look of the bedding, the old one had just scrambled out of it. He hoped the fleas went, too.

Alan knelt and laid Honor on her side. "There, sweeting. I'll have a fire going afore ye know it."

"No fire!" the ancient voice squeaked. "The soldiers!"

"Th' war's done," Alan announced quietly as he straightened the bedding and reached in his sporran for flint. He made a quick search and located a stack of peat. As he set about coaxing a blaze, he continued to reassure their host or hostess. "Rob Bruce has set the English running south. There's naught to fear hereabouts. I am Sir Alan of Strode, Lord of Byelough. I'd have your help if you know aught of birthing."

The clink of metal against stone told him the sword had been laid aside for the moment.

"I know much of it but I canna move m' leg to aid ye. Broke it just this morn when I fell from th' roof."

Alan fashioned a small torch from a broken stool's leg and stuck it upright in the dirt floor. Honor lay quietly, panting and holding her middle. Her face looked pinched and colorless but she seemed to be between pains at the moment. He brushed a hand over her shoulder and gave her a soft pat. Then he duckwalked the few ells to the pallet in the corner.

The figure reached for the weapon and Alan scoffed. "Leave off, will ye? I'll tend yer leg. I've set bones aplenty."

At closer range he could see the figure was an old woman, frizzled gray hair all awry, rheumy eyes wild as a woods creature's. He smiled to put her at ease. "Have ye a name, then, lassie?"

The crone cackled at the address. "Aye. I be Old May."

"Fair as a day in May," Alan sang in a low, suggestive voice as he examined the spindly limb he had uncovered.

A simple break with no bones showing, he thought with relief. His hands fit completely around the appendage, grasping at either side of the break and neatly fitting the bone back together. The old dame screeched once and then settled into a regular breathing of grunts.

"I've done. Don't ye move till I get it bound." He found a few old rags for binding and used the broken seat of the stool for a brace. "There now. Ye owe me, May. What must we do for my lady there?"

"Two knives," May declared. "Here, this'll do fer one." She offered the rusted sword. "Lay it under the furs."

Alan lowered his brows and recoiled from the ruined weapon.

"T' cut th' pain!" May instructed. "Now, have ye another?"

Alan pulled his *sgian dubh* from his boot and held it up. Light reflected off the perfect blade. He looked at the woman.

"Fer th' cord, lad. Ye must cut th' cord."

"Th' noo? How?" Alan squeaked, his voice breaking much as it had when he was a lad.

"Nay, ye cork-brain, after the babe comes. Fer th' noo, we wait. There's herbs fer possets and a bit o' brew for us when all's done. There be some water in th' pail, but ye mun be fetchin' more from th' burn. Get to it."

"I canna leave her," Alan said, holding his voice steady now. Steady and determined. "I will not."

The crone sighed and flapped a hand. "Drag me over by her and I'll stand watch for ye. No hurry, though. I expect she'll do nothin' much in the next wee while."

Alan did as Old May demanded. When he returned, the sound emanating from the pallet of furs made him drop to his knees and scramble forward. "Honor? Honor, don't ye die on me, lass," he ordered brusquely.

"She isna dying, ye great toad! Get some water in that pot and heat it for her soothin' drink."

Alan leapt to do her bidding, amazed that taking orders in a terrifying situation came so much easier than giving them. For the first time, he understood the blind obedience of the men he had led into battle. This was a battle of sorts, he reasoned, one for which he had no training. Best let the old wart take charge. "Well?" he asked, awaiting his next task.

"Ye sit by yer lass and wait it out. Shouldna be long by my reckoning. Ye'll have ta pull the bairn yerself, lad, for I've no' th' strength."

"Pull it?" Alan croaked.

The woman had the gall to laugh. "Catch it, then. It should come out by itself, small as it be."

He breathed a heavy sigh of relief. It must be like lambing after all. "Aye, I ken."

After what seemed hours of travail, Honor roused herself to speak finally. "I beg you bring Father Dennis."

"Nay!" Alan denied her with a harsh frown and harsher words. "Ye'll not be gettin' rites this day, woman. If ye're not shriven, ye can't die. Hear me? Ye can't die or ye'll burn in hell, aye?"

He noted her spark of anger. Her grip on his hand grew tight. Good, ire made her stronger. He feared she'd given up the good fight. "Ye can do this, Honor," he encouraged softly, "I know ye can. Ye need no priest."

"For the babe," she whispered, weakening her hold again. "Rites for the babe, sir. It will not live."

"Aye, it will so!" he thundered. "It will live and grow strong!"

She tensed again and the pain encompassed him as well

as he watched. Her low wail broke the silence. The sound prickled the skin on the back of his neck.

The old woman grunted and brushed Honor's mounded middle with one gnarled hand. Then she raked up the woolen kirtle to beneath Honor's breasts and began barking orders like the veriest commander. Alan hastened to obey like the lowliest soldier on the field.

In a matter of moments, he held a slick, wriggling handful of mewling life. "Ahh, Honor, look what ye've done here. Look!" He placed the baby on her breasts. "A lass. A wondrous wee lassie!" He felt tears streaking down his face and a fullness in his heart that threatened to unman him completely.

"Leave it there," May instructed. "Get ready fer the rest."

"Rest?" Alan hoped to God that meant surcease from this travail and not something further that he must deal with.

"Afterbirth," she said succinctly.

Resigned, Alan abandoned his admiration of Honor's tiny daughter and followed instructions to the letter. He waited for what remained inside her to expel itself and then carefully tied and sliced the cord where the old woman told him to.

Old May had scoffed when he'd washed his hands and knife in the hot water left over from the posset. A waste of time, she vowed, but Alan had sorely needed something to do whilst awaiting the birth. Evidenced by her surroundings at Byelough, he knew Honor liked everything clean. If he could but please her in that small way, he meant to do it. Following through with that thought, he now cut a spotless section of her chemise away, wet it, and dabbed the birth fluids off the babe.

For convenience, Alan slipped the child into the front

of his shirt so that it rested against his stomach's warmth, cradled slinglike against his body over the belting of his plaid. The babe stilled her flailing, but he could feel the soft squirming against his flesh that told him the wee one thrived.

Then he turned again to Honor. Her long lashes concealed the pain in the dove gray eyes. Eyes he had come to cherish in so short a time. "How proud I am of ye, my lady. Ye did fine. So fine." He brushed the tangled hair off her forehead and laid a soft kiss there.

He had kissed her in Tav's stead, Alan told himself. His poor dead friend would have wanted it so, would have wanted Honor comforted and praised for the birth of so fair a daughter. But in his heart he knew. That sweet taste of Honor on his lips had naught to do with Tavish or what his lady had just borne. The reason lay in who she was, what she was. The woman he adored beyond all reason.

Her breath warmed his neck as the soft words registered, "Take her to Father Dennis. She must be named and blessed."

"She is blessed already with you for a mother," he assured her. "Believe it, this wee'un is in no danger, strong as she be. Do not think she will die. I wouldna let her."

Honor's eyes opened as she whispered, "Father Dennis would be shocked, sir. That is blasphemy." He thought he detected the ghost of a smile in her words.

Alan grinned and tapped her chin with one finger. "Weel, wha' more would th' guid mon ken out of a theivin', murderin', fornicatin' highlander?"

She did smile then and he saw the hope in her eyes he had worked to put there.

"Rest ye now, lass. Ye've done a good day's work this morn. The bairn breathes steady and wriggles like a fish on a hook. Listen to her mew.'' He caressed the small lump curled between his shirt and belly.

"Christiana," Honor murmured softly. "Her name."

"Aha, so *Kit* it is, then! Wee Kit.'' He soothed the babe with gentle strokes across its tiny back while he watched Honor give way to sleep.

He had a family now. Never had he thought to take a wife, have a child, or a home for that matter. His older brother, whom he could hardly remember, manned the family estate in Gloucester. Their father had sent Nigel there as a lad of fifteen to learn management of it all. Then their mother had taken her youngest—Alan, himself—to her brother, Angus, in the Highlands. Instead of making Alan the heir as his father had hoped, Uncle Angus had tormented his half-English nephew and worked him within an inch of his life.

The harsh task of survival had been the making of him, Alan supposed. He had come far since leaving his uncle. He had served as a tracker and a pikeman with Alexander Bruce on two campaigns. When all the bands met near Stirling to fight the English, Robert Bruce had hand-picked several likely soldiers to train the local rabble to fight.

Alan had liked command. His "small men" had made a huge difference at Bannockburn. He led well and knew it. He also knew that event had given Bruce the impetus to knight him. That and the fact that he was to wed the Lady Honor.

A knighthood was nothing to take lightly, Alan reminded himself. No longer was he a rough-and-ready soldier, a footloose fighter with naught on his mind but the task at hand and the ale that followed. He must be worthy of his title. He must hold fast to the knightly code and all that entailed. Lusting after so grand a lady as Honor made mock of the trust Bruce had placed in him.

Sweet, gentle Honor. She looked an angel lying there so spent after her travail. He must always treat her as the virtuous paragon she was, Alan decided. It was no more than she deserved.

Chapter Six

If Sir Alan were too good to be true, he had yet to give evidence of it. In the three weeks following the birth, he remained the same patient, good-humored knight, kind to all.

Honor peeked through her lashes, pretending sleep, as she watched the sunlit scene by the window. Her husband cradled her child lengthwise on his lap, one huge hand cupping her head and the other supporting her backside. The babe issued small sucking noises, eliciting a tender smile from her temporary caretaker. The silly sounds he made in reply were just shy of real words.

And as to real words, her husband had begun speaking too carefully when he did talk to her. Though he had not yet rid himself of the highland lilt in his voice, he sounded so…well, formal now. Trying to be courtly, no doubt, but it did not suit him. Though she had taunted him about the roughness of his manner, it was that which had fascinated her. She wanted his fierceness, depended on it. And she had loved his rowdy humor.

Honor missed his bluster, his casual teasing and the roll of his *r*s. This new manner of his brought to mind the changes in her father when she was very young. When displeased with her, he had also adopted that precise and stilted sort of speech. It frightened Honor to hear it out of Alan's mouth, whatever his reasons for it.

For three long weeks it had been thus. Had she done something to warrant this treatment? He did not ignore her exactly, but he never sought her company, either.

However, Christiana drew him like a lodestone. Why did he dote so on an infant not even his own? She supposed he might feel a proprietary interest since he had been present at the birth. And there was his longstanding friendship with Tavish. Still, no man she knew would spend hours of his time this way.

Honor turned her head to the opposite side of the room to avoid seeing the two together. She felt an odd sting of jealousy. Trouble was, she could not tell for certain whether she begrudged her child the man's attention, or the other way round.

She had liked it when he hovered over her those first few days after Christiana's birth, arranging the covers, ordering the women to tend her and praising her courage. Then, as she began to spend more time out of bed than in, he had subtly absented himself. Only for the hour while she rested and he spent with the child did he come to her chamber.

Not once had he insisted they share the bed since she had delivered of the babe. "Wee Kit," he called the child. Or "our wee'un." His fascination with the infant seemed unnatural to Honor, given her own experience of men.

"Bring her to me," Honor said. She had meant to say it softly, but the demand was there. When she turned her head back to them, Sir Alan stood beside the bed and waited until she propped herself up to lay the child in her arms.

"There now," he whispered. "I'll be leavin' ye to yer meal, wee'un."

"Stay!" Honor said before she thought. Confused by her own request, she floundered for a reason. "It is not time for her to feed yet, and I...I would speak with you."

He raised one thick brow and frowned down at her. "Is aught amiss, my lady?"

"No! Nothing. Could you...would you bring me a cup of milk? There is some just there."

"It is left from this morn. I will send Mistress Nan for fresh."

"No!" Honor shifted Kit in her arms and sighed. "Sir...Alan, have I done some thing, said some thing, to anger you?"

"Of course not! What makes you ask?" He settled himself on the edge of the bed and crossed his hands over one plaid-draped knee. "Do I seem angry to you, then?"

"Not really," she admitted, "but you seldom sit and talk these days. Have you so many tasks that prevent you?"

He rotated his shoulders and leaned back his head, showing a length of strongly muscled neck. "Well, the men and I have hunted each morn. There is meat enough to last the winter months. We've seen the other stores put by as well. Mistress Nan must have told you all that. I have counted candles, shored up the weak spot in the north wall, and—"

"You make time for Christiana," Honor said, trying hard to sound appreciative instead of petulant. She wondered what it would take to have him back the way he was before. He seemed easy enough in manner, but did not sound himself at all. "You like the babe, do you not?"

"Oh, aye," he replied with a grin. "She's a bonny one! I think she must be like you when you were small, though she does have Tav's chin. Willful as he, too, I would wager.''

"Willful? Tavish?'' Honor almost scoffed before she thought about it. "I saw none of that in him!''

Alan's outright laugh made her jump. When he had calmed to a chuckle, he said, "I doubt me he would have cause to show you that side of himself. I'd bet my last groat he never crossed you once.'' Then the tenderness he had expressed toward the child returned, this time directed at her. "And why should he? Tav loved you beyond all things and would have denied you nothing.''

She ducked her head and bit her lip. Guilt held her silent for a long while. Why couldn't she have loved Tavish as she told him she did? Was there some lack inside her which held her from it? He had been a good man—the best. Had she not thought so when they first met? Had she not wished with all her heart she could wed him instead of the miscreant her father had promised her to?

Honor had wanted that so badly, she had done awful things to make it happen. She had played on Father Dennis's sympathy and then lied to Tavish just to save her wretched life. Now she felt guilty, manipulative and downright sinful to have done such things as she had.

In her heart, Honor knew she would never have survived marriage to the man her father had chosen for her. Such a life would have, at best, proved a continuance of what she had endured at her father's hand. She would have had to share the marriage bed as well, and she could not have borne lying with a murderer. With this blasted temper of hers, Trouville would have killed her, too. Then why this terrible guilt?

"Honor?'' Alan said, dragging her back to the present. "You must try to put the grief aside now. Tavish would not wish you to suffer so.'' He touched one finger to her chin and lifted it. "See how your wee lass tugs at you? She wants a happy mam. Come, smile for us?"

Before she could refuse or comply, a frantic knocking interrupted. Nan shouted, "Sir Alan! Sir Alan, come quickly! There's trouble at the gates! Hurry!"

Honor laid the baby down in the middle of the bed and tried to rise. Alan stopped her with a hand on her shoulder. "Stay here and tend wee Kit. I'll see to it."

"I am coming, too!" She shoved his hand away and shouted, "Nan? Come here and mind the babe." With that, Honor slid her legs off the bed and found her slippers. Pulling her heaviest bedgown close around her, she made for the door.

"Honor, halt!" He planted himself in front of her, his voice harsh with warning. "Get ye back to th' bed! I'll not have ye catch yer death wandering cross the bailey."

"This is my keep, sir, and I shall wander where I will! Stand away!"

His mouth tightened. Then he shook his head and threw up one hand in defeat. "Aye, well. Bundle yerself up, then." He tugged at her robe until it covered her to the chin. "Mind ye dinna overdo it, aye?"

"Aye!" She snapped. At least he was the old Alan again and not that polite stranger he pretended to be. She swept past him through the door and into the busy hall. Father Dennis rushed in to block their exit. "My lady, he has come!"

"My father?" she moaned. "Ah, no!"

"No, lady, it is—"

"Trouville? Oh, God help us!"

"Not him, either. 'Tis yer neighbor, the same man who came last month. He demands you speak with him!" The priest's eyes sought Sir Alan's for reassurance. "He wants our lady, sir. Last time he came, he meant to take her and

Byelough as well. He must have known Lord Tavish was dead at the time, though we did not. How would he have known that?''

Honor looked to Alan for an answer. ''Could he have seen Tavish fall?'' she asked. ''Could this man have been at Bannockburn?''

''Aye, 'tis possible,'' Alan admitted. ''Most everyone was. I'll go and ask him.'' With that, he set a path out of the hall, down the steps and across the bailey to the wall.

When Alan reached the wall-walk, Honor halted at the bottom of the rough wooden steps and looked up. He stood between the stone merlons, fists braced on the embrasure, looking every inch a laird, master and defender of all he could see. In that one moment, Honor knew that Tavish Ellerby had done her the ultimate favor in choosing this protector for her and their child. She rushed up to join the man whom she felt certain would keep them safe. ''Alan, you must—''

''Hist, and stay doon, lass,'' he muttered, and emphasized it with a heavy hand on her shoulder.

Thank God her rough highlandman was here without his new and courtly ways. Especially now. She backed against one of the merlons next to him and cautiously peered around it.

''It is him! You must kill him, sir. You must!''

He ignored her, shouting down an order, ''Remove that helm. I'd no' speak wi' some lowlie cowart. Where be yer colors, mon?''

''Give the orders!'' Honor demanded. ''Have the bowmen shoot!''

Alan extended his arm, his hand palm down, toward the men stationed and prepared to loose arrows. He spoke to the party waiting below. ''Who be ye and what's yer business here?''

A low voice full of laughter boomed up to the parapet, "Ian McAfee ab Shorn ab Nichols ab Gray. Don't ye know me, Alan?"

"Ian!" Alan shouted with what sounded like pure glee. "Cousin?" He threw up a hand an slapped the stone. "By God, what do ye here, ye rascally bletherskate?"

"Come to take a wife! Ellerby's dead and I wager she's need of a mon!"

"Nae more, auld son. I've th' pleasure myself," Alan said, still laughing. "But ye're welcome to come drink to our guid fortune."

"Have you run mad?" Honor questioned, horrified that he would invite the blackguard inside the very gates. "*Kill* him!"

Alan looked down at her and patted her head. "Hush now, sweeting. Ian's verra nearly kin on my mother's side. He's no threat to ye."

She grasped his hand and squeezed. "Alan, if you bear me any goodwill at all, at least make him leave. He came here with intent to take Byelough and it is not the first time. Listen to me!" She tried to stop him when he turned to speak to the man again. "Please!"

With an exasperated sigh, Alan shook his head. "Ye're overset, hinny, and canna be thinkin' straight. Ian Gray only meant to do for ye just what I have done. He fought with us and saw yer husband fall in battle. What kind o' neighbor would he be to let ye fend for yerself, eh? Calmly now, get ye down to the hall and make ready for our first guest."

Honor jerked her hand from his. She ran down the steps, across the bailey, and up the stairs to the hall. Dashing right past Nan, she rushed to her solar and bolted the heavy door.

She dragged Christiana's cradle into a corner and stationed herself in front of it. She guarded it and herself with the only weapon she could find, the broken sword Alan told her he had used to carve on Tavish's stone.

And she waited, furious, determined to defend herself and the babe, since no one else seemed inclined to do so. After what seemed hours, they came.

"My lady?" Alan's voice boomed out on the opposite side of the oaken door. "Will you come and order us a hasty repast? The rest of the folk seem glued to the floor wi' fright!"

Muted laughter grated on her ears, that of her gullible husband and the pillager Ian Gray.

Honor gripped the sword with both hands and made ready. Any time now Gray would take advantage of Alan's trust and overpower him. God only knew what treachery that one planned. All her life she had heard tales of these border ruffians and their vile deeds. They were worse than the highlandmen, her father had said.

"Come, come, Honor," Alan cajoled. "Have mercy. We hunger here."

"And thirst!" Gray added, still laughing.

"Be gone, the both of you," Honor yelled. "Drink yourselves full outside the gates."

"Och, what a sharp-tongued wench she be!" Gray declared. "I wish ye joy of her, Alan. 'Tis glad I am *my* attempt to wed her failed!"

Honor fumed. *Sharp-tongued,* indeed! She would show the dog a sharpness if only she had a decent blade.

She strained to hear Alan's reply, but the voices drifted away from the door and were lost in the sudden hum of activity in the hall.

Time crawled by. Her shoulders and arms ached from holding the broken sword aloft. Gradually, she forced herself to relax. Surely if they had not breached the door by now, they would not trouble her further. When the babe cried, Honor reluctantly abandoned her weapon and set about the feeding.

Somehow she must gain control of that mule-headed knight she had married. She could do it. She knew how to charm. Bending him to her will was surely the only means left to her. She had to use all the weapons available to hold her own. Next time she gave him an order, he must follow it without question. Suppose it had been the comte de Trouville at their gates. Alan would be dead now and she, on her way to France if not dead as well.

All the while Christiana tugged at her breast, Honor formed a plan of seduction. 'Twas too soon for such, she knew, but her new husband left her small choice. He must be brought to heel so that incidents such as this did not occur again. Alan must be made to pay heed to her when she needed an enemy vanquished.

Safety lay in his sword arm and in his ability to rally her people. He might train them to fight if only she could persuade him to do it. Yes, persuasion would be needed here.

This evening, once he had sent Ian Gray on his way and locked the gates behind him, she would proceed.

Her hour candle burned down two marks as she bathed and dressed herself. She anticipated Alan's ousting of their erstwhile guest so she could get on with her plans.

Then Honor heard a single set of footsteps approach the door. "Honor?" Alan called urgently. "Open up now. I would speak with you."

"Are you alone?" she asked.

"Aye, and we must talk. 'Tis important." He rattled the latch.

Honor slid off the bed and went to unbar the door. When it opened, Alan slipped inside, went straight to Christiana's cradle and lifted her out. He turned to Honor. "Come with me. We're to have the christening!" he declared.

"Now? Why?" Shocked at the firmness of his tone and the sense of purpose in his movements, Honor moved to bar his way. "But we set it for Sunday next!"

"Change of plan. Come along now and mind you hold your tongue. I know what I'm about here."

"Just a moment! You will tell me what prompted this or I'll not move from this spot, nor let you take her."

Alan shifted the babe to the crook of one arm and grasped Honor's elbow with the other. "Father Dennis is to christen Kit, and Ian Gray will stand godfather. Dinna worry for her safety. His men are locked outside the gates, and Ian came in unarmed." He rushed on, giving Honor no chance to object. "I asked Mistress Nanette to serve as godmother as she ranks highest save yerself. Good thing you were churched and can attend, for Ian should know you were there and approved the choice. We had best see this done. Hurry now."

Honor sputtered. "A-approved the choice? Ha! That man will never lay eyes on—"

"Aye, he will that and more. Best done whilst he's in his cups, too," Alan said, explaining hurriedly. "If he is bound to Kit's family by a tie such as this, he'll owe us his loyalty. Come an attack or other troubles, Ian will be obliged to come to our aid."

Alan tilted his head and regarded her with a half grin. "Also, he canna hope to wed Kit's mother and get these lands, even should I someday expire from an arrow to the back or suchlike."

"God forbid!" Honor quickly crossed herself at the thought. "What is to keep him from it?"

"Laws of affinity. He'll then be related to you by this canny act."

"I thought he was already related to *you!*" Honor said angrily. She had no desire to see the dolt again, much less become a relative of his, by *affinity* or any other thing.

"My mother's cousin wed one of his, I believe. Not close enough to shame him away from his plans, however. But this should do it."

"And what makes you think he will honor this ceremony and give up his schemes?" Honor asked reasonably, still balking at the idea.

"I know Ian. He might not quail at a quiet murder, but incest he will avoid. As yer daughter's godfather, to wed ye would clearly be such. The penalty for that's too great. Bruce would seize his lands. 'Tis the law. Aye?"

Honor sighed and nodded, finding no reason to argue further. She allowed him to lead her out into the hall. As he had indicated, preparations had been made. Father Dennis stood ready and a drunken Ian Gray swayed unsteadily beside him.

She noted the man's appearance more carefully than she had been able to the first time he came to Byelough. Gray stood nigh as tall as Alan, though not as broad of shoulder. He boasted no armor save the sweat-stained leathern jack of a common soldier. He wore that over a well fitted red woolen tunic edged with embroidered blue flowers. Honor supposed that garment his one attempt at looking anything better than one of his rabble. His breeks appeared torn and muddied, and his boots were scuffed.

Ian Gray's features were as rugged as his clothing, the exception there being an absolutely classic nose. Drink had slackened his mouth and clouded his eyes. His hair hung long and dark about his shoulders, small braids confining that which would have covered his ears. For all that, he was not an ugly man. Quite the contrary, some might find him quite appealing. As for Honor, she hoped never to see him again after this.

A makeshift font had been erected, actually a table upon which a small metal basin rested.

Alan went directly to Gray and deposited Christiana in his arms. Honor held her breath, terrified he would drop her. All the while Alan chattered to the man about some encounter with the English, obviously continuing a former conversation as though it had never been interrupted.

Their visitor clutched the squirming bundle handed him and looked back and forth between Alan and the babe. He appeared quite confused and not a little cross-eyed from drink.

At some signal from Alan, Father Dennis began reading the ceremony in Latin, softly, hurriedly and without a pause between words. At the appropriate time, he turned and took Christiana from the ale-flown godfather and poured water over her head. He said some few things to Nanette, then turned and asked Gray a question in Latin.

"Say 'aye,'" Alan suggested offhandedly. "Just say it, Ian, and they'll give us another cup. 'Tis good ale, aye?"

A loud *aye* and a belch greeted the fascinated assembly.

"Let us pray!" Father Dennis intoned.

Honor struggled to hold in her laughter. She knew there was nothing funny about having this man responsible for her daughter's religious upbringing, but she knew in her heart Alan would never allow him any say in that. She had to admit, Alan's trick would serve nicely if Ian Gray did not cry foul once he sobered.

Gray scribbled his *X* on the papers when Alan told him to. Then he promptly sank to the rushes as though he had been struck down.

Honor took Christiana from Nanette and retreated to the solar, wishing the man to perdition. She had an uneasy feeling they had not seen the last of Ian Gray.

Chapter Seven

Later that evening, Nanette knocked on the door of the solar which Honor had kept bolted. "My lady? The guest has gone. Sir Alan wishes you to join him in the hall."

"A great good eve to you, my lady!" Alan greeted her, raising his cup. "We hauled Ian out to his men and he is away home. I made him a good gift in appreciation of his service to us and our new kinship. A silver flagon, compliments of a dead Englishmon. He was well content. Gray, that is. I misdoubt the Englishmon was!" Alan laughed.

"You probably convinced the fellow he'd be better off dead and he likely thanked you for it in the end," Honor said dryly.

He chuckled again, took a quick sip of ale and lifted his cup in salute. "Now I think on it, he did look somewhat peace stricken. Cannot be easy, being English, anyhow."

How in the name of heaven could she manage a man whose sole aim was to please everyone, even enemies?

Then a smile crept across her face. Surely she could turn that to her advantage, make pleasing her his ultimate goal. His drink-slowed wits could be gathered up and redirected if she put her mind to it. Honor wanted him to act as the weapon she would wield when her most dangerous threat arrived. He must respond with deadly force and right quickly when she demanded it of him.

With a final pat to the braids she had enclosed in her gold-threaded caul, Honor smoothed the soft blue samite of her cotta over her flat abdomen. The chased-silver belt hung in a perfect Y over her hips, its extension swaying gently when she moved. Having her shape returned to slenderness pleased her. Hopefully, it would please Sir Alan as well.

She drew in a deep, steadying breath and joined him at table for what she hoped would be a pleasant confrontation.

"Go and take the babe to sleep with you, Nan," she ordered. With all the excitement, Honor had lost track of how much time had passed since last feeding, but the babe seemed content in her sleep. "Bring her to me later, but only if she hungers. Mayhaps she will sleep the night."

Her husband lounged on the dais in his usual high-backed chair, relaxed by what must have been numerous cups of ale. Honor took her place beside him.

"Good sir, you demanded my presence? I am here." The sweet smile she had practiced in her mirror felt strained, but she held it in place.

"Demanded?" he asked with a lift of his brows. "Nay, I'd never make demands on you, sweet one. I only wished you to come out and see that my cousin did not lay waste to the place afore he departed."

So he played courtly again, did he? Honor resolved to shake him out of that right soon. Today's events taught her that anything disrupting his concentration made short work of his labored politeness.

"Sir Ian has left us in peace for now?" she asked, keeping her tone light.

"Aye, and will in future. He's not really a bad sort, but it pays to be cautious. He fought at Bannockburn, was witness to Tav's wounding and supposed him dead of it. Few survive such. He meant well enough to give you his protection, but there was likely a bit of greed in his heart as well. No reason to kill a man for that, however." Alan smiled at his generous assessment of the situation.

Honor decided he was not drunk, or even close to it, only feeling relaxed, smug and a bit righteous.

She carefully smoothed out the frown she felt forming. "That devil ordered me to present myself when he arrived the last time. He said he had come to take the Byelough and its mistress for his own. That is no way to charm a lady, I can tell you."

"Aye, but he left when ye pelted him with arrows, did he not?" Alan asked, and then continued without waiting for an answer. "I willingly admit Ian's a mite lacking in the finer points of courtship, but he meant well enough. He only attempted what I have accomplished, Honor. My only advantage was Tav's recommendation. And the Bruce's confirmation of it, of course," he added with a wry twist of his lips. "But I don't doubt me Ian would replace me here if he could. After this day's doings, he'll serve your cause right enough if necessary, but *only* as a friend and kinsman."

Honor pressed her palms together and sighed deeply as she raised her eyes to meet his. "Then for your clever plan to protect me, I must thank you, sir. And I do."

She moved closer and laid her free hand over his where it rested on the table. A sudden warmth in her neck and cheeks told her of her blush. She had not planned that, but it would serve her cause quite well, she hoped. Becoming flustered by Alan's nearness had not figured in her scheme, but she could use that since she could not prevent it.

"He frightened me," she uttered in a small voice, attempting to sound weak. Men liked weak women, did they not?

He covered her hand and squeezed. "Ah, sweeting, there's naught to fear now, I promise you." Bright green eyes searched hers, and then his gaze traveled down her neck to her chest. It lingered there for what seemed an eternity before returning to her face. Honor breathed in deeply to show herself to best advantage should he look again. He did.

He shifted in his chair, apparently no longer comfortable. Honor imagined the effect she had on his body and quickly enhanced it by tracing her lips with the tip of her tongue. A practiced move it was, and rewarding.

Alan shifted again and leaned closer so that his mouth stopped only a hand's width from her own. Would he kiss her here in front of everyone? So intent was his regard and her reaction, that for a moment, Honor could not absorb the whispered words he formed.

And then they registered. "Best see to yer bodice, sweeting, and to wee Kit, I'm thinking."

Honor glanced down and gasped, mortified. Circles of wetness outlined her nipples, marring the costly fabric of her second best cotta. *Milk.* With a groan of embarrassment, she snatched her hand from his and fled his presence.

Tears streaked her face in hot rivulets as she rushed to Nan's chamber, a curtained, cavelike recess cut into the thickness of the keep's wall. With an angry sniff, she took the child from her maid and stalked back to her solar without a word.

So much for seduction, she thought angrily. She plopped down on the stool before the fire hole, loosening her cotta and pulling at the ties of her undergown. "Here, then," she said as she settled Christiana in the crook of her arm.

"Give thanks while you are about this that I eschewed a wetnurse, piglet. I am having second thoughts."

Round blue eyes blinked up at her, stirring guilt over her outburst of temper. Honor wanted to weep again, so deep was her frustration. "All right, little one, I am sorry. But how am I to enthrall the man when I leak like a faulty bucket, eh? What do you suggest?"

The baby grunted as though in answer.

Honor laughed, both at the babe and at her plan gone awry. "Later, then. Mam will charm him later. For now, take what you will and sleep again. I do not relish jiggling you about until the wee hours just for entertainment."

The feeding lasted longer than usual and Honor wished she had settled on the bed to do it. Just as she laid the babe across her knees to bring up the wind, Alan entered.

"May I?" he asked, even as he scooped Christiana up from Honor's lap and put her against his shoulder. A loud bubble erupted almost immediately. "Aha! She speaks Gaelic! Such a winsome child," he announced, laughing merrily. His lips brushed the babe's fuzzy head and he drew in a deep breath. "And muckle sweet, eh?"

Honor watched him sway side to side until Christiana's eyes closed. Then he sighed with contentment and laid the babe in the cradle as though reluctant to give up the pleasure of holding her. Unnatural, Honor thought. Surely fathers—especially foster fathers—did not behave so.

"She is not even your own," Honor said before she thought.

Alan's head jerked around and his look held surprise. "Of course she's my own! Whose would she be if not mine? Tav willed you to me, and she is part of you. Do you deny me rights to love her, given I did not sire her with my body?" The sad disappointment in his words and on his face tugged at her heart.

"I would deny you nothing, sir," she whispered fervently. "Nothing in this world."

Honor realized that her declaration had come, not from a calculated effort to seduce—for there had been no forethought attached to it—but from deep inside her where she had buried her hopes of ever loving fully.

The dangerous lapse frightened her. She could not allow herself to wax soft over her husband's kindness. Lord, he was kind to everyone he had met since coming here. Even Ian Gray. Kindness might be well and good for some, but not in a knight she expected to help ward off her enemies. She turned away from him and stared out the window into the starless night.

She felt him draw near as though heat pulsed in waves off his huge frame. Strong hands cupped her shoulders and made her shiver at the contact. "What troubles you now, Honor?" he asked gently. "What must I do to set your mind at rest?"

Honor leaned back against him, reinitiating her plan. He seemed in a receptive mood. She had put him there and figured she might as well take advantage of it. "I am lonely," she said.

"Ah, well, I'm not such good company." He lifted his hands from her and moved away.

"No, no, that is not what I meant," she said, turning quickly. She hadn't intended to touch him just yet, but her hand flew out to grasp his sleeve before she could think what else to do. "Wait!" Without giving herself time to think, she raised on her toes to kiss him. Her lips landed on his chin. Stubble abraded her lips as he jerked with surprise.

"What...?" he began.

Honor's heels hit the floor with a thump. Her hands fisted on his chest. "Damn you for being so tall!"

"Then damn me for this as well," he rumbled, the last word landing in her mouth as he covered it with his own.

Honor reeled with the sheer, hot pleasure of Alan's kiss. Not the slightest thought of resisting him entered her head. Her ears rang with the encouraging sounds from his throat. The soft, dense wool of his plaid tangled in her fingers, caught between their bodies. The scents of leather, wild mint and Alan himself clouded her mind until she knew nothing but his essence, wanted nothing but that surrounding...invading...

He stopped.

Honor swayed, off balance and confused. His hands gripped her arms to steady her, and perhaps to keep her away, but she desperately wanted to go on with this. All manner of reasons for that flitted through her mind, the least of which was her original plan to seduce him to her will. By the saints, she wanted this man. She wanted him to kiss her again, more deeply, more roughly than he had. She wanted him to hold her, crush her to him. She wanted him to bed her. Now. A powerful shiver of need ran through her.

"Go to bed," he ordered, his voice sounding rough with denial. "You shake with cold."

Cold? Was he daft? Her head began shaking side to side, her eyes pleading for what she dared not ask aloud. Suddenly, he lifted her and stalked across the room to the bed. *Now!* she thought. *Now he will.*

Alan deposited her on the mattress and quickly stepped away. He made a helpless, palms-up gesture, mouth open to speak. But before a sound came out, he turned about smartly. His long-legged stride had him out the door and gone before she could protest his leaving.

Honor huddled against the pillows and chewed a thumbnail. This scheme of hers had in no way gone as planned.

Tame him to her will, indeed! She had a better chance with a full-grown warhorse who had never known a bit. At least for now, she must accept that he would behave exactly as he wished. And he did not wish to bed her.

Men were such fractious creatures, she thought, pummeling the bolster with a fist. Fractious and unpredictable. She'd not yet met one as resistant to her persuasive ways as her father had been, but she feared this husband of hers might prove so. Men were all different and required different means to govern, of course.

She had handled her own father wrongly by resorting to arguments. The comte de Trouville, she had avoided altogether except for brief meetings in full company. They had had no words as yet and Honor wanted none. She feared the man above all things and held no desire to make closer acquaintance for any purpose.

But Father Dennis had gladly given his protection and assistance just for the asking. With a man of God, she had never used any womanly wiles. But she had, and still did, feed him with continuous praise for his kind heart and good works. He had responded immediately to her desperate pleas when she needed to flee France.

As for Melior, the musician, he liked her quite well, even without soft words and smiles. Though Honor had counted on his greed, she knew he cared what happened to her. If not, he would have sold information to her father concerning her whereabouts.

And Tavish would have done anything she asked of him. He had doted on her, loved her, lusted for her. By his example alone, she knew that fostering these feelings in a man provided an excellent way to gain complete control over him. Could she do the same with Alan once she found the key to his needs?

She had a scary feeling that her own needs far outweighed his, and where did that leave her? Not in control of anything at the moment, even her own unruly emotions.

For all Alan's wildness, the rough-edged manners and speech he worked so hard to alter, the gentleness in that great heart of his, and even thick-witted refusal to bed her tonight, Honor felt something she much feared was love.

As she lay there trying to calm her thrumming body and scattered wits, her worry flourished. Alan did not want her. That was it. That was why he had turned away, probably in disgust of her wantonness. A new widow, a new mother, throwing herself at his head like a trull in need of coin. Saints, what must he think of her now? Burying her face in the linen, she wept with embarrassment and frustration.

All hope was surely lost. Father would come. Worse yet, the dreaded comte de Trouville would come. The good-hearted Alan would welcome them with open arms and tankards of ale. Never mind who would save *her* from the threat of those two. Honor entertained an even worse fear now. Who in the world would save Alan?

Chapter Eight

Things were not progressing as Alan wished they would. Honor had seemed greatly troubled for many days now. Small wonder about that.

A fortnight had passed since he had stolen that kiss. A very long fortnight of forced pleasantries and careful denial of what had passed between them. *The Great Mistake*, he had dubbed the occasion in his mind, for it haunted him constantly. How could something he knew to be wrong in his mind, feel so devilish right in his heart? Obviously, Honor believed it wrongly done, and so it must be.

Her mood seemed somewhat improved tonight, however, and not so cast down as before. For the first time in weeks, he felt hopeful that she might end her sad mourning soon.

"Ye...*you* are looking bonny this night," Alan commented politely, offering Honor a sliver of tasty lamb on the point of his knife. He made a concerted effort to lay compliments at her feet whenever the chance arose. And to do it in a manner of voice that would not offend her ears. She did not like highlandmen. He struggled valiantly not to sound like one, and believed he succeeded right well. Would she never notice?

Alan wanted her so badly, he ached with it. But he did not deserve her perfection, and was loath to intrude on her continuing grief for Tavish.

He had avoided being alone with her as much as he could, though there existed little to draw him out of the keep for more than half day at a time. He trained her men, worked with her horses, and judged tenant disputes. In the hour following Mass, he attended Father Dennis in his cell and wrestled impatiently with the skill of reading.

He constantly practiced his speech, and with the good priest's corrections, managed to improve its quality so that hopefully Honor would be pleased. Still, he had too much idle time to think.

Whenever he found himself thrown together with his wife, Alan struggled to maintain a chivalrous attitude and play the quiet and serious knight. What a wearing task that was! Full battle proved less daunting and a sight more fun.

Devil take him, he had just told Honor she looked *bonny*. Surely he should be more eloquent than that. Where was his mind? He ought to have called her lovely, or beautiful, or elegant. If he voiced what he really thought— delicious, captivating, arousing—she'd know him for the lecherous fool he was.

Alan knew very well Honor would take him into her bed any time he made the overture, but he did not want her to do so simply to fulfill what she considered a duty. Or to buy his protection. 'Twas clear she feared for her safety now that Tav was gone.

She had exhibited her willingness more than once, but those approaches had been near desperate appeals. He had sidestepped none too gracefully and likely hurt her pride, but he could not take her that way. He adored her above everything. When they came together, he needed that feeling to be shared in equal measure.

Alan wanted her to want him, to love him for himself, not because he might be the only thing standing between her and whatever dangers she feared. Unfortunately, she was not ready to love again and might never be. He must face that possibility.

Oddly enough, the fact that Honor could love Tav so deeply that it reached beyond death itself, reassured Alan immeasurably. He had never thought it possible for a person to care so much for another. Certainly, no one had ever cared so for him. But he still kept hope that she would one day, and worked diligently toward that end.

The problem he agonized over now was keeping himself in line until she did feel love for him. That agony overwhelmed his good sense on occasion. Most every occasion, come to think of it.

At a glance, she set his blood to racing. Like now, he thought. Her gown of soft amber camlet dipped low in front, teasing him with a meager view of creamy breasts. The treat increased as she leaned forward to accept the bite of the meat he held out for her.

She always scented the gleaming length of her hair with flowers of some kind. He knew not the name of the blooms, but that sweet, heady fragrance, combined with her closeness, drove him wild with longing. The tips of her soft fingers touched the back of his hand as though to steady it. And she smiled. He strove to keep his countenance placid while his insides swirled like leaves in a gale-force wind.

She took the meat between her thumb and forefinger, shot him a look from beneath half-closed lids and brought it almost to her mouth. Unable to tear his gaze away, he watched her lips part. *Enticing.* Alan swallowed heavily. He could almost taste—

"The nights grow cold," she whispered, but the words

took a moment to pierce his lust-fogged brain. A quick shake of his head almost cleared it. Until she inserted the sliver of meat between the even whiteness of her teeth and teased it slightly before closing her lips around it completely.

Alan cleared his throat to cover a groan. Jesu help him, what was the woman about? He ought not to respond to this, for he knew exactly why she did it. Such a tempting woman she was, though. Honor, who was ever the lady, a lady who had recently lost her husband and borne the child of her beloved, he staunchly reminded himself. *Back away.* He leaned forward.

Alan imagined real passion, true need in her languorous gaze. That could not be meant for him. The poor lass must have no thought for the present at all. Likely memories from the pleasant past ruled her actions. No doubt she dwelt on Tavish when her eyes went all soft and her lips trembled that way.

He hastily lowered the knife to their trencher and speared a piece of cooked apple. "Here. You'd best eat more. You grow too thin."

She stared at the fruit and then turned away with a jerk. Alan ate the morsel himself and fastened his gaze on her profile. "Are ye well, hinny?" he asked gently, forgetting in his concern for her to govern his words properly. Damn.

Honor glared at him then as she had done to the apple. "Are ye daft, *hinny?*" she mocked.

Now what had he done? Alan glanced around the hall, anywhere but at her. He could not bear her anger. And she did appear to be furious for some unknown reason. What a puzzle, this wife of his. Just when he thought he well understood her, she changed on the instant like spring weather. Thunderstorms seemed likely at the moment and he languished in the open with no shelter at all.

"Have I said aught amiss?" he asked, knowing as the words left his mouth that he had erred yet again.

Her dark brows almost met and the luscious lips tightened. Fuming she was, but why?

"I've done something," he acknowledged.

"Done *nothing* is more like it!" she muttered, so low he barely heard the words. Then she spoke louder and earnestly, her anger barely banked. "Am I not to your liking, Alan? You say I am *bonny!*" Her hands fisted in the loose edge of the table linen, her voice growing emphatic as she stated, "Then you say I am thin! There is someone else you prefer."

"There is?" Alan muttered, truly confused as to what might have put that maggot in her brain. Her harsh intake of breath alerted him. Renewed ire. Doubled, at the very least.

"No! No, there is no one else!" he assured her in a rush. "I pledged faith to you and I hold by my oaths. Always! No matter what." There, how could she possibly find fault with that?

Tears tumbled over her lashes and rolled down her flushed cheeks. "No matter what? Tricked into vows, a wedding you never wanted," she whispered, sniffling. "That should matter."

"Never think it!" he exclaimed, horrified she held herself in such low esteem. "I swear by all that's holy, I am content!"

She jumped to her feet and dashed the wine goblet to the floor with the back of her hand. "Content? Content, are you? Devil take you for a liar, Alan of Strode! For a liar! You are no way content, nor in any way disposed to make this marriage real! So be it, then! Have all the maids in Christendom if you so please! But you'll have none of me, you uncouth highlandman!"

With that pronouncement, Honor stormed out of the hall, into the solar, and slammed the door. He winced when he heard the bolt fall.

Well, at least he had progressed from "ignorant" to merely "uncouth." No arguing that. She had the right of it.

Then Alan glanced around, noting the sudden stillness of the hall. Father Dennis wore a grimace of what looked to be fear. Did the priest worry his lady would suffer a beating? Nanette bit her lips together, meeting his gaze with one of wide-eyed terror. Everyone else wore similar expressions, frightened, without exception. After all this time, did they know so little of him as to think he would chastise Honor with the rod? He would cut off his sword arm first.

Then the memory of her outburst on their wedding night came to mind, her unwitting revelation of what she had suffered at her father's hands. Repeated beatings, confinement, constant fear of her own sire. Alan shuddered with anger. Still, the old man hadn't destroyed her spirit. Even now she dared words to raise a husband's wrath.

Or perhaps her recent bereavement and the pain of the birth had afflicted her mind. Poor Honor. No wonder she stayed overset. Come the morn, he would reassure her that she need not fear. For now, he had best leave her be.

He stood and slowly quit the hall, moving out into the bailey where darkness enveloped him. Those left would breathe easier, knowing he would not confront their lady tonight. Honor would give thanks he was gone. She should rest easier when Nan told her that.

Or she might think he had gone off to find another woman. Did she wish that? He thought not, in spite of what she had said.

If she were anyone else but Honor, he might have con-

strued her act at supper as an honest invitation to bed her.
Her actions again were probably deliberate. These were
dangerous times. Honor required his strength and protection and surely thought—wrongly so—that she must pay
for it, no matter how abhorrent the price. He would never
take advantage of her need in such a way.

He would not exact his husbandly rights, no matter how
much he desired her. It would be only onerous duty on her
part, a sacrifice. Alan would never bed her under such
circumstance if he must stay celibate forever. The reaffir-
mation held no comfort at all. The night felt cold and he
craved her warmth. And her love.

Never again would he share even the comfort he had
found in sleeping beside her just before wee Kit was born.
He could not, now that he had kissed her with passion. He
would not, now that the babe lay in a cradle and not inside
her to remind him that her heart belonged to Tavish Ellerby.

With a rueful shake of his head, Alan ambled toward
the stable to find his bed in the hay.

"Madame, allow me to take the little one away now,"
Nanette begged. "You are very tired. I see the deep shadows beneath your eyes. You did not sleep above an hour
the night through."

"Leave her and be about your tasks, Nan. See that you
set the others to needlework if they are idle." Honor settled Christiana beside her and closed her own eyes.

She had remained in her solar all the morning and into
the afternoon to avoid meeting with Alan. He had given
her no reason to believe he would ever strike her. She
knew he had not whipped anyone since he arrived. But he
might see fit to confine her for her impertinence. Better
that she took the choice upon herself and sought her own

seclusion. At least doing so offered some pretense of control on her part. She would choose the place. Hopefully, Alan would not regard the solar as too comfortable for her.

Nan was right about the lack of sleep. How could she rest knowing that she and her child were at the mercy of a man's idle whims? Even a man such as Alan. It did not help to know that she probably loved him. He made it very clear he did not want that. He did not want her.

Alan seemed a good man, too good to hurt anyone apurpose. He had shown no inclination toward violence in the matter of his cousin, Ian Gray. Now he even trusted him to come to their aid if need be. Trusting kin. Ha, there lay a ridiculous notion if ever there was one. She did not wish any violent tendencies he might possess to extend to herself or her people here at Byelough, but Honor knew she would soon need a man capable of violence.

Days were growing shorter, the weather colder, as winter drew near. She could surely expect her father to arrive sometime within the next month. Even now he could be in Scotland, searching. Oh yes, Melior was right in thinking Hume would come for her. She must be ready for him. Or worse yet, his friend the comte de Trouville.

Unless she convinced Alan to meet force with immediate force and prevail, only God knew what might become of her and Christiana. And Alan would be left maimed or dead.

Father would likely leave Christiana with some crofter's family to grow up in poverty. If he allowed her to live at all. He would name her illegitimate because of the documents Honor had falsified. She brushed a hand over the small head of her daughter and sighed.

"Lost in gloomy thoughts, dove?" Alan asked softly.

Honor jumped and cried out, surprised at the stealth

which allowed him to catch her unawares. "What do you want?" she asked, breathlessly.

"'Tis my time with Kit." He proceeded to lift the small bundle from the hollow beside Honor. "And with you, if you are speaking to me yet. I confess I do not know what has trammeled you so of late. You look fashed."

"Fashed? My thanks for such a pretty summary of my looks!" she said frowning. "Thin, and now fashed. I feel so much better." She regretted her foolish lapse into anger, but he had asked for it with the insult. He sounded very English today. So her last "highlandman" thrust had struck home, had it? She thought it a fair trade for "thin and fashed" and so, said nothing further.

He did not smile at Christiana or at her. While the fact that he did not failed to surprise her, her sense of loss over it did.

The slight frown he wore deepened as he spoke. "I did try prettier words, if you recall. You know well enough how beauteous you are, but I'll not lie to you even to do you kindness. You look nigh done in this morn. Did you not sleep?"

"No," she admitted, drawing the coverlet up to her neck. She watched his serious gaze travel over the outline of her body. Heat rose in her like a fever. Why did he look at her so if he did not want her?

"You do not eat enough. The babe saps you of your strength and makes you thin, whether you wish to hear it or no. Will you have a nurse for her if I find one?"

"No! She is mine, Alan. Mine to hold. Do not think to drag some woman here to take my place with her. Do not!" The vehemence of her words shocked even her. She covered her face with one hand and shook her head. "Please. I did not mean to rail at you so."

The bed sank as he sat down and laid the sleeping Kit

on the extra pillow. Large hands took hers and held them
pressed together. "I wish you would tell me what is
wrong, Honor. Do you fear me, is that what troubles you?"

"No," she whispered truthfully. She no longer feared
him in the usual sense, only his power over her life and
her child's. His tenderness confused her. Why would he
be kind to a woman who did nothing for him? If only he
would allow her to be a wife to him, she would know how
much power she could wield. She had known immediately
with Tavish. He had done everything she asked in the two
months they had spent together. But Alan seemed quite
resistant to her now questionable charms.

Could it be that he only needed more than a subtle
prompting? He had kissed her readily enough. And liked
it, too. She had felt his desire swell. What had put him off
so suddenly? Something had to be done, and quickly. She
needed Alan firmly in thrall before her father or the comte
came to destroy her life and very possibly his as well.

Honor renewed her efforts. She gave Alan her sincerest
attention, always a necessity when dealing with a man, she
had learned. "Tell me true, husband. Why do I not please
you?"

He sat back and stared at her with disbelief in his eyes.
"No' please me, lass? Ye please me well! Why would ye
be thinkin' ye dinna?"

Ah, the soft Scots returns, she thought, smiling up at
him. Fashed or not, Honor knew he had already forgotten
what he was about here. She inclined her head so that her
hair draped over one eye and then glanced up shyly. "You
called me your heartling once. *Mo cridhe* means something
like that, does it not?"

"Aye, but...I wasna thinkin' then. I hadna th' right."

Honor lay her hand on his forearm, feeling the extraordinary heat from his sun-warmed muscle. Or maybe the

sun had nothing to do with it, she thought with a smile. "You have every right, Alan. You are my husband."

For a moment, his breath stopped and he simply stared. Then he pushed off the bed and stood away. "In name. And in all ways you will ever truly need me, Honor, I am your husband. Your protector. No one will ever harm you whilst I live. This, I have promised you time and again!" He threw up an arm in a gesture of frustration. "You need not barter yourself to gain my loyalty, for 'tis yours without the asking. You know I never lie!" His lips drew into a firm line, erasing all the earlier tenderness. And her self-confidence.

His speech had altered again. Formal, dictatorial, almost reprimanding. With only the slightest hint of Scots lilt underneath his proper pronunciation, he sounded remarkably like Hume. Like her father when he grew angry.

"Barter myself?" she asked quietly, lowering her gaze to the coverlet she clutched in her fists. "In exchange for your strength? That's what you think I was about to do?"

"Why else would you offer to please an 'uncouth high-landman'?" he retorted.

"I regret those words, Alan. I do," she said. "I am sorry."

"Why? They were nothing but God's own truth. I ken what I am."

"What your father made you," she answered softly. "If not for him, you would have had your due, lived with your family in Rowicsburg Castle. You would be the gentleman you were born to be. Surely you cannot think I hold against you what is no fault of yours? I but spoke out of anger and in haste. I did not think."

Alan laughed, but it sounded bitter and his eyes were hard, glittering green. He rested his hands on his hips just below the wide leather that belted his plaid. "I could have had my due, as you call it. I could now be holed up in that same castle along with that father of mine. Or I could have been forced to follow the great prancin' Edward and his pretty knights to defeat at Bannockburn.''

He snorted inelegantly and began to pace. ''I ought to thank my da daily for his neglect. Never doubt it, lady, I am a Scot and ever will be, like it or no.''

He stopped his restless wandering by the window and looked out, his broad back to her. ''I can never be the kind of man you deserve, Honor. I know that. But I promise you I will try not to shame you. I *am* trying.''

Honor decided not to mention his attempt to alter his voice, his most remarkable feat at changing thus far. Maybe he would abandon that effort after a while if she pretended not to notice, for she rather liked the sound of his brogue.

''Since it must offend you, I'll not be wearing my breacan again after this day,'' he announced defensively. He swatted angrily at the swinging pleats. ''I had no chance to change after practice.''

''But I like it,'' she said, hoping for some kind of peace or just to ease his mind. ''It looks…bonny.'' Her gaze dropped to his strong, muscular calves. The word certainly fit.

He whirled around, face dark and eyes flashing. ''Do not mock me, wife!''

''I do not mock you, *husband!* You see? There is no pleasing you, is there? Everything I do, every word I say, you suspect some intent I never even thought upon! Go, then, stalk about somewhere else! I care not a whit what you think, you fractious oaf! Just leave me!''

He stormed out, muttering under his breath in guttural Gaelic.

Honor sighed with exasperation and fell back against her pillow. God have mercy, what *was* she to do with this man?

The odor of musty hay choked his nostrils, while the smell of dung wafted his way and added its charm. Alan grunted and turned over, trying to wriggle out a measure of comfort in the prickly bed. None to be had, he thought.

His anger increased with each waking moment. He had ridden the boundaries of Byelough that afternoon, tiring himself and his horse beyond good sense. He had foregone supper so as not to see her again this day. Hunger gnawed at his vitals. But the worst of his craving was not for food.

Damn the woman and her winsome looks, her courage, her flowery scent that spoiled him for any other.

Nay, he could not lay this coil at Honor's door. He had done it to himself. Let himself hope, right from the first, mayhaps even before he arrived here, that he could make a home for himself at Byelough, a secure place in the heart of the perfect woman.

As though Tavish Ellerby's dearest fortune might fall to himself! Tav's greatest riches had lain not in the fullness of his coffers, for he held precious little there. The real wealth, the belonging to Byelough's people and deserving the love of Honor, were the treasures Alan longed for.

What good would more gold do? He had coin enough and knew not what to spend it on. Clothes, he had, left behind by the fleeing English. They abandoned baggage wains full of rich things for the taking. Most of the Scots, intent on chasing Edward's army south, eschewed the booty. So, here he was with all he needed for a life of comfort except what he truly desired. Love. Even if Tavish had meant to leave him that, the dearest of legacies, Alan could not seem to take full possession.

He could not make Honor love him.

But his wee Kit would. No matter what her mother said, the babe was his, child of his heart. He had seen her into this world and would strive with all his being to make life good for her. Alan held that promise as sacred as the vows he took with Honor.

The people were beginning to look to him for their needs, and that boded well. Some still insisted on Honor's permission to follow his orders, but fewer did so as the weeks passed and she always agreed with his assessments. Soon, he would be lord in more than name. But what good was that if he could not gain the regard of their lady? *His* lady now, but only according to words on parchment.

He shifted again and cursed the hay chafing his naked thigh. He had promised to abandon his plaid for hose and tunic. Not that he had any real attachment to the highland garment, other than its freedom and comfort, but it symbolized what he really was. Could he become something other than that just to please Honor? Aye, he knew he would adopt any masque to win her heart.

Hadn't he already begun perfecting the way he spoke? He barely recalled how his English father sounded. Though his mother had rarely spoken the true Scots tongue in his early years, she had passed on to him the lilt he found so hard to disguise. Life in the Highlands and speaking mostly Gaelic had reinforced it. He must try harder. Maybe if he did not shame her by being so common, she would come to care a little.

With such thoughts still in mind the next morning, Alan rose and stretched his aching muscles. His English clothes were stored in the solar. As good excuse as any to see how the wind blew.

Already awake, Honor sat by the fire as Nan braided her hair. She greeted him with a frown. "You are covered with straw!"

Alan smiled at her, staunchly determined to avoid any more harsh words. "Forgive my intrusion. I have been early to the stables and have come to change."

"Would you like a bath?" she asked, sniffing faintly.

He turned to go. "I forgot." Damn, would he never learn? The burn would be freezing, and he simply hadn't thought of it.

"Alan," she called, stopping him at the doorway. "Where do you go? You know the tub is here." She pointed to the painted screen in the corner.

"T' th' burn…stream. To the stream," he said.

"And catch your death? You must be daft. Come you here and wait." She gestured to the window seat. "Nan, go tell Nial and Tofty to haul water from the kitchens. Find that soap of Tav's. 'Tis in the chest over there." She rocked the cradle with one toe to quiet Kit's fussing as she studied him. "You never bathe here. Have you been swimming in the burn each day?"

If he didn't know better, he would swear she worried for his health. Pretense, of course, but he appreciated it nonetheless. "Aye, most days. It is warmer hereabout than where I came from. Not so bad."

"Well, you are not to do that again!" she ordered. "You will come here to bathe. I will not have you freezing yourself, do you hear?"

Alan could not help but enjoy her mothering of him, pretended or not. He could barely remember such from his youth, and it made him feel warm inside to have it now. "Yes, of course. Whatever you say."

She looked triumphant, mollified and infinitely pleased with his answer. At last he had said something right for a change. Now, should he keep his tongue behind his teeth or risk more words?

"The bloom of good health becomes you, my lady." There, well said, he thought.

She raised a perfectly shaped brow and almost smiled. "Not fashed? A bit fatter, would you say?"

Now what? What could he say to that? *Yes, fatter,* and she would be angry again. *No, thinner,* and she would likely snap off his head. "You always appear beautiful to me, Honor."

"Blatant flattery, husband?" Ah, she waxed coy now, digging for more praise. Good, he had a store of that reserved for her.

"God's truth, wife." He produced his most winning smile. "Your hair brings to mind bright sun on a dark waterfall. And your skin is like fresh cream. I'd wager as sweet to taste." Och, why had he said that? Hell's fever, his plaid tented in front even as he spoke the words to her. The unruly beastie beneath it would be his undoing. He swore under his breath.

Honor's cough sounded suspiciously like a laugh. But Alan knew it was not. She would find nothing at all amusing in having him turn randy. However, when he looked up at her, she had pressed her lips together firmly and her eyes grew wider. Probably fright at being left alone with him after last night's brangle. "Will ye...will you go about your day, then? Do not let me keep you," he said hopefully.

"Oh no," she answered, employing her motherly voice now. "I would stay and assist you. I shall send Nan to see to chores. Truly, I have nothing better to do."

He colored red, could feel his face burning with it. "Kit, then. Why not take her to hall, show her about?"

"She sleeps. See?" Honor rocked the cradle again with her foot. "Ah, here is your water. Come in, lads, and mind you do not spill." With that, she busied herself adding herbs and stacking the drying cloths on the bench near the tub.

From the window seat, Alan could see behind the free-standing screen which Honor had shifted to one side. Visions of himself submerged in the fragrant steaming warmth, Honor dropping her gown to join him, water splashing in ever-increasing waves over the edge…

"Are you ready, husband?"

"Huh?" he gasped. Ready? Hell, any readier and he would burst! How the devil could he get her out of here? Nan had gone. The lads were leaving with their buckets. Except for a soundly sleeping Kit, he was alone with Honor. And unfortunately, *ready*.

"Give me your plaid and I shall have it cleaned." She offered a hand to help him divest.

"Nay!" he almost shouted. "I wish ye would leave!"

"Oh, I cannot leave Christiana unattended," she said calmly. "If you do not wish my help, then say as much. I shall sit here and leave you to yourself."

The thought of her taking the window seat in plain sight of his nakedness made him shudder with pure heat. Her eyes on his body, like invisible fingers, touching everywhere. He drew in a deep breath. "Over there!" he demanded, pointing to the bed. "Sit over there."

She smiled in acquiescence and sauntered toward the bed. Turning to face him, she braced her hands on the mattress and gave a wee hop to lift her backside high enough to sit. "There!" she said with a small lift of both brows. "Happy?"

Not anywhere close to that, he thought with a rueful shake of his head.

Committed to the bath, he moved to the tub, replacing the screen so that it stood between them. Even then, as he unbelted his plaid and let it drop, he imagined she could see.

With his back carefully turned to her side of the room, Alan stepped into the tub and sank beneath the water. The enveloping heat of it only added to his fever.

God's truth, 'twas no wonder people bathed so seldom. A bath like this each day could kill a man. And let to its natural conclusion, might soon convince his lass that cleanliness was anything but next to godliness!

Concealed at last by water up to his chest, Alan scrubbed dutifully and then leaned his head against the padded edge of the tub. He closed his eyes, intending to enjoy the warmth for only a moment.

When he woke, the water had grown chilled. He rose up, water sluicing down his body, and reached for the toweling.

The drying cloth proved no larger than a winding cloth to fit young Kit's behind. And it was then he noticed. His plaid was gone.

Chapter Nine

Honor knew the very moment Alan discovered the plaid missing. At his audible intake of breath and muttered curse, she pressed her lips together to suppress her laughter. Once he came around the screen, he was hers.

He did want her. It had been there in his eyes the moment he entered the room this morning. She had seen it before, of course. Why he had refused to act on it no longer mattered. He would today. Honor no longer cared what he thought of her reasons, or of her wantonness. The time had come to make this marriage real and she meant to do it. Last evening her self-doubt and temper had made short work of her intentions, but she had herself well in hand now. No more delays.

Her body rippled with anticipation. With desire for him. He kindled that all too easily, but Honor knew that was all to the good. If what she felt for Alan of Strode was truly love, she meant for him to return it in kind.

She arranged herself in what she considered a provocative pose, the bed linen barely covering her breasts and exposing a fair length of one leg. Surely he could not pretend to misunderstand *this* invitation.

She had taken away his clothes and removed her own.

While he had bathed, Nan had come to take the sleeping Kit to her own chamber. They were alone, undressed, with the door bolted.

The plan lacked any semblance of subtlety, but thus far that trait had gained her nothing with this man. She would be as direct as he always was. He suspected her motive and had even stated it outright, but she could alleviate that suspicion.

In the next few moments, she would convince him that only love for him had prompted her actions. She could do this. She had done it before when it was not even true. That guilt aside, she would do it again, this time with truth on her tongue. He must grow to love her, or he would not fight to keep her when the worst happened.

Honor wet her lips, summoned a smile and made ready.

He stepped around the screen and immediately fastened his gaze on her. Honor couldn't stifle her sigh. She had seen him unclothed before, but not when he returned her regard.

His expression revealed nothing, not anger, not lust, not humor. A shiver of apprehension skipped along her spine. She allowed the sheet to slip lower, but his eyes did not follow the movement. They were locked with her own.

"You have finished your bath," she commented, nearly breathless at the sight of him. His hair, darkened by its wetness, gleamed like burnished copper. Wind-tanned skin held a damp sheen, and muscles appeared gilded by the morning light from the window.

He had not bothered drying or covering himself with the small cloth she had borrowed from Kit's changing basket. Neither did he display any sign of embarrassment at his rampant reaction to her. He merely stepped forward so that he stood in the middle of the room, seemingly at ease except for the state of his rather impressive loins. She held her breath.

"The water is barely warm," he said, pronouncing each word carefully. "I shall order more for you."

Honor swallowed hard. "No, I have already—"

A loud clattering of hurried footsteps outside interrupted, followed by a frantic pounding on the door. "My lady, my lady, he is come. He is by the gate, demanding entrance!"

Alan rushed to the door, heedless of his natural state, lifted the bolt and jerked it open. Father Dennis almost fell inside the room, his eyes on a level with Alan's evident readiness. "God save us!" he gasped, eyes wide and mouth agape. "You are—"

"Aye, more's the pity. Who has come?" Alan asked calmly, brushing aside the priest's shock.

"Lord Hume!" Father Dennis exclaimed, now staring at the ceiling. "My lady's father! He has found her!"

Alan turned away and went for the clothing chest in the corner. In seconds, he had donned smallclothes and tied up the points of his woolen hose. He shook out a long-sleeved tunic.

The nightmare had come true. Father was here. Whyever had she sent Alan's plaid below with Nan? He looked so much fiercer in that than in these English clothes. Honor quickly banished her shock. She cursed herself for bothering with mundane thoughts when disaster threatened.

Scrambling from the bed, she grasped Alan's sword from its wall mount. She held it ready as his head emerged from the neck of his tunic.

Alan raked her body with a sharp green gaze, which then flew directly to the doorway. He hurriedly stepped between her and Father Dennis, shielding her from view.

"Get to the gate!" he barked at the priest. "I'll be there directly to deal with his lordship."

Honor grasped his arm. "Alan, wait!"

"Go!" Alan ordered the priest, and the door slammed. Sandals clapped on the hall floor outside. "Dress yourself, Honor, but remain here until I send for you."

She slammed a fist on his upper arm. "Listen to me, Alan. Heed, for this will not wait!"

He paused in buckling on his belt and glared down at her. "Aye, what is it then?"

"My father has not come here for a visit. He has come to return me to France. To take me away. Do you understand? He will have brought men with him to enforce this."

The green eyes narrowed. "He cannot know Tavish is dead. Once we explain—"

"I ran away," Honor hastened to explain. Now was no time for lies. She could only hope Alan would uphold her decision and forgive her deception of her family. And of Tavish. But best he not know that much yet.

"I escaped a marriage I did not want for one which I did. I ran to Tavish and he wed me without my father's consent."

A frown drew lines between his brows. "You defied your father?"

"Yes! He would have wed me to a lord who had already laid two young wives to rest. A cruel man! They are both cruel! Please, I beg you, do not return me to him. Anything, I will do anything you ask, only—"

Alan placed the tips of his fingers over her lips. "Say no more. You are mine and what is mine, I keep."

A sob of relief shook her as she grasped his sword between her breasts. She leaned forward, resting the top of her head on his chest. The cold steel of the hilt against her skin felt comforting. "And you speak true, always. Thank God you are here," she whispered against the silk. "You will have to kill him."

"Nay, I'll not." Alan held her away with both hands on her shoulders. "Wear the amber kirtle. It becomes you." With that, he released her, lifted the sword from her hands and quickly left the room.

Her heart thundered in her chest. She stood naked, alone, and terrified that her life and that of her daughter would soon be shattered, if not forfeit. And the man she had grown to love would surely die did he not act quickly.

The mounting terror threw her into action. Mumbling curses under her breath, Honor snatched up a chemise and slipped it over her head. The amber cotta did nothing to alleviate the chill of fear as she settled it over her body. She fastened a gold-linked belt around her hips and twisted her loosened fall of hair into her golden mesh caul.

If she must face her father, she would never give him the satisfaction of knowing that his very presence undid her. She never had and never would admit to his face that she feared him, no matter the cost. Alan would save her. He must. But would he be able? Could he even save himself?

Alan watched the man who called himself Lord Hume. The prancing white steed he rode, comparisoned in silver and black, danced side to side, as impatient as his master looked. The man busily issued orders in French to his hulking second in command.

When he had finished, Alan made his presence on the wall-walk known. "I am Sir Alan of Strode and hold this keep. What purpose brings you here?"

Hume looked up toward the battlements. Anger and frustration lined the otherwise handsome face. The resem-

blance between father and daughter was not too remarkable, Alan thought, but was apparent nonetheless. A few
features in common, evident determination, proud carriage,
but there it ended. Alan could see malice in these eyes,
where none existed in Honor's.

She had the right of it, too. Hume had brought men with
him to enforce his will. Many men—at least two score—
and they looked to be orderly and well trained. Certainly
well dressed and mounted. Weapons abounded. No home-
whittled spears for these lads. Helmets shone even in the
weak autumn sunlight. Pennons flew Hume's black and
silver, adding their wind-flapped clicks to the clink of har-
ness and squeak of leather trappings. No other sounds invaded the silence as Hume glared upward.

Finally, the man deigned to speak. "Where is Ellerby?"

"Dead."

"By your hand?"

"By an English sword."

"Where is my daughter?" Hume demanded. "What
have you done with her?"

"Wed her," Alan stated flatly. He worked hard to prevent showing hatred for the man. It would do no good
allowing his knowledge of the man's cruelty toward Honor
to cloud his reason.

"I would speak with her," Hume demanded.

"Fine. Dismount, divest yourself of weapons, and enter
alone," Alan answered.

Hume laughed. His men did as well. Then the man sobered and inclined his head. The smile he offered would
have frozen the loch clear down to the dirt, Alan thought.
"You take me for a madman, Strode?"

Alan smiled back. "I take you for my lady's father,
come to wish her well. Unless you reveal another cause
for your presence here."

"I have come to collect an errant female who has shamed her sire. She is betrothed to another."

"She is wed to me. Where is this man if he is so hot to have her? I would see him."

"I come in his stead to retrieve the faithless jade. 'Tis a wonder he wants her still, but there you have it." Hume shifted in his saddle, looked away and then back again. "You have the keep here and whatever else belonged to Ellerby. Send out my lass and I'll be off."

Alan shook his head once. "Ah, but she's my lass now."

"We will take her if we must," Hume warned, all pretense of good humor fled.

"Ye can try," Alan countered. And possibly succeed, he thought to himself. Even if he armed every adult within the keep, they were still outnumbered. And outmatched, even were that not so. The men with Hume were professional soldiers, probably some mercenaries and freelance knights, in addition to sworn liegemen who wore his colours.

Hume leaned forward, resting his forearms on his pommel. "We will make camp. You have until tomorrow noon to hand her over."

"And should I refuse?" Foolish question, but lack of an immediate answer would give them a little time.

"We will take her, of course," Hume avowed. "And this place. We will leave you with nothing. Think on that."

When the force turned in unison and rode off toward the edge of the woods, Alan descended the steps into the bailey. He found Honor, standing stock-still as though she had frozen to the bottom step. "Well, wife, it seems your finery is wasted on him. Your father declined our invitation."

Honor did not move until he took her arm and threaded

it through his own, leading her back to the hall. Her pallor
and stillness gave witness to her terror, but the set of her
shoulders belied it. What courage she had, he thought
proudly. What mettle in the face of her fear.

The vision of her, naked as a newborn and holding his
sword for him, filled his mind. She had Hume's strong will
all right. What pluck she had to refuse her father's choice
of a husband. And then to choose one for herself.

Perhaps Tavish had put her up to the adventure once
they found themselves in love, but she had obviously carried through with it. He wished Tav had told him all of
their story. Alan had assumed until this very day that they
had wed with the baron's eventual blessing.

When they reached the hall, he situated her on the settle
by the fire hole and dragged over a stool to sit directly
before her. Her hands felt like ice as he pressed them between his own. Softly, he broke the silence. "You had best
tell me the whole of it, sweeting. Tell me how you became
Tav's wife when your father was dead set agin it."

He knew the moment her courage deserted her. Her
shoulders rounded and her wee chin quivered a bit.

"Oh, Alan, please do not be gentle! Please do not," she
said. Her voice broke. "I ne-need you to be fierce for me.
For us and for our people here. Father will destroy everything if you let him!"

His heart ached for her, so sorely that he could think of
nothing save easing her mind.

"*Gentle?* Me? Ah, lovey, dinna greet. Yer auld da's got
oats fer brains if he thinks he can wrest away a highlandman's lass! Ignorant of niceties, I may be, but I've a few
tricks I do well. Fightin' for what's mine bein' what I do
best!" He tipped up her face to his and kissed her nose.
Then he looked deeply into her tear-filled eyes. "And ye
are mine, hinny. Never, never doubt it."

"Alan," she said, hesitating as though something had just occurred to her, "I am wrong to expect this of you. I must do something to stop Father. What if you cannot prevail no matter how well you fight? He will lay waste to everything."

"Not whilst I live," Alan promised.

"I know that! But after he has killed you, then he will!"

Her words were earnest. Her gaze held regret and anguish. "Listen well to me, husband. If he learns of Christiana, he will get rid of her somehow when he takes me. If you bear me any pity and her any love at all, you will hide her existence for me."

"He will never take you," Alan promised. "Nor harm our Kit."

She sucked in a deep breath and squared herself as though for battle. "I have decided it's best I go out to him and leave willingly. That way, you and all here should be spared. I pray you take my daughter to someone kind who will care for her."

She twisted her hands to grasp his, palm to palm. Her fingers twined with his and squeezed. "Do not try to soothe me with promises. I am certain Father has a small army with him, and I am no witless fool. Byelough is strong, but not invincible. Our people are not fully trained to warfare and have never withstood siege. Let me go out tomorrow."

"Not if I must tie you here," he declared, and smiled.

"Let me do this!" she cried. "I want my daughter to live! I want *you* to live!"

"She will live and so will I. Here, with you." Alan felt his temper loosening its bonds and his voice rose accordingly. "Do you heed me now, wife. Since my seventh year, I have had nothing. No family to speak of. No possessions save what I could hide or defend with my blade.

Now my brother of the heart entrusted all he owned and bade me hold it dear, as he would have done had he survived. You think some prickly-arsed ex-Scot can mince into these hills and snatch it from me with threats? Not with thrice that number of sheep in helms! Bleatin' fools followin' a fool and no mistake!'' He shoved her hands away. ''Now hie yerself to the solar, woman, and see to the bairn. I've plans to make.''

He stalked away, angry with her for her doubting his abilities. And even more furious at the thought of her sacrificing herself, either to his lust in exchange for protection, or to her father to save him and Christiana.

Suddenly, he stopped and whirled around, shaking a finger. ''And do not think to leave that chamber! If you move from that room, I will have you locked below. In the *oubliette*.''

The new and greater horror that suffused her face did not bear watching. Only then did Alan recall that her father had betimes locked her away. The urge to recant his threat and give her words of comfort did not override his prudence, however. If she feared imprisonment that much, surely she would not dare his wrath by trying to leave the safety of the keep.

He quit the hall and hurried to the bailey to find Father Dennis. A plan had formed in his mind, the only solution he could imagine for this dilemma. But it required a swallowing of pride that would likely choke him with its bitterness.

If he'd retained any doubts that he loved this contentious woman he had married, this thoroughly destroyed them all. When he first vowed on his soul to do anything to keep her, he never imagined God would test him like this. He looked up at the heavy clouds moving in and imagined he heard a rumble of laughter.

"Well, then, if Yer goin' ta make me crawl through the dirt like a whipped hound, Lord, the least Ye can do is give auld Hume a braw soakin'!"

It began to rain.

On the morning of the third day, Alan paced the battlements where he had spent most of that time. Hume and his men looked settled in for a siege. Tents lined the edge of the small area of woods that lay just out of bow range. Smoke from their cook fires spiraled upward through the light mist.

The sounds of hammers and axes echoed through the hills. Soon Hume would order the ladders they were constructing to be laid against the walls. A battering ram would test the strength of the oak portals of Byelough.

Hume had sent two knights to escort his daughter to him that next day at noon. Alan gave them the expected refusal. Formal threats ensued, but thus far only the village had been damaged. Hume had fired two cottages and promised to burn more today unless Honor presented herself. The villagers had wisely abandoned their homes and probably sought refuge in the caves that riddled the nearby hills.

Alan searched the trail that wound out of the valley hoping against hope to see the relief he had humbly requested.

"Will he come, sir?" Father Dennis asked softly as he joined Allen on the wall-walk.

"I do not know. Are you certain the player can find Rowicsburg?" Alan remembered the musician's assurance just before he wriggled into the bolt-hole.

"Oh yes, Melior will find it. He will present your request. Question is, will your father heed it?"

Alan wondered that, as well. Never had he asked his

sire for anything. They had not spoken, nor communicated
with each other since Alan had been sent to his uncle in
the Highlands at the tender age of seven.

The man lived, Alan knew, and still served as sheriff
and warden of the border before the decisive battle at Bannockburn. He believed the castle at Rowicsburg remained
in English hands for the moment, but the good baron may
have taken himself off to England when he heard of
Bruce's victory. Only time would tell, time Alan had little
of.

If the musician had located a mount to purchase and
ridden hard, he would have arrived in Rowicsburg in little
more than a day. Counting the day's ride back, today
would be the very earliest Alan could expect help to arrive.
If it came at all.

It galled Alan to ask anything of his English father, but
where else could he turn? Despite his comradely treatment
of his cousin, Ian Gray, Alan did not truly trust the man.
Since Ian was now related by law and could not wed
Honor, he might be willing to join forces with her father
for the reward of Byelough and its lands. And Gray could
not hope to win an outright battle with Hume's men any
more than could Alan and his meager force.

He could not depend on the king's help. Bruce was
chasing after Edward and laying waste to England. And
good King Robbie would never spare men for a personal
favor anyway. Bruce might do so to protect Byelough itself. He seemed to consider the holding important, both
for its location and the secret caves nearby. But Alan knew
he could not depend on that, even if Bruce could be found
in time.

His father was the best chance for holding Byelough
against Hume. He no doubt had a full purse and could hire
every freelance in and around Rowicsburg if need be. For

a personal battle such as this, political loyalties could be laid aside for the nonce. 'Twas not an uncommon thing at all.

Alan found he was not above employing guilt to bring the old man running. Family was family. If Adam of Strode had any honor at all, he would come to the aid of a son.

It did seem strange to pray that Rowicsburg had held out against the Scots forces. Alan did have hope there, since most of that army was now rampaging through the north of England. Yet it made him feel disloyal to Scotland to wish they had failed to take so important a place, just so his father would come here and lend his aid. Alan was and ever would be Scot.

He reached to smooth the folds of the plaid Honor had urged him to wear. ''Makes you look invincible,'' she had said when he went to the solar for fresh clothing this morn. Alan smiled. She did like a highlandman, after all. At least when it came to facing down her father.

Morning gave way to evening, and evening to night. Constant knocking from the builders' implements ticked off the moments. Intermittent taunts from Hume's men drifted from the distant camp. Alan waited, hopes for reinforcements dimming by the hour.

Long after full dark, he abandoned his vigil, gave orders to the guards, and returned to the hall.

''Bid our lady join me,'' he said to Nanette, who sat near the fire hole with her sewing.

The birdlike Frenchwoman nodded and rushed away. Moments later Honor appeared. ''Has my father gone?''

Alan chuckled without humor. ''Would that such fortune blessed us. Nay, he squats nearby and makes ready for our wee war. Are you well?''

''Well? As well as any prisoner can be, I suppose.'' She

dropped into the chair next to his own and signed heavily, wringing her hands. "You must let me go, Alan. Someone will die if I do not."

"Then someone will die," he stated. "Have you eaten?"

"I cannot think of food." Her eyes pleaded with him for her release, but Alan would never grant her that. She would not go out these gates and disappear from his life forever. Even if he knew she would be well treated by her kin, he would not allow it. He certainly could not send her home with a man who abused her.

Her selflessness warmed his heart. That she would sacrifice herself for Byelough's people, for him and for her daughter, proved her goodness of heart. But the fact that she would do it so willingly also fostered an anger against her that he could not suppress.

Just as he turned to her to chastise her for it, a commotion at the hall door snared his attention.

Father Dennis and one of the guards rushed toward him from the stair that led from the kitchens below. Sandals and boots slapped against the flagstones and the two men panted as though they had run all the way.

"Sir! Melior has returned. He and others are emerging from the bolt-hole even now!"

Alan jumped to his feet and made for stairs. Honor grasped his sleeve to keep pace.

"Stay here!" he ordered without halting. She let go of him, but he sensed she followed.

Once they reached the kitchens, they entered the storeroom just as Melior came through the low doorway. He smiled sadly. "Sir Alan, I have brought him with me, but—"

"My father is here?" Alan dashed the skinny musician aside. Between the sacks of grain and chests filled with spices and supplies, Alan spied a portly figure assisting someone from the small opening at the back wall. A baby wailed.

Alan felt glued to the spot as he watched a woman emerge from the opening. The man held her arms to support her and a small, very angry face peeked over her shoulder. As she straightened, he saw that the bairn was strapped to the woman's back in a sling. He stepped forward then to help the trio through the maze of stores piled around the tunnel's opening.

His father turned and gazed at him from near equal height. The brown hair had grayed with age. Adam Strode was just past the half century mark, after all.

"Alan? My Alan?" he whispered. "It *is* you!"

"Da?" The familiarity slipped out unheeded as Alan searched the features for the man he had once known. Changed, certainly, but not to an unrecognizable degree. "You came."

The older man looked away and snorted. "Well, of course I came. Years of your angry silence could not alter the fact I am your father! Did you think I would not come?"

"My silence? What do you mean? 'Twas you who—"

"Hist!" a feminine voice intruded, "Could ye take each other ta task a mite later? I'm bent wi' th' weight of this wee beast. And he's devilish hungry."

Alan jerked his attention away from his father to the woman. She appeared near his own age, covered neck to toe in a rich cape of gray wool trimmed in what looked to be marten fur.

Her smooth, handsome face contorted with a grimace of pain as the bairn let go with a screech and yanked with both fists at her disheveled hair. "Get 'im off me, would ye?"

Both Alan and his father rushed to her back. Alan untied the sling and Adam lifted the child free. "I'm Janet," the woman declared, and held out her hand to Alan. With a nod of her head toward the noisy child, she continued, "and this is yer fractious brother, Richard."

Alan stared at the squirming baby. "Wh-where is my mother?" When no answer came, he jerked his gaze to his father. "Da?"

"Your mother's been dead these last six years, Alan. Did you not know? Did Angus not tell you?"

A fist of pain struck Alan's chest and he backed away. He dropped heavily to a sack of grain and buried his face in his hands. "Nay," he whispered. "Nay." His mother, dead.

"A fever took her. She was quickly gone," his father said, but Alan barely registered the words through his haze of grief.

Truth told, he could scarcely recall the face of the woman who had borne him, but the feel of her soft hands on his brow, the musical voice with its sweet lilt, remained steadfast in his mind. He had clung to the sensation and the sound of her almost every night since last he'd seen her, near twenty years ago.

He felt Honor's hands on him now. Her soft, small fingers kneaded his shoulders, brushed over his hair. He heard her quiet orders. "Take everyone above, Father Dennis, Melior. See to their comfort for a while. We shall join you anon."

Feet shuffled through the rushes. The baby's whine dimmed as everyone ascended the stair to the hall.

Alan turned and buried his face in Honor's middle. Tears worked their way through his tightly closed lids as he held his breath. He clutched her hips, his hands fisted

in her robes. Without words, she gave him what co̶m̶f̶o̶r̶t̶
she could. He embraced it in near desperation.

His mother. Dead. Soft arms cradled his head as he wept
silently for other arms he would never feel about him
again. For goodbyes he could never say. For forgiveness
he could not yet offer, even did her shade appear to ask
it.

When he finally released her, Honor knelt before him
and kissed away his tears. "I am so sorry, Alan. I grieve
for you," she whispered.

He nodded and gently set her away from him so he
could stand. "Aye. But we've no time for this now. I must
speak with my father. His men must be camped nearby
and we need to plan our strategy."

She made some murmur of agreement and led the way
out of the storeroom. By the time they had crossed the
kitchens and climbed the stairs to the hall, Alan had recovered himself. He put thoughts of his mother away.

Honor must be his first concern.

Chapter Ten

Alan's father, the new wife and child, and Father Dennis sat grouped around the head table with two chairs left vacant for Honor and himself. Alan sat and immediately downed a full tankard of ale without glance or greeting for his guests.

When he had finished, he turned to his father. "Where are your men?"

Adam Strode lowered his gaze to his wooden trencher, his large, capable hands flat on the table on either side of it. "There are no men, save myself. David Bruce had the castle surrounded. Janet, Richard and I happened to be in the town when the Scots arrived. Lord Witherington will have surrendered Rowicsburg to the Scots by now."

"How did Melior find you?" Alan asked, resignation settling about him like heavy chains.

"By chance. He stopped at the alehouse and asked how he might send word to me from my son. The alewife is a good friend to Janet and knew where we were hiding."

Alan looked at the woman his father had taken to replace his mother. She shifted the sleeping babe in her lap and glared back. "So you've no help to offer, then," Alan stated.

His father grunted. "Only my wits, such as they are."

"English wits. Well, we know how sharp they are, do we not?"

"They have kept your body and soul together!" his father declared. "Had I not made a Scot of you, you'd be heading south now with that puling king of mine or else rotting in that bloody bog near Stirling."

Alan smirked. "Protected me, did you? Admit it, Da, you did it to straddle the border. To rule lands in both countries through Nigel and through me."

Then Adam sighed with defeat. "Aye, that, too. Look, son, I offered my loyalties to Longshanks, as did your brother Nigel. That Edward was my true king. I am English and I make no apologies for it. That's what I was born to be. But I would not have had two sons bound to Edward the Second as he came to power. As eldest, your brother had to go to Gloucester. I am glad I did not have to sacrifice you as well."

"Sacrifice?" Alan asked. "What do you mean?"

His father looked up at him, the sad wrinkled eyes bright with tears. "Nigel is dead."

"No," Alan whispered, running a hand through his hair and shaking his head. "Mother *and* Nigel?"

"Aye. Your brother took an arrow through the heart on one of the expeditions into Wales last year." After a long silence, he sniffed and shoved back his chair. "Enough talk of death. What's to be done here? The jongleur says it is Lord Dairmid Hume, your wife's father, who lays siege to you. May I ask the reason?"

"He wants her back," Alan stated succinctly, "for another alliance he has in mind."

"Ah, I see." Adam frowned and worried his beard with his fingers. "You have only a handfast and he won't wait out the year, then?"

"No," Honor interrupted. "We were wed by my priest!"

Adam smiled at his daughter by marriage. "He cannot simply null a union that has been blessed and duly consummated, now can he? Where's the worry?"

Alan and Honor exchanged wary glances.

Adam rolled his eyes and slammed his palms against the table. "Well, you've said the priest blessed it, so you've left the other undone, eh? Jesu, Alan, didn't that sheep-shagging uncle of yours teach you *anything?* Do you not know a marriage is not legal until...? Oh, good lord!"

Alan rose and kicked back his chair. "This is not a matter for discussion, Da."

Adam laughed bitterly, "I should say not! 'Tis a matter for action, I'd say. *Immediate* action."

"For mercy's sake, Da, Honor has just birthed a child," Alan offered in a low voice.

"Not yours, I take it?" Adam asked. He snorted. "No, I guess not. When?"

"She bore Tavish Ellerby's babe some...six weeks past?" He looked to Honor for confirmation of the time and she nodded.

His father nodded once and took the sleeping child from his wife. "Point me to our chamber, Alan, and get you to your own. Methinks you have business to attend, and Janet and I need some rest."

Honor guided the couple to the stairs leading to the upper chambers. Alan could not see her face, but knew it must be the bright red color of his own. Damn the old man.

Consummation. He'd not once considered that lack of it might endanger his right to keep Honor. Her women-in-waiting would know that he and Honor had not lain together as husband and wife. He had only slept once in her bed and she had been too great with child then to accomplish anything. After Kit's birth, he had bedded down in the hall, or sometimes the stable. And if Diarmid Hume took Byelough Keep, the women might feel compelled to admit as much to him in order to regain Hume's good graces.

Alan felt he had no right to ask Honor to lie with him. Not that he didn't want her. God's bones, he thought of little else. But he knew she still loved Tavish. Alan did not want her to come to his bed only to gain his protection, but he must protect her at any cost. And he must be a husband in truth in order to do that. He must own her legally.

Then all he need worry on would be preventing her widowhood.

Honor rushed ahead of Alan's father and Lady Janet, wanting to be done with settling them in for the night. She pushed open the door to the guest chamber and stood aside for them to enter.

She regretted the lack of a bedstead, but guests usually brought their own. Gesturing toward the thick, wool-stuffed pallets her women had hastily laid, she assured them, "We shall have a bed constructed for you on the morrow. Shall I have one of the women attend you, lady? Or take your child to sleep with them?"

"Nay," Alan's father answered for his wife. "We shall fend for ourselves this night. We be so weary, I think we could sleep upright against the walls."

He turned and took one of the hands she was wringing against her waist. "Be easy, girl. Does my hulk of a son put fright in those lovely eyes of yours?"

"Oh, no!" Honor answered, surprised that he would think such. "My father is the one I fear." And her betrothed, but she would not dwell on that worry. Father must be trying to repair his plans without involving the comte de Trouville. Thank God.

"Dairmid Hume," Lord Adam mused, still clasping her hand. "I met your father once, you know. He traveled to London with Balliol during the peace talks. We were scarcely more than lads, but he had a nose for politics even then. Didn't think much of England, as I recall."

"So he always said," Honor elaborated. "He sold his lands near Edinburgh and has lived in France since his marriage to my mother. He is somehow in Robert Bruce's employ concerning matters of the French court." Honor slid her hand from his and began backing toward the door.

She wanted nothing more than to get to her solar and comfort Alan in his grief. His mother's and brother's deaths might have been well mourned by these two, but the tragedies were new to her husband. She recalled his quiet tears in the storeroom and how staunchly he put them away for later, turning his concern to her.

"Bruce's man? Hmm, that could complicate matters here. Or it might possibly help." He shrugged. "So our Tavish found you there in France?" the Baron asked.

Honor ducked her head to avoid his eyes. "I wed him here, my lord. We were married for two months before he joined the Bruce."

"And so, died, leaving you to Alan's care," he concluded for her. "I begin to see how this goes. Is this marriage not to your liking, little one?"

"Sir Alan is all that's kind and honorable, my lord."

The baron smiled, and Honor could see Alan's future countenance in the sire, no less handsome for the added years. "You love him?" he asked.

"I hold great respect for your son, my lord," she replied, avoiding a direct answer to his question. "He is very loyal. Alan promised as Tavish lay dying to look after me. Us,'' she corrected. "My daughter, Christiana, and myself. Tavish did not know of the babe, however.''

"But my son accepts that your girl is now his to care for?''

Honor nodded emphatically. "He does, Lord Adam. He dotes on her, more than is wise, I think.''

"And you as well, I'd reckon,'' he said, scratching his head and shaking it. "But he would not intrude on your husband's memory, is that the truth?''

"Tavish was his friend,'' she explained. "I believe he holds that dearer than his own desires. He is a good man, my lord.''

Lady Janet scoffed as she tucked furs around her son. "Lord deliver us from *good* men, eh? I nigh had to drug this one to get his clothes off. That faithful to his wife, he was. Even with her dead those three years!''

"Hush, Janet!''

She laughed and hopped up from the pallet to slide her arms around his waist. "Listen to him growl! Such a fearsome bear. And he knows I mean no disrespect. I loved his lady almost as much as he. Only right that I look after him for her,'' she tweaked his beard as she crooned, "as he grows old and toothless.'' Janet chuckled again when he grabbed her hand and nipped her fingers.

"Well, ah, I should…'' Honor began, completely at a loss in light of the couple's easy affection.

"Aye, you really *should*,'' Adam agreed with a meaningful lift of his shaggy brows. "'Twill be our first line of defense.''

Honor hurried to the door, blushing to the roots of her hair. Just before she reached it, she felt his hands on her shoulders.

"Daughter?'' he said softly against the top of her head.

"Do not go afraid. Alan's heart is in his eyes when he looks at you."

Honor nodded quickly, felt him release her, and scrambled out of the room as though the devil pursued. What did the man mean? *Alan's heart was in his eyes?* Did the baron believe Alan loved her? She had certainly worked toward that end.

If he did love her, and in light of what she felt for him, Honor knew she should confess to Alan what a charlatan she really was. That she had never loved his best friend at all. That she used Tavish's affections. Of course, he would hate her then, toss her out to fend for herself. Not to her father, perhaps, for he was not cruel. But how could a man called Alan the True bear to live with someone he knew to be deceitful? How could he love her?

But lovers they must be—at least in body—if she planned to ensure this marriage was legal. Lord Adam was right in that. Her father might have undone her marriage to Tavish because she had used the altered documents and wed him under false pretenses, but this union with Alan would be infinitely harder to set aside.

It had genuine documents to commend it, and the blessings of not only the priest, but Robert Bruce himself. Her father did work for the Bruce, keeping abreast of things at the French court. Invoking the Scot king's name might dissuade her father from killing Alan. She had not thought on that until Lord Adam put it in her mind just now. Robert Bruce had ordered her to wed Alan. Now she must put the seal to it and honor those vows tonight. Will he nill he, Alan must agree to that.

Despite the reasons for the event, Honor did look forward to it. She had never seen a finer figure of a man or one with a sweeter disposition. Considering all he had endured, he might have turned bitter and raged against life.

But no, he had survived it all—abandonment, neglect, abuse, the rigors of battle—and still smiled at the world with a glint of humor in those wonderful green eyes. How could she not admire him?

She did not need to entreat him to love her, Honor knew that now. He either did or did not, no matter what she did to alter matters between them. Alan would keep her as safe as he was able in either event. She did love *him*. That would be enough, Honor told herself. More than enough, and they would add the physical pleasure of the marriage bed. Even if he did not really love her, he did desire her. She knew that for certain now. And Honor meant to make him infinitely glad they had wed.

The baron was right. She *should*.

Alan paced the solar while he waited for Honor's return. He tried pushing thoughts of his mother and brother to the back of his mind. They were nigh to strangers, after all. Nigel, he could barely remember. A tall, fierce-looking fellow at fifteen, he had been eight years Alan's senior. Da had packed him off to England shortly before Alan's own sojourn to the Highlands.

Their mother had wept, that he did recall, and it had frightened him. Not three months afterward, she had shed more tears as she left her youngest in her brother's care. Alan had been beyond fright that time. Terror absolute had held him in its grip, a terror called Uncle Angus.

Could he forgive her, now that she was dead? Later, he would try. Later, when the present trouble lay in the past and he could think straight. He would grieve then, as well, for the mother he both loved and blamed. And for the brother he had scarcely known.

Tonight he must do what he craved and also dreaded. Part of him relished the thought of possessing Honor. He had dreamed of it, sleeping and waking, since their first meeting. She would submit, probably even pretend to like his attentions, but later in the night, he would hear her weeping for all she had lost. Weeping with regret for Tavish, his friend, the husband of her heart. How could he do such a thing to her?

How could he *not?*

Back and forth he trod the tightly fitted oaken planks that bore not the slightest trace of dirt or dust. Honor's penchant for cleanliness drew him nearly as much as her grace and beauty. Perhaps the squalid life he had led, sleeping either in a filthy hall amongst clansmen who cared naught for fleas and filth, or outside in the dirt itself with warriors of like ilk, made him yearn for the sweet scents of his early youth. The comforts.

Though he had bathed scrupulously since coming here, he wondered if any soap could fully scrub away the sheep-dung smell of life with Angus MacGill, or the odor of battlefield carnage.

He did not deserve to lie with a woman such as Honor. But he must, and he would. Even knowing how she would quail inwardly, probably hate herself and him for the necessity of it, Alan could not completely suppress his joy at the opportunity to have her.

"Alan?" she said softly, "Are you all right?"

He turned and worked up a stiff smile. "Aye. I'm well enough. Everyone set for the night?"

"They are too tired to mark the lack of comforts," she admitted, seeming distracted. "I stopped by Nan's chamber and fed Christiana. She sleeps." Honor drifted toward the bed and pulled back the covers. Hesitantly, she looked back at him, a question in her eyes. He noticed her hand on the furs tremble slightly.

"Ah, sweet Honor, dinna be afraid," he whispered, not

daring to approach her yet. "We need not…" He couldn't finish that. No, he could not deny himself this, despite her qualms. And his own.

She let the coverlet drop. "Why does everyone think I fear you? 'Tis time, Alan. You know it as well as I. All must know for certain this is no marriage made of words alone. I am not unwilling to do this, as you must have guessed by now."

He shrugged, unsure that he could even accomplish a decent mating knowing how she must feel inside. "I know you were willing the day your father came here, and even before that. I'm not so thick-witted that I didn't notice. But I also knew your reason and I misliked it. I still do."

"Could we not speak of that?" she asked, turning away.

Indecision gripped him again, and an unfamiliar foe it was, too. Alan hated it. Should he take her or not? Probably not, since he could better bear a frustrated body than a heart full of guilt.

He knew what she wanted to hear, so he forced it out. "After what my father said at table, all will believe the deed done tonight. You are no virgin bride. They cannot prove we did nothing. No one will know for certain."

"You and I will know," she chided. "Could you lie to my father if he asks directly? You, who are known for your honesty?"

May be that he could. Anything to prevent her feeling she must betray her vows of love for Tavish. Anything to save her tears. Though it meant abandoning truthfulness, practically the only virtue he had left, Alan considered it.

Honor sighed and shook her head, "No, Alan, I do not think you could, and I would not ask it of you." She began to unlace her kirtle. "Will bedding me be such a chore, then?"

He laughed. "Daft. I knew ye must be lacking somewhere. 'Tis yer wits. How could anyone not want ye? I do, with all my being, Honor, but I ken—''

"Do you now?" She raised her brows, shot him a side-long glance, and let the kirtle drop. Her softly pleated chemise glowed in the candlelight, draping the curves and hollows of her body like a beckoning veil.

Her lips parted as she ran her small pink tongue along her top lip. Fascinated, he watched it disappear. Wanted to follow with his own. Desperately wanted to.

How had he gotten to her side without walking across the room? He squeezed his eyes shut and shook his head to clear it. When he looked again, she pulled away the headpiece of woven mesh that held her rolls of hair. The shining waterfall tumbled down her shoulders and over her breasts.

Unable to resist, he reached out and lifted a handful of the spun silk to his lips. "So beautiful." He moved the strands against his mouth, inhaling their flowery scent, tasting their texture.

She moved closer so that the fabric of her chemise brushed against him. Her fingers tangled in the neck lacing of his sark and pulled it free. "You do not need this," she whispered softly. Her breath stirred the hair on his chest, stopping his breath as effectively as the blow from a quintain.

"Or this," she continued, removing the round silver pin and sliding away the length of plaid draped over his shoulder. His lungs filled with a rush, his hand fisted in her hair when she began to unbuckle his belt. The heavy leather dropped to the floor with a soft thud.

She smiled up at him, a knowing smile gone almost wicked. The fingers of her right hand plucked at the shoulder of his unlaced sark. "Will you remove it?" she asked.

He could not speak. Instead, he turned away slightly and

awkwardly tugged the sark off over his head. He watched it hit the floor beside her kirtle. Her chemise now lay in a pool atop the amber wool. Alan kicked off his boots and slowly raised his eyes. Honor stood carelessly draped in the ells of his now unpleated plaid.

"Your breacan," she said, her slight French intonation giving the word a softer sound. She smiled wider and smoothed the loose gathers over her breasts. "Remember when you said you would not wear it again? I thought to steal it for myself even then. It does make you look invincible."

Alan thought she must have lost her courage and sought to cover herself as well as change the subject. Too late for that now. She had gone too far. Here he stood in nothing but the skin God gave him, thanks to her. And though she was not looking down at present, she must surely sense he had passed the time for self-denial. "So, ye wish to be the invincible one now, do ye?"

"Ah, and under your plaid, I am so," she murmured softly. "Dauntless. Indestructible. I feel it. Nothing can harm me here."

Alan nodded slowly and rested his hands on her shoulders. "Aye, 'tis glad I am ye ken that."

He only wished to God it were true. They both knew it was not. She had been right to doubt his ability to keep her safe from her father. The old man might well conquer the keep and all within. But not this night. For now she could pretend, and he with her. "There's magic about it, ye know?"

"Show me," she whispered, her gray eyes languorous, silvered by the candlelight. He watched in amazement as she held open the familiar brown-and-green folds in welcome.

For a long moment he stood there, held in thrall by the

sight of her perfection. Full, rounded breasts lifted and fell
softly with each breath, their dark rose peaks beckoning.
Her slender waist fanned out to sweetly curved hips and
in again to well-shaped thighs and legs. Her ankles and
feet seemed small even for her wee size. A fairy child, a
pagan sprite, surrounded by the colors of the highland for-
ests. Enchanting as a druid queen on Samhain Eve.

"I want you so," he breathed out the words on a wave
of need so great it almost drove him to his knees. He
surrendered gladly, sinking slowly to the floor, sliding his
arms beneath the plaid and gathering her to him. He lay
his cheek against her, turning slightly to taste the curve of
her hip, the softness of her belly, the sweetness of her skin.
"Feast of dreams," he whispered, touching his tongue to
the smooth, tender place above her mons.

She made a sound in her throat, of desire or denial, he
knew not. Cared not, for slowly she sank before him so
that they knelt knee to knee. She raised her eyes to his and
he imagined hunger in them, wished for it so hard he found
it there. With a groan of sheer animal pleasure, Alan
claimed her mouth. Ravaged it, seeking to erase all vestige
of any other who had so much as admired it from afar.
She was his. Everything, everyone else be damned; Honor
was his own and his alone.

Still raining hot kisses over her face and neck, Alan rose
to his feet, gathered her, plaid and all, into his arms and
lifted her to the bed.

When she made to speak, he covered her mouth with
his and crawled up beside her, surrounding her in a hold
so fierce, she'd dare not say him nay. She had not pushed
against him in protest, but beyond that, Alan did not deliberate whether she liked what he did. She might only
pretend, or she might only endure. He could not bear

knowing, either way. Honor had foregone her chance to escape.

Part of his fevered mind told him to slow his advance, court her with touches and soft words. Another, more insistent part warned him this was best done now or it would not be done at all.

He rolled her beneath him and parted her legs with his knee. The wine-sweet, heady taste of her kiss banished all thought as he reached between them and touched her. To his surprise, she arched into his hand as though eager. Ready.

He drew away from the kiss and looked down at her, fully expecting gritted teeth and tightly closed eyes. Instead, her face was fraught with something like wonder, open and trusting, wanting. The sight undid him and he thrust into her like the veriest half-grown virgin he felt.

She cried out, but not, he thought, in pain. Her open-mouthed smile stole any remaining wits he had, along with his heart. Her body rose to his as though he'd trained it every night for years. The pleasure of its fit around his own made him worry he would spend himself with the very next foray, but he held back. No power inside him would force the end to this just yet. Not until he savored a full measure of the miracle that was Honor.

He slowed apurpose and tried to regain his usual control. But he had not reckoned with her well enough. Honor's small hands grasped his hips, slid down to draw him to her, squeezing, raking his skin with her nails. The sensation, combined with his tentative grip on reality threw him right over the edge. He hurled endlessly against her like North Sea breakers pounding into the caves of Wykshead.

Every feeling in the world collected in the space where they joined, the tight cling of her passage around him, the wet friction, the pull of her womb.

Ah, saints, he could not last. The shudder and keening cry might have been his own. But her body rippled around him, held him fast for what seemed a flash of a moment. Or eons. Time mattered naught for he burst forward with all his life force and felt he had died of it. Hoped she had as well, for he never wanted to part from this woman in any way or form.

Honor.

Breathing her name was his last waking thought.

Honor wriggled out from beneath Alan and then cuddled next to him, pulling the tail of his plaid over them both. If she'd had any reservations about consummating this marriage, they were well laid to rest now. She had never imagined an experience such as the one she'd just had.

Lovemaking with Tavish had been pleasant enough that she had missed it when he left, but doing so with Alan proved extraordinary. *Magic,* he had said, and so it was. She should have known he would never lie, but that had to be the truest word he had ever spoken.

Her lips stretched into a wide smile and she sighed against his shoulder. Thoughts of nights such as this one stretching into a limitless future made her shiver with anticipation. Yes, love or not, this feeling between them would definitely be enough.

"Honor?" the gruff whisper interrupted her musings.

She moved her head so she could see his face. He looked worried. "You slept," she said, resorting to an inane observation to avoid voicing the intimate things she would really like to say. *Would you kiss me again? Would you hold me, take me, make my body weep with pleasure?*

No, it was probably too soon for him, and he would think her wanton beyond redemption. Mayhaps she was.

He shifted to support himself on one elbow, his head

resting on one hand as he looked down at her. "Are you well?"

"Well married, that is a certainty!" she said, laughing softly. She knew she blushed; she could feel the heat in her cheeks.

He sighed and brushed her tangled hair off her face with his free hand. "I fear I might have been overly rough with you."

"No bruises. I told you no harm could come to me." She flipped up the corner of his plaid. "Invincible. Magic."

His smile warmed her heart. She sensed he wanted to say something serious, but held himself back. For a long time, he said nothing, just stared at the fabric, thinking.

Then, when he finally spoke, it had naught to do with what had happened between them. She knew that was no oversight, but deliberate avoidance to cover either regret or embarrassment. Honor suspected he seldom let lust take him unawares such as it had this night.

"See this small thread that runs through, the lighter one?" He traced a line of gray that crisscrossed the brown and green. "This makes my breacan different from all the others old Moriag wove for the clan."

"Because you are part English?" she asked.

"Nay. Aye. I dinna ken why." He rolled to his back and laced his hands beneath his head, staring at the overhead drape on the bed. "When my mother left the Highlands, I stood watching her ride away, too frightened to weep. My uncle shoved me at Moriag, the main weaver, and ordered her to outfit me with a breacan and beat the English out of me. She took me in hand then and we went to her cottage. 'Twas little more than a bothy, but larger than the rest in order to hold her looms." He smiled at a memory and was quiet for another while.

"Did she make you this?" Honor fingered the raveled edge of the plaid.

"Aye, but that was not the first. I sat for hours watching her weave that day. She fed me, of course, made me a pallet in the corner. Long into the night, I listened to the clack of her loom. When she had finished, she stripped me of all save my sark and taught me how to belt it on."

"Hard to do?"

He laughed softly. "Aye, there is a trick to it if ye havena a ghillie to help. But I got the hang right quick." Then he took the cloth from her fingers and again traced the small gray stripe. "Moriag pointed this out to me. Said it was an added thing, a prophecy. She had the sight, so she said."

"What did she predict?" Honor asked.

"That the blue thread running through would be the color of my lover's eyes."

"Was it?"

"Ach! I was seven, pissed with females because of my mother's leaving, and in no mood to hear such drivel from a barmy old woman." Then he grinned down at her and raised one fiery brow. "But later on, when I was twice that age, I chased every blue-eyed lass in th' glen, bonny or nay."

"Did you catch them?" Honor queried with an answering grin.

"Fleet o' foot, our highland lassies. Not every time." He looked thoughtful. "In this last plaid she wove me, just before I left Uncle Angus to make my own way, she made me note the thread again. 'Twas not blue as before, but gray. When I asked her why, Moriag said this was the color of my *true* love's eyes."

Alan pulled on the corner of the plaid, draping it next to her cheek. "Gray as a dove's wing," he whispered.

"Aye. She has the sight, does old Moriag." His hand held the cloth against her face as he lowered his mouth to hers and kissed her softly.

Honor held still, Alan's words registering in her mind even as his taste teased her lips. *True love's eyes.* Gray, like mine, she thought. Her heart skipped and she firmly attributed it to quickening desire for the man who could make her body sing.

She was no green girl who needed practiced love words to make her a willing wife. Mayhaps he even meant them. Alan probably did love the woman he thought her to be. She could fix that with one conversation, one she never hoped to have.

How could she love him and still deceive him? Did that mean she did not love him after all?

Trust, that she knew she felt for him, and admiration. Appreciation for his strength, his wit, his beauty and his passion. Oh Lord, his passion! Even now she could taste it in his kiss, feel it rising like the loch in a spring flood.

Already she felt this overpowering need to confess it all to him, but therein lay disaster.

Honor could not afford love if it caused this kind of grief. And, no matter how dear Alan held it, she certainly could not afford truth.

Chapter Eleven

Alan roused Honor's women from their sleep before dawn and demanded they heat and haul water for her morning bath. "Hurry yourselves," he urged the maids. "Do not make your lady wait."

He left them to their task and went out to see whether he could divine what happenings his wife's father might have planned for the day.

Honor still lay abed, burrowed in the tangled bedcovers. He wanted her women to see her rosy, well-loved countenance before she donned robes and assumed the serenity she usually wore. There should be no question at all what had occurred in the solar last night.

He bore mixed feelings about that occurrence. Two occurrences, he corrected, fighting an uprush of renewed desire. Remarkable, how sweetly she had welcomed that second, unnecessary coupling in the predawn hour. Well, it *had* been necessary as far as it concerned him, but she might have said him nay on grounds that their goal already stood accomplished. Why had she not? Still fogged with sleep most likely.

Would she prove angry when she woke fully? Would she feel guilty? If so, her guilt could never equal his own.

Tavish's shade teased the fringe of his troubled thoughts. Would he haunt Honor as well?

"'Twas duty, Tav. Hers and my own. Ye wished it on us," he muttered darkly as he crossed the bailey. But Alan knew in his heart he had wished it on himself with a single-mindedness he had never before applied with such fervor.

"Ho, Alan, lad," his father called down from the wall walk. "Come see this!"

Alan rushed up the steps and joined Adam. "God ha' mercy, he's fired the whole village!"

"He has that. Looked to be empty, though. Not one villager running and screaming that I could see or hear. Nor any livestock. Your folk must have taken to their heels aforehand, God be praised."

Adam leaned forward between the merlons and squinted. "Look, they gather for some purpose over there by that hillock." He pointed through the lifting mist.

Alan nodded. "Aye, their machines will be taking shape there. Hume plans to move on us soon with the ram and ladders, I expect."

"Can we withstand?" his father asked, turning to him with hands on hips.

"For a while. They outnumber us heavily and Hume has a goodly trained force. Look to be men of some experience, around forty of them. A good many of them mercenaries."

"Why does he go to such trouble? This is no light undertaking, dragging a retinue of this size across the channel just to claim one errant daughter. They had to bring all of their victuals, mounts, everything. Very costly. Most men would simply take the loss and damn their luck."

"She pricked his pride, most like," Alan said.

"Could be that. Or he believes he can still barter her for more wealth than he is spending on this enterprise."

"Hume will make no further bargains for *my* wife. That I vow."

Adam chuckled, fingered his beard thoughtfully, then looked back out across the field. "Speaking of vows and such, how went the night?"

"First defense in place," Alan answered evenly, refusing to allow the old man to ruffle his feathers this morning. His father seemed to delight in causing him embarrassment. Two could play.

"How went yours?" Alan countered. "Find comfort, did you? Or do you but content yourself by urging others to the deed these days?"

To Alan's chagrin, the old fellow threw back his head and laughed uproariously. When he caught his breath, he landed a hard slap on Alan's shoulder and crowed, "Ha, you have grown sharp as a dagger, boy! I knew you would! Your mother early warned me I'd suffer my own barbs out of your mouth one day. By God, she knew you well!"

"Not near well enough," Alan remarked, "else she would ha' known I'd earn her brother's wrath by yer trainin' me up to such outspokenness." He could not help dishing up a bit of guilt over his parents' abandonment.

With satisfaction, he watched his father's face darken with poorly contained rage. "Angus strapped you often?"

"Regular as he ate oat parrich."

Adam cleared his throat and swallowed hard before speaking again. When he did, his voice sounded gruff, forced. "It was the making of you, I expect. Good thing, too. I'd not have had the heart to do it myself."

"Ye failed to answer my question," Alan said, leaning a shoulder against the battlement. "Do ye comfort yourself on this...woman?"

His sire cocked his grizzled head and regarded him with a narrowed gaze. "Aye, I do. Sadly lacking as your education under Angus must be, you surely know we did not find your little brother under a bracken bush."

Alan straightened and crossed his arms over his chest. "She may well have *found* him there for all I know."

His head snapped to the side with Adam's sudden blow.

The ringing in his ears almost obliterated the low ominous growl of his father's words. "I do not defame *your* wife, sir. Do not insult *mine!*"

Alan looked long into the flashing green of eyes that mirrored his own. He saw no guilt and no apology. His gut roiled with rage and shame. Rage, for his mother's sake and at his father's defense of another woman. Shame at his own pettish strike at a female he did not even know. The shame won. "I do beg your pardon, my lord. And...hers, as well."

"Well then. Best forgot." The large hand that had once guided his first steps and just now scrambled his brains, extended toward him. Hesitantly, Alan grasped it.

"Angus has no patch on ye for strength in a backhand, Da. Seems ye do have the heart for it after all." Alan rubbed the side of his face, which felt numb.

Still clutching his hand, Adam pinned him with a steady gaze. "I will not defend my actions to you, Alan. I loved your mother well whilst she lived, and love her still. But I am now wed to Janet. Love for the one takes nothing from the other. If you do not understand this, at the very least, respect it."

"Aye, tha' I'll do," Alan promised.

His father released his hand and turned aside, rolling his eyes. "For God's sweet sake, boy, why do you insist on sounding like a bloody sheep-thieving highlandman?"

"That's what ye wanted me ta be," Alan said with an

evil grin, intensifying his brogue. "That's what I am. Have ye got somethin' agin sheep, Da? I ken ye keep harpin' on the wee buggers."

"You do that apurpose, sounding just like that bloody Angus," Adam accused. "And you can speak civilly when you choose! I've heard you do it!"

Alan turned away from his father and braced his hands against the closest embrasure, looking out. "Leave off, Da. We have bigger problems to ponder than my manner of speech."

"We do that! Such as why you never answered our letters. Not once did you. Not a word, and it broke your mother's heart!"

"You sent none to me," Alan said in a flat voice. He continued looking at the smoke filled sky.

His father gasped. "We *did!* Many!" Then he groaned. "Angus. I will kill him." A silence fell between them and lasted too long. "I cannot believe you'd not even question the lack, Alan. When you grew older, why did you not write to us to ask why?"

"I could not," Alan whispered, his voice almost lost in the wind. "I simply could not." Then he turned to his father and smiled. "Let it go, Da. 'Tis done and done."

"By God, no! It is *not* done!" Again a tense silence fell. "But you are right, we must lay this issue aside for now. You have enough on your mind." He laid his hand on Alan's forearm and squeezed. "Let me keep watch, son," he offered in a brusque, but conciliatory tone. "You go below."

"Verra well." Alan left him there. He had more pressing things to do than hurl accusations at his father. And besides, it was not half as satisfying as he had thought it would be. Whether there had been letters or not mattered little now. His father could have come to him or brought him home if he really cared. The damage had been done. Nothing had changed between them this day, nor would it.

He entered the hall still scowling. First thing, he saw the woman called Janet breaking her fast. Curious in spite of himself, he approached the fire hole where she sat toasting her stockinged feet and munching on a scone.

Her untidy hair trailed over one shoulder, the other half tucked haphazardly under a wrinkled kerchief. Alan had to admit the old man had an eye for women. His mother had been a beauty. Everyone had said so. Though he could no longer see her face in his mind, he knew it to be true.

This Janet boasted an earthy, tumbled up kind of loveliness herself. Her features were right saucy, her body full-figured in all the right places. Here was a woman he might have chosen himself before he met Honor. At least to while away an hour or so. God knew she was around the right age. Too young by half for an old stoat like his father.

The little lad they called Richard stood between her legs, dimpled elbows on her knees, head lifted and mouth open. Alan watched as she pinched a good-size crumb of the scone and popped it into the boy's mouth. The child had green eyes and dark red curls. No bracken bush by-blow, this little fellow. He definitely was a Strode.

His stepmother looked up then and grinned wickedly at Alan. "Good morn! You have a merry look about you. All went well, then?"

Alan pinched the bridge of his nose and sighed, shaking his head. "God's truth, does no one think on else? Aye, 'twas done and done. Are ye content wi' that?"

Her laugh belonged in the alehouse where his da probably found her. "Question is, son, is *she* content with that?"

"Do not call me *son,* woman! You presume too much!"

"Save all that bluster for someone who fears it, *laddie*," the woman advised, her voice strident. She plucked off another bite of bread for her babe. "You're but an older cut of this'n here. All three—you, Rich and the old man—alike as three beans in a pod. Holler and stomp, rail and fuss. Gives a body hives, it does. Sit you down and pour a cup." She nodded toward an empty stool.

Alan sat. Why, he couldn't say. He wanted nothing to do with this trull. 'Twas the boy who held him there, he decided. His brother. "How old is he?"

"Nearin' two," she answered in more congenial tones. "Spiteful little beast!" she accused the child when he nipped her finger and giggled. She rose and set the boy in front of Alan. "Mind him whilst I find the jakes, would you?"

Before Alan could summon an answer, she swept away and left him alone with the babe. "Richard, eh?"

One fat little hand tugged Alan's sleeve as the chubby body launched itself against him. A string of loud babble as unintelligible as gutter French poured forth from the little imp and ended with a resounding, "Da!"

"Nay, I'm not yer *da*." Alan lifted the boy and held him so they were face-to-face. "I'm yer brother, lad. Alan." He repeated his name several times while the wide green eyes searched his.

"Awan!" preceded another spate of curious sounds. This time culminating with *mik*.

"That much, I understand," Alan said and stood, intending to carry the child to the kitchens where they had goat's milk aplenty. He rather liked his brother's directness.

For a moment, he recalled an early happening in his own life, tugging on a much larger hand, demanding a drink or some such. Had it been Nigel's hand?

He looked into the face of this brother and felt tears sting his eyes. "You and I will know each other, Dickon. That, I do vow. You won't need to ask yourself the question, was it my brother's hand I held?"

He supposed, in order to effect that promise, he must try and get on with the so-called lady wife of his father. But he did not have to like her.

All in all, the morning had not shaped up as he would have wanted, yet was not far removed from what he had expected.

"Husband?" came the quiet query. "Father Dennis wishes to speak with you before you gather the archers."

Alan suddenly recalled the daily practice he had instituted and should be supervising even now. He handed Richard over to Honor with a warning. "Have a care. He bites."

She laughed merrily as she hefted the child onto one hip. Alan didn't think she looked at all upset by the night's events. Wouldn't do to begin discussing that here and now. Maybe never. Why not just go on as they were? Women tended to talk a thing to death anyway.

Guilt notwithstanding, he fully intended to employ his husbandly rights unless she strongly objected. He could not help but stand in awe of her composure. She made no demands this morning, no accusations. And she exhibited no regret whatsoever for what they had done, either by word or expression.

"Honor," he said without thinking, "aptly called. You are all an honorable lady should be, and I hold you in higher esteem than any person I know."

Embarrassed by his unexpected declaration, fearing the tears that quickly welled in her eyes, Alan fled like a boy caught red-handed stealing sweets.

Whatever had possessed him to say such? he wondered,

as he stalked back out into the bailey to look for the priest. He had meant it, of course. He never lied. But it must have hurt her somehow to hear him say it.

Doubtless Tavish had offered like praise at one time or another. It would have been like him to do so. That was what had brought her tears. Memories.

He cringed inwardly to think how inept he must sound, spouting his rough compliments, when Tavish had accustomed her to the smooth, practiced words of an educated nobleman. Alan felt his heart nigh break then, knowing he could never hope to compete with Honor's cherished recollections of Tavish.

And who had he to blame for that lack in himself? None but the parents, who relegated him to the care of a rogue uncle whose idea of courtly words consisted of, "Bend over, lass, and I've a copper for ye."

Damn them all.

Father Dennis approached with less than his usual grace. Melior followed him like a curious shadow.

"Sir Alan, we are woefully short of arrows, I think. The archers wonder if there will be even enough for a second volley."

Alan considered for a moment and laid a hand on the good father's shoulder. "We must tell them to make every one count."

Melior edged his way between them. His soft, musical voice intruded. "I could sneak out, perhaps gather materials to make more. Or go somewhere else for help?"

"Nay," Alan said, appreciating the offer. "We know not where Hume has men stationed. If one discovered the tunnel's opening, they would be on us from the inside."

The songster grimaced and struck his small fist in his palm. "Is there nothing that we can do, then? Must we simply wait until they overrun us?"

Alan laid an arm about the thin shoulders. "You can keep up our spirits with your tales and songs. And I can teach these knaves to aim straight. I'll not let Hume take our lady. We'll fight him to the last man standing."

"As you say, sir," Melior agreed quietly. "Have I leave to attend your father on the wall-walk?"

Alan nodded and slapped him on the back. "Aye. Keep him company if you like. Only mind he doesna teach ye any English lays to sing over my supper, eh?"

"What if we concoct a tune wholly Scot, sir, with a touch of French guile?" Melior asked cryptically, "Something to swell the heart with hope of victory. How would that be?"

"I say, go to," Alan replied.

So, the men—even to the bard and the priest—rankled with inactivity. Alan accompanied Father Dennis to the area where straw-filled targets awaited the chance arrow. He noted the twenty-odd villeins gathered with their roughly hewn bows.

Remember Bannockburn, he told himself with a determined nod of his head. *Outnumbered, half-trained, well-led and victorious.* Then he turned to Father Dennis. "Got a prayer for us, Father?"

Later that evening, Honor presided over the table, nodding the maids in and out with the sparse three courses she had ordered up for dinner. Meager fare for guests, but with a siege imminent, prudence won out over the need to impress.

Alan's countenance did not bode well for a pleasant evening. He looked fit to kill something. No amount of cajoling could rouse him to a better mood, so she gave it up.

Janet threw her several sympathetic half smiles. Honor

quite liked the woman. They'd had pleasant enough conversation that afternoon, and had begun a tentative friendship despite their obvious difference in upbringing. As far as mothers-by-marriage went, Honor knew she could have done worse by far than Janet Strode.

When they had finished their stewed apples and cheese, everyone quickly made their good-nights and took to their respective chambers. No one even suggested a game of gammon or a song from Melior, much to her relief. She felt in no mood for entertainment, at least not of the kind more than two could enjoy.

The solar seemed chilled, despite the hearty blaze of the fire. She wondered whether Alan would suggest bedplay this night. Likely not, given all those frowns and glares. She supposed he and his sire had quarreled, or else he had simply worried himself into a stew about her father's threats.

Were it the latter concern, he certainly did not suffer alone. But he had said he would protect her and she had to believe it. That was her only hope. Pray God her father's men could not breach the gate or the walls of Byelough.

Surely the siege force would run out of food long before the castle stores were depleted. Then they would have to leave. Nothing more could be done at present in any case.

Once she had fed Christiana, Honor instructed Nan to take the babe away to sleep with her. She watched as Alan leaned forward on the stool by the fire, carefully honing his sword. The thing must be sharp as a carving knife by now. She made ready for bed, leaving him to his chore.

When she lay covered to the chin, he finally put the blade away and divested himself of his clothes. Not once did he meet her interested gaze or speak. He climbed into bed beside her as though she did not exist.

"Art weary, Alan?" she asked as she reached out and brushed his arm to show concern.

"Aye," he answered, pulling away from the touch and turning away from her.

So, it was to be that way, was it? They might not have many nights left to hold each other, and Honor badly needed to be held tonight. She suspected Alan did as well. Something was very wrong here.

Had he guessed by her actions that she had never loved Tavish? Perhaps he thought her disloyal to enjoy their loving so. Had she been too bold in her seduction last eve? Did he hate her for it now that he had thought on it a while?

He would never trust her, never believe her constant with regard to himself if he discovered she had played Tavish false with lies. She sniffed and wiped her cheek, unaware until then that she wept.

At the sound, he quickly rolled over and stared at her in the candlelight. "What's amiss?" His voice sounded gruff with irritation.

"Nothing," she said with a curtness that belied the words. "I would not have you angry, is all."

"I am not angry!"

"You are!" she insisted, kicking herself for beginning what she knew would grow into a confrontation she did not want.

"Nay, Honor. Leastwise, not angry with you," he whispered, his voice softening with what sounded much like regret. "This waiting for attack plagues me."

"Is that truly what troubles you?"

"Well, that and more. It angers me that I have naught to offer in return for all you give to me. Were I very wealthy, well connected, or nobly inclined, your father might well leave us be. You are so perfect, and I...I know I am not the kind of man—''

"And how are you not? You won many riches with that sword of yours and a king troubled himself to knight you. Better than that, you are the soul of kindness," she argued, brushing away a long strand of hair that fell over his forehead. "See how you have always handled Christiana? Think how you deal with our people. What can you mean, not my kind of man? There is none better that I know."

He stared at the top of the bed curtain, avoiding her eyes. "I speak of other things, Honor. Things I should have learned at my mother's knee, at my father's side," he said, closing his eyes and sighing all forlorn. "At a tutor's hand. You should have more than an ignorant—"

"Unlettered," she corrected. "There is a great difference as you once pointed out. Can it be you pity that young fellow you once were, after you staunchly forbade me to do so?"

That earned her a twisted smile that grew into a short laugh. "Aye, you've the right of it, I fear. I have been wallowing in self-pity, have I not? 'Tis a new experience and I cannot say that I like it much."

Honor leaned over and kissed his cheek. His days' growth of beard scratched her lips and made them tingle. He turned his head slightly and brushed his mouth across hers. "What a treasure you are."

The warmth of his words suffused her body. She wanted him. Dared she become the aggressor again? Without further thought on it, she settled her mouth on his and deepened the kiss. He drew away and stared into her eyes for what seemed like hours.

When he spoke, his sincerity frightened her as no angry act could ever do. "Honor, my heart, I need you. I know you cannot love me, but I need you more than my next breath.''

"I am yours," she whispered. In that moment, Honor knew she had never spoken truer words than these three. He would take them at face value, of course. Her body belonged to him by law and he could do with it as he willed. But she could admit to herself, if not to him, that he held more than that in his power.

Dread mingled with elation as he drew her against him and began to work the magic she craved.

She loved Alan of Strode. There it was. Against her will and against her better judgement, but she loved him none-theless. And even if her father could not manage to take her from Alan, her own perfidy regarding Tavish would surely destroy any tender regard he had developed for her.

More deceit was the only answer.

Even as Honor returned Alan's caresses full measure and gave herself up to the pleasure he offered, remorse over her deliberately continued dishonesty weighed heavily on her heart.

Eventually they slept, wound about each other like vines intertwined, sated and content. At least for the night.

Scratching on the door gave way to loud knocks as Honor tried to come awake. Alan had already roused and was busy lighting the candle that had guttered out earlier.

He quickly unbarred the door and opened it, standing in the opening to shield her from view.

She heard David the Younger, whom Alan had chosen to lead his guard, speak breathlessly as though he had been running, ''Attack's begun. Ram's in place, sir. They sneaked it up under cover of dark. We just heard 'em.''

"Archers to the parapet?"

"Aye, sir. Gettin' there."

"Oil vats tended?"

"Hot as hell, sir."

"Pikers watching for ladders?"

"In place."

"Take yer station. I'm right behind ye." Alan wrapped his breacan round his waist, buckled his belt, and slung the excess fabric over his bare shoulder. Grabbing up his sword, he ran barefoot after David, bellowing orders as he crossed the hall.

Honor jerked on her bedrobe, snatched up his boots and hurried after him.

Chapter Twelve

Honor ignored the pebbles and grass stubs pricking her own feet as she carried Alan's boots across the bailey. He couldn't fight barefoot.

In the light of the torches brandished by latecomers running to man the wall-walk, she spied Alan's large form ascending the steps near the front gates. Without further thought, Honor dashed after him.

The first blow from the ram pealed like thunder. She stopped in her tracks and looked toward the portals in time to see the thick timber vibrate. Deafening shouts ensued. Battle cries echoed off the surrounding hills.

She ducked her head and ran for the wall steps, tearing up one side, shoving against others making their way to the top.

Alan yelled above the crash of the ram and taunting bellows from both sides of the wall. "Choose targets. Do not shoot wild!"

A crossbow quarrel flew past his head, arced downward and stuck in the dirt. Honor froze, shocked at his close brush with death. *Her father's men would shoot him! He had no care for his life up there.*

"Alan!" she screamed. "Alan, get down!"

He turned then. She knew the moment he saw her. Green eyes narrowed with anger, he shouted, "Get back to th' keep, lass! Make ready for wounded!"

When she opened her mouth, he drowned out her words with his order. "Go now or I'll open the buggerin' gates and let him have ye!"

She dropped his boots and ran. Never had she seen a man so riled! Would he do it? Would he turn her over? Never. 'Twas merely battle fury that made him threaten.

Another bolt from a crossbow landed inches from her foot. She jumped and screamed. With all the haste she could make, she tore up the steps to the hall entry and bolted the doors behind her.

"Good lord, they are mad, all of them!" she said as Nan ran to her. "I never thought it would come to this."

"You knew. That is why you wanted your husband to kill him first," Nan reminded her. "Come, feed the child and drink some wine. You are beset."

"Right enough!" she agreed heatedly. "Beset and scared witless. Gather linens and the basket of simples. We may—no, *will*—have wounded ere this is done! Hasten!"

Honor pushed Nan toward the kitchens and made for the alcove where she knew Christiana would be waiting.

For what seemed half the day, screams, shouts and the battering of the ram filled the air at Byelough. Even the stout doors of the keep itself provided an inadequate barrier to the awful sounds.

They opened the doors to admit wounded though there were only four of those after all. Each time the call came to open the portals, Honor cringed with fear that Alan would be among the men felled by arrows or bolts. Her father must not own many bowmen or she suspected it would be worse.

When silence descended, everyone halted what they were doing and glanced fearfully at each other. In a few moments, she heard Alan's voice. "'Tis done for now. Let us in."

Honor hurried to remove the heavy bar and fell into his arms as he entered. Alan squeezed her once, then promptly set her aside. He stalked toward the tables where the wounded lay. "How bad?" he asked her.

"Two with shoulder wounds. One lost an ear, of all things. Old Hamish had the worst of it. We had to cut a bolt from his chest. He will live, I think." Honor said. "What…what about the others, my father's men?"

"Worse than ours. They carted away nine or ten. A few burned, three shot, most hurt when the ladders fell." He smirked, still not looking at her. "Your father's well enough. Never came close."

"Will they come back?" she asked, hating how weak her voice had become.

"Sure as the sun rises. I think not today, however." He turned quickly and left the hall to return to the men outside.

Honor swiped at her cheeks, wet with either sweat or tears. She didn't know or care at this point. Exhaustion drew her to the nearest stool and she sat with her elbows on her knees.

"Are ye ill?" Adam of Strode asked softly.

"Yes," she answered, not bothering to look up at her father-in-law. "I am sick to death of all this. I have never witnessed a battle before."

"Battle? Hell, daughter, this was but a slight argument to what will happen on the morrow. I think we but tweaked their anger."

"They will take Byelough, will they not?" she demanded, standing up then and facing him squarely. "I must go out to my father and stop this madness."

He took her by the shoulders and shook her gently. "Hold on, my girl. It will not be necessary to do that. You leave things to old Da, eh?"

She scoffed. "And what can you do?"

The smile he gave her looked so like Alan's, she nearly wept again. "What I should have done already. Why don't you have a nice rest now?"

"Good thought," Janet agreed as she appeared at his side. "Come, Lady, and let us see to the bittie ones. They're like to set up a howl the likes of which we've not yet heard today if they don't get fed soon."

She hugged Adam's arm to her breasts and winked up at him. "See you wash off that stink afore I see ye again, eh?"

He laughed and tapped her nose. "That mouth will be your undoing one day, you sly wench."

"Mayhaps tonight," she cooed suggestively.

Honor left them bantering and went to refresh herself and feed the baby. Adam and Janet made her long with all her heart for such a closeness with Alan.

Given his attitude today, it did not seem likely. Despite their loving the night before, Alan had distanced himself. Did he resent her for bringing on all this trouble?

No further attack occurred that afternoon. Alan remained out with the men, readying Byelough for tomorrow's assault, she assumed.

Supper was catch-as-catch-can, broken meats and stale bread, dried apples and chunks of cheese. Most ate standing around the hall, picking at the dishes covering the one table not in use as a bed for the wounded.

The men gathered in groups to discuss the next morning's plans and the women remained subdued. All retired early with the expectation of another dawn exactly like, or worse than, the one they had just endured.

Someone had remarked on the fact that the supply of arrows and boiling oil had diminished dangerously. He had been quickly hushed, but not before Honor heard and divined exactly what that meant. Tomorrow Lord Hume would take Byelough Keep. Tomorrow, she would likely become a widow unless she surrendered herself.

Once Alan and Honor were abed, she said as much.

"You will not go out to him," Alan said, his voice low and hoarse from shouting orders. "I will not let you go."

"I must," she insisted, pleading with her eyes for permission to stop the fighting. To save him and to save Christiana.

"Nay," Alan said simply. "If they take the keep, your priest has orders to hide you and Kit in the bolt-hole. I will distract Hume and his men while Father Dennis takes you out to the caves where the villagers hide. Once he returns to these parts and hears Byelough has been taken, Bruce will come. You must stay hidden until then. The king will protect you if I...cannot."

Honor shook her head and grasped his hands, desperate to persuade him to let her go. "Father will kill you."

"The whole of Edward's army tried to kill me, sweeting. Yet here I am."

He dropped one of her hands and pinched out the candle by the bed. Her other hand he brought to his lips. "Go to sleep, Honor. I dare not love you tonight, for I would be too fierce."

Honor rested her palm on his heart until she felt the beating slow. He slept. She wondered if she ever would again.

A knocking noise awakened her. Surely it wasn't dawn already! Alan leapt from the bed and opened the door.

David the Younger stood there, his rushlight illuminating his excitement.

"Sir, they are come back!"

"Attack?" Alan swung around, almost knocking the candle stand to the floor in his hurry to dress.

"Nay, sir, not th' soldiers."

"Then who? Back from where?"

"The bolt-hole, sir. Melior said summon you in all haste! They've done it!" David stuck the torch in the holder beside the door and ran back into the hall.

Alan pulled on a sark and reached for his plaid. "Stay here until I see what this is about," he ordered Honor.

By the time she had thrown on her bedgown and reached the hall, Alan had halted beside the group gathered around a form on the floor. Her father-by-marriage hooked a booted toe under the body lying on the floor and flipped it over on its back.

"Your nameday is next week as I recall," he said to Alan in a well-pleased voice. "Brought you an early gif-tie!"

"God ha' mercy, Da! 'Tis Hume himself!" Alan coughed out a laugh of disbelief. "How—?"

"Well, Melior here thought of it. We dressed us up so," he said, brushing a hand over the dark woolen clothes he wore, "and took ourselves out to the woods behind their campsite. 'Twas merely a matter of waiting until nature called him."

"You've killed him." Honor whispered, not altogether grieved.

"No, no, no," Adam assured her. "Just gave him a sound knock on the head. He'll come about right soon, I expect. Of course, then he could die of embarrassment."

Alan laughed again, this time with pure delight. "This is too good to be true. Tell me I am awake!"

"You are awake, else we are all dreaming," Honor said. "Now what will you do? Kill him?"

Alan did not answer her, but spoke instead to David, the guard. "Bind him securely. Throw him in the small storeroom. Lock and guard it with your life."

"Why not the *oubliette?*" Honor asked. Dropping her father in a deep dark hole dug under the floor of the keep seemed fair enough after all he had done.

"There's a thought," Alan said. "But come the morn, I want him close at hand."

"Will you beat him then?" Honor asked, still staring at her father with rapt fascination.

Alan looked at her curiously. "Would you want me to?"

Honor covered her mouth with her hand to hold back the words. God help her, she did want him beaten. She wanted him very soundly beaten.

Her gaze flew to Alan's, then to his father's. She had asked if they would kill him, and they thought she wanted them to. Did she? What must they think of a daughter who would wish such things on her own father?

Without another word, she turned and ran to the solar to bury herself in the bed. No more would she say. Not one word to damn herself further in their eyes. She had seen the censure, felt their rebuke.

They were good men, and kind. They would not understand how she felt. How her father had once made her feel. How terrified she was of him even now as he lay senseless on the floor.

She had brought all this on the people of Byelough, on Alan and his family, on Christiana and herself.

Honor knew she could not place all the blame on her father's head for what had happened. If she had played the dutiful child, none would have been wounded this day. No one would be in danger now but herself.

If only she had done what she ought.

Alan did not return to the solar. Honor needed time alone tonight, he reasoned. Seeing her father had upset her terribly and he did not know what he could say to alter that.

Hume had beaten and misused her over the years. For that alone, Alan wanted to kill him. He might do it yet.

"A bit like holding a wolf by the throat, having Hume within the keep," he said to his father.

"Better here than out there, don't you think?"

"Aye, but it was a mad thing you and Melior did, Da. You could have been captured. And if I refused to trade his daughter for my father, he might have killed you."

His father laughed and shook his head. "*If* you refused to trade? You mean *when* you refused. You'd never have exchanged her for me, nor would I have expected it."

Alan lay down next to the fire and curled his plaid around him. "Go to bed, Da. We'll tend to Hume come the morning."

"You will sleep here in the hall? What of Honor? You would leave her all alone in there after what has just happened?" He pointed toward the solar door. "What will she think?"

"You tend to your wife, old man. I'll tend to mine." With that, he closed his eyes and dismissed his father.

Before he slept, the thought occurred to him that Honor still might try something foolish. What if she attempted to see her father? Suppose she got some notion of going out to Hume's men to prevent another attack in the morning. He didn't think she would. But just the same, he got up and repositioned himself across the threshold of the solar.

Just before dawn, Alan rose and went to fetch Hume from the storeroom. He hauled the man upright and dragged him through the kitchens, up the stairs and back into the hall. There he deposited him in one of the two chairs.

Alan sat on the corner of the nearest table, swinging one leg and observing while his prisoner gathered his wits. Here was one Scot gone soft, Alan thought. Too much of the good life. That needed fixing.

"Where is my daughter?" Hume demanded.

"'Tis naught to you. I'd say ye've greater worries at the moment."

Hume glared at him and remained silent.

"We're going to speak with yer men at first light," Alan said conversationally. "And ye will order them back to France."

"Ha! And leave me no chance of rescue? I am no madman!"

"A matter of opinion, that, and 'tis certainly not my own," Alan said. "Yer actions thus far make me think ye're quite daft. Who but an addle-pate would spend so much effort draggin' an unwilling daughter—a well-married one, ta boot—back to a home she fled in terror?"

"The ungrateful minx betrayed me!" Hume shouted.

Alan backhanded him across the face, splitting his lip. "Have a care, Hume. I hold yer life in these hands."

"You dare not kill me. My men will take this place apart stone by stone, burn what's left and spit you over the coals."

"I canna fer the life of me think why they would do that, Hume. Knowin' as they do there'll be none to reward 'em for it," Alan replied. "For ye see, I'll be slitting your throat before that ram of yers makes another dent in my gates. Instead of burning oil, yer own life's blood will be pourin' over their heads as I hold ye by the heels. I'll do it, Hume, make no mistake. I never lie.''

Hume grunted in disgust. ''Then why would you cozen a lass who does so with every breath? She lied to me, at long last pretending to agree to the match, and so to the man I betrothed her to! She likely lied to Tavish Ellerby as well. Otherwise, he'd not have wed her without my consent. Do you trust a woman with such a false tongue in her head? Why the devil would you want her?''

Alan cocked one brow and pretended to give that thought. ''Why the devil would you?''

''I told you! I have plans for her. The comte de Trouville still expects to wed her and I—''

''That he'll not do. And she canna wed him, for she is wed to me.''

''Numbwit! She will be a widow ere I leave this place!''

Alan smiled. ''Ah, but she'll be an orphan first.''

Hume said nothing further, and refused to meet Alan's eyes. He shifted in his chair as though to make himself more comfortable.

A prickling on the back of Alan's neck told him someone approached from behind. When he turned, he saw Honor's pale face. He reached out and took her hand. ''Go back to bed, Honor.''

She shook her head, her eyes trained on her father.

''So, here is the faithless cat come to gloat, eh?'' Hume growled. Blood dripped from his split lip. ''Are you happy now?''

Honor stared at him and then at Alan. ''You hit him?''

''Aye, I did,'' Alan admitted. ''Apparently no' hard enough for his mouth still works.'' He smiled at her and caressed the back of her hand with his thumb. ''Why don't ye go see to the babe?''

Her hand jerked from his and flew to her mouth as she moaned. "Oh, no!"

"Babe?" Hume croaked. "You have a babe? Whose babe?"

"Mine," Alan answered smoothly. "We have a daughter." He thought he saw a brief flash of wistfulness in the older man's eyes. Surely a trick of the firelight, but mayhaps not. It wouldn't hurt to know just how soft Hume was inside that hard shell of his.

Alan continued, "She is a lovely wee bairn, much like her mother. Ye have a fine granddaughter, Hume. Would ye like to see her?"

"No! Never!" Honor cried and dashed from the hall to the alcove where Kit slept with Nan.

Hume's eyes followed her, a look on his face that Alan found unreadable.

"'Tis time. We'll go out and await yer men," Alan said. "I advise ye to do exactly as I say, else this'll be the last sunrise ye see."

Honor watched from behind the curtain as Alan and her father left the hall. A few moments later, Adam descended the stair and followed. The men who passed the night on pallets along the perimeter of the hall must have gone out earlier. The one man seriously wounded still slept.

Her fear gave way to curiosity. What would Alan do once her father's men arrived? A bigger question, what would her father do? Would he demand they attack despite the risk to himself? It would be just like him to do such a thing. She had to know.

Striding across the hall with determination, Honor let herself out and hurried down the steps and across the bailey. She stopped at the foot of the wall-walk steps and waited.

The creaking of wheels upon which the battering ram rode broke the silence just as the sun shot its first rays into the gray-pink dawn.

''Halt there!'' Alan shouted loudly in French. The creaking stopped. Someone below roared her father's name.

''We hold your lord. He has orders for you,'' Alan's voice boomed out in the stillness.

Honor stepped back so that she could see what was happening on the parapet. Alan held her father with a long blade against his throat. Father Dennis stood close, ostensibly ready to shrive the corpse.

Again Alan spoke, this time in English, ''Tell them, Hume, or I'll kill you here and now!''

Never had Honor heard so chilling a tone. Not at his worst, had her father sounded so threatening as did her husband. Here was a man she did not know at all. Vicious, cold and deadly. Frightening. Had she truly wished him this way?

His sudden language switch made Honor aware of something. The words he had spoken to her father's men were not the broken phrases of a man speaking a strange tongue. Alan had lied to her. His French had sounded perfect.

''Go...go home! Leave,'' her father called out.

''Not without our pay, my lord. We have no gold to buy our passage back.''

Father Dennis stepped up to the wall and dropped a sack that clinked when it hit the ground outside.

''Take it and go,'' Alan demanded, again in their language.

Honor heard the buzzing of heated conversation outside the walls. Then a deep voice questioned, ''What of our lord Hume? Will you allow him to leave with us?''

After a whispered conversation with the priest, he answered, "He stays!"

"Do we have your word you will not harm him?" the voice boomed.

Hesitation, a brief consultation, and then, "You have my word that he will die if you are not gone by noon. Once he is dead, you may take him."

The voice demanded assurance. "If we do leave, will you release him later?"

Alan remained silent, his knife steady beneath her father's chin. Honor wished she could see over the wall. Were they going as Alan had ordered?

Alan's father quit the wall-walk first. When he saw her standing there, he took her arm and led her across the bailey and back to the hall. "They are riding away," he muttered as they walked.

Honor said the first thing on her mind. "He speaks French."

Adam turned to her in surprise. "Who, Alan? Of course he speaks French. Latin and Gaelic, as well. Even picked up a bit of Italian from our minstrel. Always liked English best, though. Our Saxon blood, I suppose." His chest swelled with pride.

Honor pressed her lips together to hold in a curse. Lord Adam opened the door for her and they entered the hall. Honor kept walking, head down, deep in thought. When she did speak, she tried to sound unconcerned. "All that accomplished by age seven? Remarkable. I would wager he had no problem at all with his letters, either."

"None at all! Could write and read, though we had no books about to give him much practice. Taught him myself."

"I see," she said. "Would you excuse me, my lord?"

"*Da.* Why don't you call me *Da* as Alan does. Unless

you call your own father that...oh, sorry. For a moment I forgot...well, never mind.''

"You can talk about him, for heaven's sake. He is still my father. And the names I have called *him* would burn your ears." With that, she left him, entered her solar and slammed the door behind her.

Her anger knew no limits in that moment. Alan had played her like a fish on a string! Her own lies held no candle to his! She knew now who had written that letter ordering her to marry him.

Devilish beggar probably never knew Tavish well at all. Likely tricked Tavish into signing that paper and then filled in the rest in a shaky hand to disguise his own writing. Lord, could she trust no man in this world?

All his prattle about never lying and how honesty meant everything to him! That was but smoke to cover his own foul tricks. And to think how he had preyed on her sympathy. How her own guilt had eaten away at her because he was so damned *honest!*

Well, at least he dare not take her to task for the things she had done when his own dealings were so much worse. She had only lied to escape a dreaded marriage. He had lied for the sake of greed, pure and simple. He had wanted Byelough Keep, and had taken it by guile.

And now he had her in the bargain. He would soon wish he had found someone other than Tavish Ellerby to swindle, she vowed to herself. He had yet to guess what lengths she would go to in order to look after her own interests.

Alan of Strode was due a rude awakening.

Chapter Thirteen

Alan escorted Hume back to the keep. No one spoke as they entered the hall.

Lady Janet sat before the fire holding young Richard, who was wrapped tightly in a blanket. Hume slowed his step to regard the woman and child with open curiosity. He must have marked the child's age and decided it was too old to be Honor's, for he looked disappointed.

Alan delivered a push that sent the man on to the kitchen and into his storeroom prison.

"I'll not bind you again, but you will remain here," Alan said, ushering him inside. He withdrew his dagger and sliced the ropes from Hume's wrists.

The man bristled as he rubbed at the red welts on his arms. "I will not abide this, Strode. Surely even you know that nobles are allowed freedom within the walls so long as they give assurance they'll not attempt escape. Will you not accept my word?"

"I'd not accept a crust of bread from ye were I starving to death," Alan replied. "Think on how yer daughter must have felt when ye locked her away. With rats fer company and the walls closing in." He gazed steadily at the man and raised one brow. "She must ha' dreaded each beating ye threatened as well."

Hume drew himself up and threw out his chest. "You would not dare beat me!"

Alan smiled his most evil smile.

"B-but that is unconscionable!" he sputtered, "To put lash to a defenseless man is—"

"Not quite so wicked as thrashing a wee defenseless lass, is it now? Dwell on yer cruelty to her, Hume. Regret it to yer last day."

With that admonition, Alan slammed the door and bolted it. He grinned at the stream of foul curses clearly audible through the sturdy oak panel.

For the moment, he had dealt with Hume. He had purposefully given the man the wrong idea about his fate just to make him worry. No lies exactly, but close enough. Alan felt no guilt over that, surprisingly.

He did wonder just what he really would do with the man. If he turned him out, Hume would only gather his forces and strike again, this time harder and with full knowledge of the secret entrance and the sparsity of fighting men within Byelough.

If he did kill or even beat Hume, there could be repercussions. As he understood it, Hume provided information on the workings of the French court for the Bruce. Alan doubted King Rob would appreciate the loss of Hume's services.

The only thing Alan could think to do was detain him until Bruce returned from England and could settle matters. Alan and Honor *had* wed under Bruce's direction, after all. Surely on orders from the King of Scotland, Hume would hie back to France and leave them be. He was still a Scot, after all, and subject to obey his sovereign.

For the rest of the day, Alan trained his triumphant

troops, saw to the remaining stores and planned how he would go about rebuilding the village.

He delayed the confrontation with Honor because he feared hearing what she might demand with regard to Hume. Would she want his execution? Unfortunately no law he had ever heard about supported such a punishment. Though it should, the mistreatment of a daughter held no dire consequences at all.

The thought that Honor truly might wish Hume's death gave Alan pause. How could such a soul as she—so gentle in all other respects—desire the death of her own father?

He had once hated his own sire for destroying a seven-year-old's trust, but loved him nonetheless, simply because he had given him life.

Honor wanted retribution for her hurts, but Alan doubted she could bear the guilt that ensued once she saw it carried out. Whatever Hume had done to her, he was the only father she had. What a coil, this love-hate thing for an errant parent.

Alan counted himself more decisive than most, but he could think of no ready solution to his own contrary wishes, let alone those he feared Honor entertained.

Honor remained in her solar all day, pacing angrily and rehearsing the diatribe she planned to inflict on her husband for his venality. She tried and discarded numerous alternatives.

Her first thought—an outright attack on his person with a blunt weapon—certainly would not work. Neither would railing and gnashing of teeth. He would likely laugh at either tactic. Weeping and instilling guilt held possibilities. Tears undid him. Unless that reaction was merely a pretense of compassion.

The only thing concerning Alan of Strode that she held

as a certain truth was his desire for her. Men could not pretend about that. But denying him her body would prove a less than useless endeavor. He could simply take her and have done with it.

Suddenly Honor knew what she would do. Her response and affection increased his pleasure. No doubt of that. She would withhold both. He would find a cold bed this night and every other, a stiff and unyielding bedmate who offered only scorn for his efforts. Her anger surely would douse any desirous feelings on her part.

The decision boosted her spirits and gave her at least a small sense of control over her life. If there was anything she hated, it was the idea that a man—any man—could assume full power over her. How could she have forgotten that, even for a moment? Her weapons against it might be few and paltry, but use them she would and right diligently.

She would let him know she knew of his deception. If he understood French so well, then she would give him something to understand. Nothing would she hold back. He would not be able to reprimand her for her accusations and insults to him without admitting he knew the language. And that alone would prove the truth of his perfidy. The liar. She wished she knew how to curse in Latin, for that would give her twice the pleasure.

What did she have to lose? Alan had already done what she wanted. He had trained her men to defend the keep, few though they were. Thanks to his making Ian Gray Christiana's godfather, Honor no longer stood in danger of abduction by that cousin of his. And Alan had rendered her father harmless.

Her only other worry, the comte de Trouville, did not even know her whereabouts. Honor was certain her father had not involved him in any way or the comte would be here now, exacting his revenge.

When she thought on things in that respect, her machinations had proved quite successful thus far. She had what she wanted. Safety.

She could deal with the small problem of deceiving a husband who had deceived her first. At least he did not resort to cruelty. Even as she thought that, the picture of Alan holding a knife to her father's throat, his voice filled with deadly venomous threats, set her quaking. And Alan had struck him as well, she remembered. While he was bound.

She shook off the qualms and took a steadying breath. Alan would never strike her. He would never lock her away. Her heart beat faster. But had he not threatened to do just that when he thought she might leave the keep and surrender herself?

Well, she would deal with it if he turned his meanness toward her. She would find a way. If she had outwitted Lord Hume, king of backhanded blows and master of intimidation, she could certainly handle one ignorant—not illiterate she knew now, but ignorant—highlandman.

Alan waited until all were abed to approach the solar. He had delayed this as long as possible. Honor had not appeared in the hall for supper. Nor had she eaten a bite of the food Nan had taken her. Only then had he truly begun to worry.

Obviously she felt more trammeled over the morning's events than he had thought. Did she fear for her father's life? Or was she in there planning how to celebrate his death?

Alan found he knew little of the woman's mind when

he had thought he knew it as well as his own. A female was a riddle no man should attempt to answer.

She lay abed, covered to the ears, her hair coiled over the pillow like a length of twisted satin. The uneven rise and fall of the coverlet told him she did not sleep. "Honor, are ye well, hinny?"

"*Non,*" she answered, and followed with a spate of French too rapid for him to comprehend. Her voice sounded raspy as though she were ill. Or freshly emptied of tears. Poor mite.

He did not ask her to repeat what she had said since it did not sound like a question. He quickly undressed and slid into bed beside her. Encircling her with one arm, he pulled her back against him and breathed in her glorious scent. She held herself rigid and her body trembled when he slid one hand across her middle.

"Go to sleep, sweeting," he said. "I'm too weary myself for loving tonight."

Another unintelligible, almost angry, expostulation, preceded a loud sigh. Then she shoved his hand away, turned on her stomach, still facing away from him and lay quiet.

Pity he couldn't have Father Dennis standing near to interpret and prompt answers as he had on the battlements this morn. Poor Honor, so overset she could not think but in her mother tongue. Well, he should simply let her rest tonight and not trouble her more.

"*Bonne nuit,*" he murmured, thinking to soothe her with one of the few French phrases he did know. He ignored her exasperated groan, attributing it to her continued desire for solitude. Sleeping on the floor yet again did not appeal to him, however, so he simply closed his eyes, wriggled out a comfortable spot, and fell asleep.

As he woke, dawn offered a weak glow through the oil-skinned windows and revealed Honor's absence. Alan rose without hurry and donned a fresh sark and his breacan. He spent an inordinate amount of time working his leathern boots to soften the stiffness caused by yesterday's mist. He pulled on thick woolen knee hosen, the slightly damp boots, and drew the laces round his calves.

All that time—and he spent more than twice his usual in dressing—he wondered how Honor fared this morning. Had a good night's rest restored her sweetness? Or had her mood grown darker, even more troubled? What must he do to ease her mind if that was so?

Full of questions for which there were no ready answers, Alan entered the hall to break his fast.

Honor sat at table conversing with Father Dennis. He took his seat, noting he received not so much as a nod of greeting from her. Unwilling to force the issue in company or to interrupt the two, he downed a full cup of ale and wolfed a portion of bread and cheese.

When he had finished and still had no attention, he turned to her as he rose from his chair. He made her a perfunctory bow and spoke as formally as he knew how. "I bid you good morn, then, and take my leave."

She shot him a look, narrow-eyed and rather frosty. He got his nod, but no more than that.

Alan motioned for the priest to follow him. He would get to the bottom of this. As soon as they reached the steps leading down to the bailey, he stopped and turned laying a hand on Father Dennis's arm. "What's amiss with my lady?"

The priest's eyebrows flew up with an expression of innocence. "Lady Honor? Why naught that I know, sir. She seemed fine just now. A trifle excitable I admit. Chattered more than her usual, now that I think on it."

"About what?" Alan asked anxiously.

"Rebuilding and the like. She is worried about the villagers and the coming winter. Right that she should, she is their lady.''

''Aye,'' Alan agreed, ''but more than that's awry. She acts as though she's angry.''

''And are you not?'' Father Dennis asked reasonably. ''Our people face a harsh time if we cannot replace the stores they lost and put a roof over every head before the weather turns.''

Alan nodded and sighed, glancing out toward the hills. He clapped the good father on the back and went to gather the men. No point wasting the day wondering over a woman's megrims when he had work to do. Likely the priest was right anyway. What lady would not be vexed in such circumstance?

The next day and the next brought no change in Honor's attitude. Alan retired both nights to a silent chamber. Every time he touched Honor, she would shift away and utter a curt spate of French.

When he awoke to an empty bed and joined the company in the hall, Honor immediately took herself away from the table, ostensibly to see to the babe or speak with the kitchen staff. Never once did she meet his questioning gaze or answer in aught other than her mother tongue.

He knew he should leave her be. Approaching a woman in such a mood boded ill for any man with good sense. But damn the mood, he was her husband. The aftermath of such happenings as Byelough suffered should draw a man and wife together, not drive them apart. Alan needed her and he suspected she needed his comfort as well.

She was so unlike herself. This night, he promised himself, he would get to the root of this coil of theirs, set her to rights and get his sweet and gentle Honor back.

Honor heard his heavy-soled boots outside the solar and quickly arranged herself so as to feign sleep. How much longer she could maintain this fiction, she did not know. Thus far, he had shown more patience than she expected. Would he simply go on humoring her as though she were some touchless puzzle? He had remained silent, still pretending not to understand her, giving her no answer at all to her reproaches about his hoaxing. He did not intend to explain it, she decided. He must think men were above all the rules of fair behavior.

Did he not yet realize she punished him for his misdeeds? She wanted him to know it, by heaven. She wanted him to suffer with the loss of her affection, not act as if it meant nothing.

She had almost rather be beaten than ignored. Almost. Her loud and frustrated sigh gave her away.

"You do not sleep," he accused. "Why do you pretend?"

"I do not wish to speak with you," she replied in French.

"Well, at last, something I ken! But ye will speak, by God, and in Scot or English, an ye please!" he declared. "Enough's enough!"

"Oh no, not near enough!" she said, abandoning the French and scrambling to her knees on the bed to face him. She wanted absolute understanding between them now, despite whatever results she might encounter.

He wanted reasons? She would give him reasons. "You are a lying, despicable lout, Strode! Coming here with a *deathbed wish* of Tavish's!" She twisted her lips in a snarl. "A foul trick is what it was! You wrote it yourself. Tricked me into marriage and gained to yourself all I had worked for!"

He looked stunned. "Ye've lost yer reason," he whispered, shaking his head with the shock of it. "What ha' done this to ye, hinny?"

"Ah, lapse into your brogue, will you! Be what you are, you stupid savage! Bloody murderer! You killed Tavish, didn't you? Killed him to get what was his!"

She sucked in a terrified breath when he approached the bed, grabbed her arm and shook her. He *would* beat her! How rash to provoke him so. What was she thinking? She knew in her soul he had not killed Tavish. Tricked him and stolen from him, surely, but never murdered the man. Why in God's name had she said such a foolish thing?

His voice came low and grating. "If I thought ye truly believed all o' that, wife, I would as soon leave this place tonight, take what I came with, ride out and ne'er look back." He stared straight into her eyes, unblinking. "Aye, I would."

"Go, then," she mumbled, afraid to raise her voice when his huge fingers clutched her arm fit to break it.

"Nay, I cannot. Bruce wishes me to hold this place even if you do not. What devil's got into you, Honor, that you should accuse me so? I did not kill your husband. He was a friend in my youth and I loved him well. As a knight and a man, I admired him above most."

"You wanted what was his!" she dared in a small voice.

"Aye, Tav was blessed and I admit to envy. But I never thought to have it until he forced it on me." His hold lessened. He turned his head aside and blew out a long breath. "'Twas Tavish played the trick, not I."

"Liar!" Honor said, fuming, no longer caring if she roused his fury. Let him do his worst, she thought recklessly. "You forged that letter as surely as I altered my marriage documents! Don't you dare deny it, Alan, don't you dare!"

He looked at her as though she had grown horns. "'Tis true ye did that, then? Changed the words?"

"Aye, but for the good of all I did so," she admitted hotly. "But you...you did it for theft, plain and simple. Greed and lust for what Tavish owned and you did not!"

"You loved him that much," he stated.

"I feared my father that much!" she shouted. "Tavish meant protection! Escape! I feared for my life and ran as fast as I might to the only man who had ever given me a moment's worth of kindness!"

"Ye never loved Tav?" Alan asked. He held himself very still as he spoke, his hand hovering near her arm. "Never?"

Honor drew back against the headboard, looking everywhere but into the accusing green eyes above her. "I...cared very much."

"But ye never loved him?"

"He fathered my child! Treated me with concern! I *cared* for him!"

He grabbed both her arms then and gave her a firm shake. "Answer me, God witnessing, Honor. Did ye *ever* truly love him?"

She dropped her chin to her chest, overwhelmed by grief and guilt. "No," she admitted in a broken whisper. "I wanted to, and I would have...given time, I would."

Alan released her with a shove, turned on his heel and left the solar without another word. Honor curled herself into the pillows, dragged up the covers and wept.

How had all this gotten so out of hand? He was the villain here and making her out to be worse than he. She buried her face, scrubbing it into the linen. But she *was* a villain, as surely as Alan of Strode. All this ire of hers, 'twas only a means of distributing the guilt so that she did not bear so much of it. Shame coursed through her, an ugly river in her veins that washed waves of pain through her heart.

She could never forgive herself. But she would not forgive Alan, either. Hateful knave. At least *she* had not preached truth and honesty at all and sundry while making such a mockery of it. At least, she was no hypocrite. *Alan the True,* indeed!

In his grief, Alan sought solitude. Since there was none of that to be had within the crowded walls of Byelough, he saddled his horse, ordered the guard to open the gate and rode out.

The crisp night air heightened his senses, bombarding him with the scent of damp heather and the lonely silence of the sleeping hills.

The bitter taste of disappointment lay thick on his tongue. He could not reconcile the deceitful, caustic woman in the solar with the sweet and perfect lady he had wed. How could he have misjudged her so drastically? She had sorely wounded his pride and broken his heart in one conversation.

All this time, he had imagined her purity of heart, her rare ability to love unreservedly. What was even worse, Tavish had imagined it as well. The poor man had died thinking himself a cherished husband. Alan almost envied him that. At the moment, he wished he had not uncovered the blackness in her soul, that he had died defending her before the truth came out.

With a harshness he seldom employed, Alan kicked his horse into a ground-eating run and raced across the valley. Through the narrow pass they thundered and into the next open vale toward the burn and Tavish's resting place. Lathered and blowing, the mount obediently slowed to a walk between the rushing waters and the grave. Alan kicked out of his stirrups, swung his right leg over and slid to the ground.

Angrily, he scooped up a fist-size rock and plunked it on the growing pile of stones and muttered a perfunctory prayer as was custom.

That done, he paced back and forth before the cairn. "Lucky devil, ye are," he muttered. "I want ye t' know that!" Alan kicked at a loose rock, sending it onto the pile placed there by others who had happened by or come there for the purpose. "There's another for ye! That's for her! She'd not ha' prayed with it, neither."

Anger increased with every step. "Ye thought she loved ye, wanted ye, missed ye, aye? Welladay, there's a woman for ye, Tavish. Fractious, conniving, meddlesome creatures. Best do wi'out 'em." He added with a toss of his head, "For some things anyway. But if a mon's lookin' fer heart's ease, he'd best find th' plant o' that name. And chew on a mess of it till he drops doon dead!" Alan shot a quick glance of apology at the grave. "Nothin' personal in that. 'Twas just a thought."

Alan alternately stomped around the cairn and by the burn and stopped to heave stones into the water just to throw something. Suddenly, all energy left him and he sank down onto the bank. "Ah, Tav. I curried such hopes, y' know? I curried such great hopes."

He rose then, tossed a last rock into the tumbling waters and turned toward his horse. His ire and disappointment had not diminished in the least, but now smoldered in his breast, likely to break out into a raging conflagration.

Best that woman not give it cause with that tongue of hers, he thought darkly. Best she not, or he'd show her the rough side of his own. Deceiving Tav. Making sweet with himself. Mayhaps her father had no choice but to thrash her to try to cure her dishonesty.

Then Alan cringed inwardly at the very thought of it. In his mind's eye, he pictured Hume with a stick and wee Honor cowering with a wall at her back, her soft gray eyes wide with fear. "Nay, then. Not a beating," he muttered. "Never that."

But he'd not forgive her. Not for the lie she had lived with Tavish, and not for her grand pretense at caring for himself, Alan decided firmly. And there she was accusing him of untruths. She had only pretended to believe him when he first came here. Now she named him a grasping liar. The worst of insults.

The woman mocked the honor she'd been named for, and that was not a thing he would excuse under any circumstance.

His heart lay heavy with its load of anger and despair as he rode slowly back to Byelough. He envisioned the future stretched out before him, long years filled with the bitterness of doubt and suspicion.

When he passed the old dame's cottage where he had helped to birth wee Kit, daughter of his heart, Alan sighed. Here lay another concern. He could not permit Honor to taint the bairn. She might teach Kit to lie, if not apurpose, then by example. But how could he take a babe from its mother, especially this child whom Honor held so dear?

At least this quandary need not be solved today. But why not tell Honor of his thoughts on the matter? Aye, there would be a punishment to fit the misdeed. Let her stew in the juices of consequence for her wicked foolery.

"No!" Honor screamed, covering her face with trembling hands. "Oh, no, please, Alan. Please, I beg you do not!" She sank to the floor before him, weeping.

"You shall have her until she needs you no more," he assured her through gritted teeth. "I only hope Kit will not draw character along with the milk. Count yourself privileged I do not put her to another's breast anon. Fortunately, you will bear no more children, leastwise not by me.''

"Beast!" she cried, beating the floor with her fists until he thought she must break some bones. But he held himself erect, staring down at her with all the disdain he could muster, willing back a sudden wave of sympathy. "You are a beast!" she repeated in a tear-filled whimper, "and I hate you!"

"Aye," he admitted. "'Tis truth you spit now, wife. How does that taste in your mouth, eh? Strange and foreign, I'd wager. Best grow accustomed to it, for if I catch you in another falsehood, however small, you may rest assured there will be no friendly ears around you to hear another. Not your daughter's, not your maids', no one.''

He left her huddled in the midst of the solar, the violent shakes of her sobbing tearing at his sanity. God help him, he must not relent in this. 'Twas his only recourse to make her understand the wrongness of what she had done. Her only hope of redeeming herself by holding to truth hereafter. Tears blurred his vision as he firmly quelled a wish to go back and offer comfort. He must not.

Honor roused herself after a while and rose on leaden limbs. She washed her face, straightened her gown, and repinned her braids. With head held high, she slowly walked into the hall and across to the fire hole where Nan sat rocking Christiana to and fro. "Give her to me," she said softly.

"She sleeps, my lady. 'Tis not yet time for her to feed," Nan replied with a smile.

Honor reached down and took her child from the maid without another word. Then she strolled about aimlessly for a few moments before making a roundabout path to the kitchen stairs.

The guard, David, sat on a three-legged stool between the storeroom where her father was imprisoned and the other which housed the entrance to the bolt-hole. A quick glance around revealed no one else save the spit boy idly turning a joint of meat over the fire.

"David," she said, "would you go and show that lad the proper manner of that? He's like to char our supper if he continues to lag."

The guard nodded and grinned as he rose to do her bidding. Honor quickly slipped through the door when he wasn't looking and laid the sleeping babe on a sack of grain. She pulled another bag away from the opening to the escape tunnel, and then retrieved Christiana.

The child awoke and blinked up at her when Honor hugged her a bit too fiercely. "I shall find us a home, dearling, never you fear. No kine-thieving highlandman will steal you from me, my lambkin. Never, so long as I live!"

Once in the tunnel, Honor hurried through the absolute darkness, trailing her free hand along the wet stone walls, feeling loose rubble crunch underfoot. She felt no fear of either the darkness or what lay ahead. It could bode no worse than what she had left behind.

Chapter Fourteen

Alan wrestled with his conscience the whole day long. He barked orders more sharply than his uncle Angus had ever done. He watched his troops—villagers and crofters unused to a harsh lord—struggle to hold their courage in the face of his fury as he put them through their paces. Weaklings, he called them. Grass crunching conies.

They shamed him with their cheerful acceptance of his taunts and their doubled efforts to please. But that shame held a poor light to the self-reproach he already bore.

Time and again he assured himself that he'd had no choice in the matter of Honor's comeuppance. She deserved to weep. She deserved to worry. Why, then, did it twist his heart into knots to think of her doing so? Soft, he'd become. Soft as parrich.

He had promised to take away her child, her wee Kit, whom he loved more than her own life. Bitter justice, he concluded. Better that Honor should have considered what her wicked dissembling might incur before she had acted. Would Tavish not have done the same had she confessed her lies to him?

Nay, not in ten thousand years, his inner voice answered.

"Hell and damnation," Alan swore under his breath. He looked up and realized the menfolk staggered with exhaustion because he had completely forgotten to call halt to the sword practice. They dragged their wooden blades in the dirt, then hefted them up with sluggish thrusts. Sweat poured from their brows and stained their sarks.

"Cease!" he shouted. And contritely added, "Well done, lads!" He waited until they dispersed and then slowly headed for the keep.

Honor had not appeared for the noon meal. Not surprising, he thought. She surely felt keen shame now that he knew her for a liar. And likely dread, as well, that he would take the babe from her too soon.

Mayhaps he should admit to her now that he would wait a year to do so. Or two. Kit would need her that long, surely. He would make it three to be on the side of safety. Infants thrived best with their own mams, he was sure of it. Three was not such a great age, four might be better. Who knows, by that time, Honor might well have learned the value of truth.

People could change. He had done so and right quickly. He almost never lapsed into his highland speech now, Alan thought with pride. Not unless he was somehow vexed or did it apurpose. Honor could be different if she tried. Surely she would see that she must, given the alternative.

He would go and tell Honor that now, so she would not sicken herself with tears all day. He would give her a goal to work for and she would be happier, knowing the reward in store.

Alan hated thinking how much he longed to see her smile again. A false smile it would be if directed at him. He cursed himself for craving it all the same. Perhaps with time, he could make it real.

"Sir Alan," Nanette cried across the hall as he entered. "I must speak with you! Now!"

"Pray wait, lass," Alan stalled, and kept a steady course for the solar. "I have urgent business with your lady."

"Oh, but she is not here! That is what I was about to tell you!"

"What do you mean, not here?" Alan asked, his gaze darting hither and yon. Everyone stopped what they were doing and regarded him with wary looks. Nan glanced toward the stairs that led to the kitchens and on down to the cells below.

"Where is she?" Then he sighed loud and long, his lips tightening with frustration. "She has locked herself in a makeshift cell, like Hume's, I'll wager! Aye, courting sympathy. Choosing her own punishment so that I'll relent and not take—"

"Non, she has not!" Nan whined as she tugged at his sleeve. "She took Christiana and she has gone away!"

He stared at the scrawny, pinch-mouthed female. Her dark eyes were pitch cauldrons, roiling with worry. "Gone? Where, woman? Where did she go?" Alan demanded.

Nanette released his sleeve and wrung her hands together. His eyes fastened on her soft white claws, amazed that she had dared to touch him at all. She had never liked him, this one. Had she conspired to secret Honor and Kit away, somewhere out of his reach? He leveled her with his most fearsome look. Were all French women as devious as his wife?

Nanette's nasal voice cut into his troubled thoughts. "I know not where she is now! She came out soon after you quit the solar. Just after dawn. She took the babe from my arms." Nan paused, shaking her head sadly. "She acted strangely, so I meant to leave her to her thoughts. All the day I thought she had retired to the solar. When I went to take her food this eve and relieve her of the child, neither of them was anywhere to be found. I am so worried! Why would she do this?''

Alan knew very well why. He clasped her shoulders and gave her a shake. ''You have searched the whole keep?''

Nanette sucked in a breath and held it for a space, then blew it out in a rush. ''And the bailey. David believes she must have crept out the bolt-hole. The door was ajar and the provisions moved aside.''

''What!'' Alan thundered, furious as hell. God only knew what mischief would assail her outside the wall! ''David!''

The guard came running.

''Why did you not tell me immediately she left, eh?'' Alan yanked the fellow off his feet by the front of his sark and shook him.

''We...we only found her gone th' noo!'' David stuttered. ''She musta...nay, had to o' left when she came to th' kitchens this morn. She tricked me away from ma guardin', sir! Tol' me ta see ta th' spit boy and then—''

''Never mind that! Have ye sent anyone after her?''

''Nay, there's no' been time,'' David said, balancing on his toes and trying not to choke.

Alan released him with a muttered oath. ''Assemble the men.''

''Morgan, Neil,'' he barked, pointing to two of the men with minor wounds who still hung about the hall, recovering, ''take torches and go through the tunnel. If she's hiding in there, one of ye bring her back. The other, meet me at the outer end to let me know. If she isna in there, go on through and join me. We'll look fer tracks and search the wood. *Move ye!* 'Twill soon be dark!''

Alan tore out of the keep and ran at full speed toward

the stables, shouting for the gates to be opened as he went. He had to find her before something else—or someone else—did.

God, what had he done? Frightened her witless, of course, and sent her running. He should have waited until it was necessary to take Kit away from her to tell her so. With a bit of patience on his part, he might never have had to tell her that at all. Damn her for taking this mad risk, and doing it with a bairn in arms. Damn himself for making her do it.

By the time he saddled his horse, five of the men were preparing their own mounts to join the search. "Bring two extra beasts for Neil and Morgan. God only knows what she's got herself into."

"Do you think Laird Hume's men might still be about somewhere, sir?" One of the men asked as they cleared the gate.

"They are bound for the coast," Alan stated firmly. Then added under his breath, "I hope."

Alan located Honor's tracks immediately at the tunnel's exit. Another small-footed set accompanied hers. He supposed she had taken one of the women with her. The moment Morgan and Neil appeared, the search party began to follow her trail south.

"Sir! Sir, wait up!" Father Dennis shouted. His sandaled heels prodded none too kindly, urging his puny mount forward to join the group.

Father Dennis reined in, cleared his throat and straightened his shoulders as if preparing for a blow. "Melior is gone, as well."

"That thrice-damned jongleur stole my *wife?*" Alan could scarcely believe the pompous little songbird had such a powerful death wish.

"More like guided her, I would guess," the priest said.

"Melior was widely traveled before he ever came to Lord Hume's employ in France. He brought her to Byelough, a very difficult place to find without directions. If you recall, 'tis why I advised you to send him to Rowicsburg to get your father. He knows the countryside well."

"She's heading south. If she didna change direction, she coulda gone ta Dunniegray. Naught else save England lies in this direction," Morgan offered tentatively. He exchanged a worried look with the priest.

Alan shook his head in disbelief. "Gone to Ian Gray? Ha! When she once begged me ta kill him? But if she has, would Melior know where the place lies?"

"He would," Father Dennis affirmed. "His livelihood once depended on knowing the location of every keep with a coin to spare."

"Damn his hide!" Alan cursed. He'd kill the little snipe when he caught him. Strangle him with a damn lute string.

Beyond the wood they lost all sign of the tracks as a heavy rain began to fall. "God's cursed me," Alan said, sighing, "I dinna think He wants me to find her."

"That is blasphemous," Father Dennis remarked distractedly, as though performing an automatic duty.

Alan looked down at the treacherous footing, picking a careful trail past the bogs where a man or beast could disappear beneath the ooze in moments. He refused to think what might be buried in that muck now, never to be found.

If Honor and Kit had come to harm, he could only blame himself for it. He had used his anger and pride like weapons against her, and against the truth he must have known deep inside himself. Honesty had been the one constant in his life. Why then had he threatened Honor with something he must have known he would never do?

He could no more separate Honor from her daughter

than he could sever his own arm. He loved her—loved them both—too much to hurt either in such a way. And yet, they might both be dead beneath this very bog because he had to satisfy his need for retribution. Because in a fit of fury he had hidden the truth from himself and from the woman he loved.

It dawned on Alan then that Honor's lies alone had not caused his wild disappointment in her. The grand and enduring love he had envisioned her having for Tavish did not exist after all. The love he had hoped she would transfer to himself one day. Disillusionment. That was Alan's problem with all of this. His wife fell short of perfection. She was merely human, and he had foolishly expected more.

More truth, Alan suddenly felt a bit of relief in the realization that Honor did have faults. He only wished one of them was not this confounded streak of independence. Even though she had succeeded at it once, striking out on her own this way could prove extremely dangerous.

He said a silent prayer for Honor's safety, and prayed he had not come to his senses too late.

"Ah, here he comes, my lady!" Ian Gray crowed, rubbing his palms together. "The noble Strode! I do vow he's as full of himself as any lad I've ever seen. This will entertain us much better than that wee singing worm you brought."

Honor approached the shoulder-high edge of the battlement. She cuddled the sleeping Christiana close as she peered out at the riders picking their way through the boggy terrain.

She had a strong feeling tonight's entertainment would consist of the public flogging Alan would give her for leaving Byelough. No doubt Ian Gray would open the gates to him. But then, he had little choice in that matter.

Dunniegray consisted of only two towers joined by crumbling walls at front and back. A poor keep, to be certain, hardly strong enough to withstand any determined attack for long. Not a siege, either, for there were few provisions here. She had asked.

Her only hope had been that Alan would not find her here, that he would discount the possibility that she would seek shelter with a man she had once feared. Had Melior not followed her and suggested they go to Dunniegray, she would never have thought of it.

Little did he know that she feared Alan of Strode above the devil himself. A pummeling she knew she could stand. He dared not murder her. She didn't consider that a possibility anyway. But if he took her child away, it would kill her then and there. That he would do, for he had promised as much.

"Please," she whispered to God.

"Oh, you needn't plead, Lady Honor," Gray said with a jovial smile. "I ken what must be done. Go below to your chambers where 'tis warmer, and see to the bairn. Bring her and join us to sup in half an hour. And see you keep quiet when you do. I'd play this my own way, eh?"

"Show me a way out of this place, Ian Gray," she demanded.

He smiled down at her and gave her shoulder a reassuring squeeze. "No need for that. Trust me."

Honor rolled her eyes heavenward and expelled an exasperated breath. "I suppose I have no choice."

"None," he affirmed cheerfully. "Be off now."

Honor saw little point in making any fuss that would anger Gray. Pleading their new kinship, she had asked for sanctuary and he had supplied it, such as it was.

Alan might pull Dunniegray Keep down around their ears before this matter was settled, but her host must have some sort of plan to prevent that. Why else would he be smiling like a cream-fed cat?

Best she spend the next half hour hiding Melior from the certainty of Alan's wrath, and concocting a plan to escape it herself.

Supper came all too soon and still she had thought of nothing that might remove her from this predicament. Losing Christiana would destroy her. She supposed she must cry mercy, for all the good that would do.

Her husband stood in front of Gray, the sparsely provisioned table between them as Honor approached from the rear. She kept her eyes downcast and avoided looking at him directly.

"Sit here, my lady," Ian ordered when she arrived. He indicated the rough-hewn chair beside his own.

Honor sat, holding Christiana in the crook of one arm. She felt Alan's burning green glare, but could not meet his eyes for fear she would either fall to begging like one condemned, or else lose her temper and worsen her fate.

"So, Strode, you say you'll pay me for the lady here?" Honor knew Gray asked the question to bring her up to date on the discussion they had just been having.

"If need be," Alan said. She could almost hear his teeth grind. "But if you ask ransom for a kinswoman, you shame yourself, Ian Gray. I had thought better of you."

Gray laughed merrily as he toyed with his eating knife, flicking his thumb over the blade. "Aye, well, many have made that mistake. But I have not said I would demand anything for her release. 'Twas you who offered."

Honor dared a look at Alan. He had spoken very deliberately to Ian, biting off each word. Though he appeared deadly calm at first glance, she noticed a muscle tic near

the hinge of his jaw. His usually open and friendly gaze
had narrowed. The predatory stillness about him frightened
her.

Thankfully, he stood alone across the wide trestle table
so that she remained well out of his reach. And, praise
God, none of the men who rode with him were present in
the hall, else they might have taken the place then and
there.

Gray's men looked as well-ordered as Dunniegray itself,
which was not well at all. Small wonder he coveted Byelough.

Centuries worth of fires had smoked this hall, its stone
walls free of any coverings or whitewash. Mounds of
bones from countless meals lay about their feet, too many
for his lazy hounds to bury. The rushes lay trampled near
to dust. No self-respecting insect would bide there, she
thought.

The chamber Gray had shown her to had appeared little
better. A warrior's keep with never the touch of a woman's
warmth, was Dunniegray.

Could she really remain here? Did she want Alan to
allow it? A beating might be preferable. But if he meant
to take her babe from her, she would stay and right gladly.

"You refused to send her out to me," Alan said calmly,
breaking Honor's musing. "I assumed you brought me in
here to set a bargain."

"No ransom, cousin. I would keep her," Ian stated with
a flash of white teeth.

Honor cringed. Ian Gray might be near as finely formed
as Alan, but the coarseness of the man made her husband
look a genteel courtier by comparison. Still, if she must
stay here in order to keep Christiana, then she would do
it. Gray would not harm her. He could not take her to wife

even were she free, since he stood godfather to her daughter.

Her anger at Alan's cruelty had not abated one whit. Love him, she might, but not enough to welcome suffering such as he intended for her.

She opened her mouth to tell him so and felt Ian's strong fingers bite into her thigh. A warning? He had said to be silent. She closed her lips and waited to see what he meant to do.

Alan had sucked in a deep breath and his gaze roamed the hall. *No chance without your men,* Honor thought. Alone, he had not a prayer of taking her and Christiana and escaping this place. And he knew it.

If Ian allowed him to leave, Alan could prepare an attack or seige to reclaim Christiana and herself. But he had no way of knowing whether this place also had a bolt-hole. Indeed, if it did, and if Ian permitted her to leave by it, she could well be in France before Alan gained entrance again. France was the last place she would attempt to go, but Alan could not know that for certain.

He would do whatever he intended to do immediately, she believed. Honor only prayed he kept his wits and did not force Ian Gray to kill him.

She noted a flicker of desperation as Alan exhaled slowly and assumed a mask of indifference. "You cannot wed her, Ian, so what is your plan?"

"Och, I know that! I must marry for wealth, anyway, and all that she owned is already yours. Bruce wants you to have Byelough and so you must," he said reasonably. "'Tis only right.

"However, since you do not want the lady, I'll keep her. She'll make a right fine *châtelaine,*" Ian said, wriggling his eyebrows and leering at her. "I'm certain you have no objection there.'' He speared a sliver of greasy mutton and offered it to Honor. She politely refused.

Alan paused as if he considered Ian's plan. When he answered, he seemed totally at ease, almost bored. But Honor marked the way his forefinger drummed against his thigh. ''Nay, I must have her back. There is Tavish's bairn, which is mine now.'' He nodded toward Christiana.

Ian rose immediately, lifted the swaddled babe out of Honor's arms before she could think to protest it, and laid the wriggling bundle on an empty trencher. This he slid across the table in front of Alan. ''Then have it, cousin. Enjoy!''

Alan straightened and stared down at Christiana. ''But you cannot—''

''Aye, I can!'' Ian exclaimed, very precisely. ''You may go now since you do not seem hungry.''

Alan slammed a fist down on the table beside Christiana. ''I'll no' leave wi'out my wife, Ian. Damn yer hide!''

''Ye'll leave wi'out yer damned hide if ye dinna mind yer manners!'' Ian mocked. ''See there, you've gone and made it scream. Och, what lungs! Take it away and be-gone.'' He made a dusting motion with his eating knife.

Alan scooped up Christiana and laid her to his shoulder, patting her bottom until she quieted. When he spoke, his voice was tense, contained. ''Ian, think. A bairn needs it's mam.''

''Get you a wet-nurse,'' Gray suggested, popping a piece of meat in his mouth and chewing heartily.

''I canna do that,'' Alan argued softly, jiggling Christiana a little. ''Look, the babe's not too well, aye? She must have her own mother to see to her. Have ye no pity, mon?''

''No more than yourself, apparently,'' Ian returned, squeezing Honor's leg again. Another silent message?

Well, he wasn't groping for pleasure. She thought she knew what the fellow was about now and hoped to goodness he succeeded.

Her husband wanted her back. And not just for Christiana's sake, either. It would be all too simple to hire a replacement to nurse the babe. Several women at Byelough had babes and could easily accommodate another. Even his own stepmother could, and would do so gladly. No, Alan wanted *her*. Possibly he did so only so that he could punish her for this escapade, but she hoped he had another reason. If so, if he did desire her, he might one day forgive her.

Ian's trick might force Alan to promise she could keep Christiana with her. She had told him everything in order to explain her unexpected arrival. Would Gray help her that much? He never seemed to take things seriously. To him, this was probably just the evening's entertainment he spoke of earlier. Honor knew it must be killing Alan inside to grovel to his cheeky cousin.

"Ian, I want my wife. Do not make me kill you."

"Fine boast for a man with but six lads outside the walls and no weapons on you. Besides, she is unwilling to go and I'll not force her."

Alan leaned forward. "Honor, tell him you wish to go home."

She remained silent.

"Damn you, woman! *Tell* him!"

Honor glanced from Ian to Alan, worrying her bottom lip with her tongue. Then she inclined her head and studied her husband for a moment. "I will come with you, sir, if you promise not to part me from my daughter."

He gave one succinct nod. "Done. She will remain with you until she is of an age to foster."

"Until she marries," Honor bargained. "And I shall have right to approve her match."

"Nay, you will not!" he argued.

"Then I shall accept the hospitality of Dunniegray," she stated flatly.

Alan turned away and lowered his head. She did not want to think what muttered curses Christiana might be hearing sotto voce. "Verra well," he mumbled.

"Louder please. 'Tis a vow, I am asking of you," she declared.

"Aye, then, I *vow!*" he nearly shouted. "Ye can keep her! And have say to her disposition! Are ye satisfied?"

Christiana gurgled, as though to add her own demand.

"And you will not visit any punishment on Melior for his aiding my flight from you. Promise," Honor ordered.

Alan glared, shaking with poorly restrained rage.

Honor looked from one man to the other. Ian sat with his arms crossed, tongue in cheek, eyebrows raised in question. Alan looked fit to burst on the instant.

She dared not provoke him any further, but some devil made her do it anyway. "Have I your oath, sir?"

"I will not kill him. My word on it."

"Not quite enough, sir," she said softly. "Melior only followed me to keep me safe."

He pulled in a quick, deep breath, and released it slowly before answering gruffly. "Have your way of it then. I'll not punish the fool!"

Ian laughed and clapped his hands. "Great God, I love this!"

"You," Alan promised ominously, "I *would* like to kill."

"But not tonight!" Ian said, laughing even harder.

"Come, Honor, let's begone from here," Alan said,

turning toward the door to the hall, surely knowing she would follow since he still held Christiana.

"'Tis full dark now," Ian mentioned. "You are both welcome to bide the night."

"Not for a promise of paradise would I stay in this hell-hole," Alan said over his shoulder.

"As you will, then," Gray conceded with utmost politeness. "Do come again!"

Honor threw Ian a smile behind Alan's back. She had made a friend by coming here, she thought. Ian Gray was a rogue of the worst sort, a wily rascal who obviously loved a good jest. As near as she could tell, he made a jest of everything. That he used her and hers for his own merriment bothered her not in the least, considering the results of it. Not daring to speak aloud, she mouthed her thanks.

He nodded and winked, still toying with his eating knife. Just as Alan reached the doorway, the blade thunked into the wood only half an arm's length from his head.

Alan jerked around, murder in his eye. Unarmed and holding an infant, Honor knew there was little he could do. Before he could speak, Ian ordered, "Do not mistreat her again, Strode."

"Go to hell, Gray!" Alan said, tugging the knife from the door with his left hand. With a pointed glance around the littered hall, he added, "Though I canna think the accommodations there would be much worse."

With that, he returned the knife. The point embedded itself in the front edge of the chair arm between Ian's second and middle fingers.

Ian's whoops of glee followed them out the door and down the wooden outer steps to ground level. Even after the sturdy gates were closed behind them, she could hear him.

She made no objection when Alan handed Christiana to

Father Dennis. Then he lifted Honor to the saddle of his warhorse and mounted behind her. "Hand Kit to me," he instructed the priest. Alan settled her babe in her lap and encased them both in arms that felt hewn of oak.

On the ride home, Honor wondered whether Alan would ever soften toward her again. Would he ever hold her as he had done before and be the tender lover she had come to care for? Mayhaps not, but she did know she could trust his vow not to take Christiana away from her or to harm Melior.

She wished she had extracted Alan's promise not to beat her while she was about making her demands. A thrashing was not her greatest concern, however. She had simply lost all control over her life, if in fact she had ever had such to begin with.

If only she had kept her wits about her and not told Alan the truth about tricking Tavish, he might have kept respect for her. All she had needed to do was say that yes, she had loved her husband. Unfortunately, she had found she could not lie outright to Alan about that.

Now he, just as her father had once done, directed the disposition of her body, her possessions and her future. Never again would she feel herself mistress of her own fate.

But at least Honor had gained something she never thought to have. She had the choice when Christiana came of age to wed. Her daughter would never have to lie, steal and seduce a rescuer to avoid a dreaded marriage as Honor had done.

She supposed that was no small victory for a woman, however it came about.

Chapter Fifteen

Alan's outrage shrank to fairly manageable proportions as they rode away from Dunniegray. Then picking his way through the perilous bog after dark required his concentration for a while. Until this moment, he had hardly suffered at all from holding Honor close. Now, on more certain ground, he encountered another problem.

Without danger to distract him, he had little to think on but how soft she felt, how delicate and perfect the body resting so trustingly against his own. Alan wished he could bury his nose in her hair and draw in her sweet scent, but pride prevented that. Consequently, his own sweat, that of the horse and the odor of wee Kit's fouled nether cloth totally occupied his keen sense of smell.

Honor had not uttered a word since they set out. He knew she feared what he might do when they arrived home. Strange that she had not thought to protect herself by making him swear to forgo her own punishment. Did she feel she deserved it?

Alan believed she did need a penalty. Not anything truly hurtful, of course, but something to prevent her doing anything so foolish again. He decided to allow her to worry on it a while longer. That in itself should serve as proper chastisement. His arm tightened around her waist. She need not know just yet that it was desire that prompted it. That, added to a healthy measure of relief that she did not lie dead in the bog.

They rode through the gates of Byelough where nearly every inhabitant of the castle and a number of village folk greeted them with rushlights and cheers. One of Honor's women reached up for the child the moment Alan halted his mount.

He got down first, and as soon as he set Honor on her feet, a crowd surrounded her. They hustled her away and into the hall so quickly, he had no chance to protest it. He would not have done so anyway.

Protecting their lady spoke well of their people, even if their purpose *was* protecting her from him. Alan smiled wryly and shook his head. Devious and calculating, Honor might be, but she commanded the love of everyone around her. His love, most of all.

Even Ian Gray had been smitten. That struck a harsh chord of jealousy in Alan. But it also alleviated some of his distress that she had duped him so roundly with her innocent smiles and pretense at perfection. Fool Alan might be about her, but at least he was not the only fool.

Thoughts of fools brought Melior to mind. By rights, he ought to have the man's head on a pike. Wisely, the player had remained at Dunniegray for the nonce. Likely, he would venture back when Ian assured him Alan had vowed not to kill him. Honor had enticed that particular fool to do her bidding for the second time.

She had, by hook or crook, drawn both Melior and Father Dennis away from their good living within her father's household. Then she had seduced Tavish with words of love and the false marriage contracts. Turning her charms on an unworldly fellow such as himself must have hardly challenged her at all, Alan reckoned. Then Ian had turned up sweet for her. A cartload of addle-pates, the lot of them. His residual anger continued to dissipate as he began to see the humor in it.

"I should order us all to don jester's garb," Alan muttered laughingly to himself.

"Pardon?" Father Dennis questioned as he fell into step beside him.

"Bells," Alan explained with a chuckle. "We should be wearin' bells on our caps. And motley."

"Ah," the priest remarked, clasping his hands behind him, head bent in thought. "You think we need to entertain our lady, sir?"

Alan laughed. "I do not doubt she was well entertained this eve, bells or no bells. 'Twas a right good comedy. Ye must have heard Gray cackling as we left."

"All went well inside Dunniegray, then?" Father Dennis asked, unable to hide his curiosity about the confrontation inside Gray's hall. "You looked so preoccupied on the way home, I hesitated to ask."

"There were harsh words passed. I could tell ye all about it in confession, come the morn," Alan teased with a sidewise glance.

"And argue with me about any penance as usual," the priest grumbled, his brows knit with aggravation.

"I'll have a head start on the prayers," Alan said with a wry grin. "Lady Honor has already brought me to my knees."

Humbled, he was. And weary, too. Surprising then, how light of heart he felt now that he had Honor out of danger and home where she belonged. Or perhaps he was only light of head. By rights, he should be furious with her still.

Nanette met them at the hall door. "You may not use a rod thicker than this against her," she announced as he

and the priest entered. She shoved an ell's length of cedar
at him. "Do so, and I shall bring charges of cruelty! I
know of this law!"

Alan flexed the switch, measuring its width against that
of his thumb. He pursed his lips, fighting a smile. So Nan
thought English law held any sway hereabout, did she?

He tapped the side of his right leg gently with the
knobby branch. "Too thin," he judged. "Ye'd best bring
me another more to size."

Ignoring her glare, he stuck the limb under his arm and
walked around her, making his way to the table that had
been set out with cold meats and bread. He slapped a slice
of venison on a crust and wolfed it, washing it down with
a half tankard of ale he'd snatched out of Morgan's hand.

All the while, his eyes roamed the room. "Where is my
lady? If she's gone off again, I'll do murder."

Morgan jumped. "Solar, sir. Davy's standing guard."

"Oh well, now there's a real comfort," Alan remarked
with sarcasm. He set the tankard down and took the switch
Nan had brought him in his hands again. Slowly he strolled
toward the chamber where he had first met Honor.

Memories of that meeting assailed him, renewing his
feelings of disappointment and darkening his mood. He
had believed her so faultless then, just as Tavish had described her.

The only good thing to come of that realization was that
he need not keep up all the tedious attempts to improve
himself. She could damn well take him as he was. A dispirited sigh escaped him as he pushed open the door.

Honor stood ready for whatever he had come to impart,
lecture or beating. Her chin raised a notch when she spied
the thick switch he had bowed between his hands. Her
fingers clutched together so hard, her knuckles turned
white. "Sir," she greeted him.

"Where is Kit?" he asked. He had not thought she would part with the babe for any reason, at least not for a while.

"With Lady Janet," Honor explained. "I did not want her to witness…any unpleasantness."

Alan noted the small cauldron hung over the fire, full of heating water. Another cold bucket wept rivulets on the hearth, waiting its turn. The tub had already been half-filled in preparation for a bath. Hers, obviously. His, now, however.

Without further words, he laid the switch aside and began removing his clothes.

"Wh-what are you doing?" she asked breathlessly.

"Taking a bath," he replied. "I doubt I could rest whilst reeking of sword practice, a round-ride through the bogs, and exposure to Gray's dung heap of a hall. Get my own soap, would ye? I dinna relish smelling flowers the night through." Unless the scent came close up from her own person.

Well, that was hardly likely unless he forced the issue. He knew he could, and she would submit. Honor would not dare refuse him after all she had put him through this night. But he still felt a bit too much anger at her to be a tender lover.

Alan watched her scramble through his supply chest full of English booty. He rather liked the fact that she jumped to so quickly. Making amends for bludgeoning his pride, no doubt. Aye, he could deal with that.

"Bring a larger length of linen, if ye please," he added. She snatched one off the stack on the nearby stool and plopped it down closer to hand. Apology in action, he decided. Very good.

He sank into the lukewarm water and leaned his head

forward. "Scrub my back, would ye?" She did so almost
savagely, but it felt satisfying to be obeyed, nonetheless.

"Now wash my hair," he demanded, warming to this
order-giving mastery of her. He enjoyed the furious scratch
of her short, rounded nails against his scalp. Stimulating.

Lather dripped down his forehead and seeped over his
face. He brushed it with a wet hand, making matters worse.
She had complied thus far with everything he had told her
to do. He could get to liking this.

At last he understood. A man needed to take a firm
hand, but do it kindly. All Honor had required was direction. Trouble was, he had been too in awe of her to provide
that. No more, however. No cause for reverence now
where she was concerned. Flawed he might be, but so was
she.

Wickedly, Alan considered having her wash all of him,
but he knew exactly where that would lead given the day's
happenings and the fact that he already felt painfully
aroused by only this casual touching. If he made love to
her right now, he knew he would forget any quarrel he
had ever had with her. And he was not ready to do that
just yet.

"Well? There's soap in my eyes," he announced with
a sniff.

Suddenly, icy water sluiced over his head and back.
"Aarrgh!" he howled, slinging his head about. Still
blinded by soap, he twisted around and grabbed for the
bucket. Another freezing slosh blanketed his chest, chilling
the warmth that engulfed his nether parts. "Damn!" he
shouted, "Are ye tryin' t' freeze it?"

A heavy wad of linen hit him square in the face. "Shall
I dry you, sir?" she asked innocently, without a hint of
remorse.

"I think not!" he answered curtly as he examined the

toweling, expecting stinging nettles or some such. Her sudden act of rebellion confused him. She had seemed so docile, meek as a lamb, eager to do anything he asked of her. Now *this!*

He thought longingly of the stick Nan had given him, even knowing he could never bring himself to use it.

"Get ye to bed!" he barked, unwilling to have her see him still erect and ready despite the chilly dousing. She would think him weak-willed indeed if he rose out of the tub, randy as a goat, and did not act on it. And he would not act on it, he told himself firmly. Not tonight.

Who is it I'm punishing here? he wondered.

However, Alan knew better than to follow his instincts in this. His heart would soften toward her once he took her in his arms. He'd give her anything she asked, do whatever she wanted, forgive her worst transgressions. Tempting, but not a right husbandly thing to do at this point. Honor needed discipline, to know who called the tune in this awkward dance of theirs.

Alan dried himself, his back toward the bed, and then wrapped his lower half in the bath sheet. He need not have worried that she watched. When he glanced over his shoulder, Alan saw that Honor had turned away, curled into a ball and practically hung onto the far edge of the bed.

He tossed away the toweling and crawled into bed beside her. This would not be an easy thing, sleeping here without demanding his rights, but he would manage.

"Good night," he wished her gruffly.

One of them might as well have one, Alan thought with an inner groan as he blew out the candles by the bed. It sure as hell would not be him.

Honor carefully slid her legs over the edge of the bed and sat up. The mattress rustled gently and she held her breath. She had thought he would never sleep.

For what seemed hours, she had lain there, hardly daring to breathe. Her breasts ached for want of nursing. Her legs hurt from walking all the way to Dunniegray and then riding home on that beast of Alan's. The muscles of her arms were sore from carrying Christiana. And her heart ached for all that might have been and might never be.

Fortunately, she had no bruises to add to her pains. Though he had brought a stout stick with him tonight, Alan must have felt too tired to wield it. Tomorrow, he would, probably in the presence of everyone to further shame her.

She would not protest it, for she had courted punishment at every turn, by running away, taunting him in Ian Gray's presence, and later dousing him in the bath.

Why did her temper fly so wildly? She could just imagine how the comte de Trouville would have reacted were he her husband. She would be dead and buried already.

For now, she would go to Christiana and do her duty as a mother. More relief than that, she could hardly expect.

She would not try to get away this time. Honor felt justified that she had planned an escape from her arranged marriage to Trouville. She had possessed no means to stay there and fight against it. Yesterday, she had run again out of fear she would lose her child. In that, also, she had seen no option. But now she had Alan's promise that she could keep Christiana. She would not run again.

Whatever her husband planned for her, she must endure, for she had nowhere else to go. Returning to her father's house would not be possible. Even though Hume was here now, Alan would have to release him eventually, and she would be right back where she began a year past. She could not flee again to Ian Gray. Alan had already threatened to kill him for giving her shelter. She did not want that man's death on her conscience, for he had treated her very kindly after all.

All those reasons aside, Honor wanted to stand her ground here. This was her home and where she wanted to be. Alan of Strode might never love her back. He probably would not suffer her foul temper without retaliating, but he would treat her fairly enough. Certainly better than she could expect at any other man's hand.

Honor almost made it to the door when Alan's weary voice halted her. "Where is it ye go to now, wife?"

"To nurse the babe," she answered quietly, hoping he would roll over and go back to sleep.

"Fetch Kit back here," he said. Not a suggestion.

She nodded.

"Honor? Come directly back or I shall come after ye. I want ye *here!*"

Though his words were sharp, Honor detected the flash of vulnerability in them. As suddenly as that, she realized that her abandonment had injured Alan deeply.

Never mind that he had precipitated her flight with his threat, he obviously felt himself wronged by her leaving. His mother had deserted him and also left scars. Honor had no desire to hurt him further. She simply wanted peace.

"You do not understand, husband," she said softly. "I discovered your games when I had just begun to trust you, and I do admit that made me angry. However—"

"Games, Honor?"

"But I want you to know that my leaving was nothing to do with that, or even the hatred you had for me. I have lived with hatred before and can do so again. I only went away to prevent Christiana from suffering exactly what you once endured, the separation of a child from its mother. I would do anything, anything at all to keep her by me.''

He said nothing, but she could hear his unsteady breathing disturb the near darkness of the chamber.

She went on. ''Now that I have your promise not to take her away from me, Alan, I'll not leave you again.''

''Can I believe that? Ye've lied before, Honor. Just as my mother lied when she said she would come back for me. Just as my father lied when he promised she could stay with me in the Highlands. You were not honest with your father, or Tavish, or with me.''

''The price of honesty was too high,'' she said sadly. ''Set your guard to me, if you will. Withhold your trust and despise me, since it pains you that I am not perfect. But know this one truth, Alan. Given like circumstances and despite the guilt, I would do the same again for all it has brought me.''

She left the room and quietly closed the door behind her, knowing she had also closed another, stouter door between them.

When Honor returned, Alan had propped the pillows high for her and held the babe while she settled herself for the feeding. He watched the procedure without comment, the same soft look on his features he always wore at such a time.

When she finished, he took Christiana from her and laid the babe against his bare shoulder while Honor righted her shift.

''My thanks,'' she muttered when he had put the sleeping child in her cradle near the hearth.

''My pleasure,'' he replied. ''She is so fair. Very like yourself.'' Honor did not wonder that his voice sounded so sad at that thought. Especially if he considered more than Christiana's appearance.

"I trust she will become a better person than I," Honor said wryly. "And I pray she will never have cause to do all that I have done."

"I wish I could understand why you did what you did," Alan admitted with a sigh. He covered Christiana and patted her gently. Then he came back to the bed, leaned back against the heavy bolster, his hands laced behind his head.

Since he did not stare at her accusingly now, Honor felt comfortable enough to attempt an explanation. "My father simply created an untenable situation, which I sought to avoid. I delayed the marriage as long as I could. When the time drew near, I thought of Tavish, recalled his proposal and made my plans. Wedding the comte de Trouville might have meant my death and I was afraid. The man has buried two young wives already. I had no wish to be the third."

"That doesna tell me why ye deceived Tavish," Alan said.

Honor wondered what more she could tell him. Surely he knew why she had.

"Had ye told Tav your reasons, no doubt he would have moved heaven to save you that fate. He loved ye."

"Ah," Honor said with a nod, "so did I know it, right from the first."

She turned to Alan and propped on one arm so that she could face him directly, willing him not think her so foul as he did. "You see, I meant to make it true. I fully meant to love him and I would have done, had we more time. 'Twas only two short months, Alan. Only two. Never did I say him nay, not once. I gave Tavish all I had in me to give."

"Gratitude," Alan muttered. "Small sop."

"It was gratitude, but more. I cared for my husband, wanted him to be happy, looked forward to his return,"

Honor said truthfully, feeling the tears on her face. "I mourn him, Alan. I do! He was my friend."

"But ye did not love him."

"Not as I love—"

Alan's gaze whipped to hers, a warning. She bit off the word she would have spoken, appalled at her stupidity. For long seconds, neither spoke. Then he turned his back to her and settled himself as though to sleep.

Honor felt the rebuff as deeply as a sword thrust. Nothing she could ever say would make him believe her. And the horrible truth was, she could not expect him to.

Later, when sleep nudged insistently, Alan's words roused her. "Honor, I would have yer sacred vow never to lie to me for any reason hereafter."

She thought long and hard about his request. There might be worse consequences along the way if she acquiesced. Dared she do so, knowing she might discover a need of employing subterfuge again? Somehow, she knew that she could not lie to Alan anyway, whatever the reason.

"I do promise," she said, with as much sincerity as she had ever said any thing.

"On Kit's head, swear it," he demanded softly, turning to face her in the weak light thrown by the fire.

"On her very soul, I swear," Honor replied with conviction.

He hesitated a moment, then asked, "When we spoke of Tavish, were ye about to say that ye loved *me,* Honor?"

She bit her lips. Here was the first test of her vow. "Yes," she admitted.

"Could ye say it now that you have sworn truth on yer daughter's soul?"

"Yes," she said, uncertain whether he wanted the actual words.

"Then say it," he urged.

"Why?"

"Because I wish to hear it."

Honor closed her eyes, willing God to make him believe. "I do love you. With all my heart."

"Did ye speak thus to Tavish? These very words?"

Honor took a deep breath, her vow still ringing in her ears. "I did."

He blew out his breath from between clenched teeth. "Ye have no reason to love me or even to say that ye do," he said with a remnant of accusation in his words.

"But I had *every* reason to love Tavish and to say so," she replied. "There is the difference, Alan."

His tongue clicked against his teeth and he covered his eyes with one hand. "Go to sleep now," he advised, "'Tis late."

Honor laughed bitterly. "If you think I could sleep after this conversation, you must be mad!"

"Aye," he said. "I truly must be."

She regarded him carefully, wondering if she dared say exactly what she thought. He had not hit her yet and she was heartily sick of wondering when the blows would come. Might as well have done with it now, for she intended to have an answer.

"You never troubled yourself to explain why you deceived me so. May I ask why is it you hold me in such contempt for lying when you have done so from the outset?"

"I?" he asked, plainly shocked by her accusation. "I *never* lie! Truth was all I had to hold to for years, I treasure it above all things. I have told ye this!"

"Oh, you did that right enough! Time and again," she said, gaining courage. "No education at all, you said. Then how is it your French is so flawless, I ask you?"

He slapped the knee he'd drawn up under the sheet.

"Bless me, the good father will have to compliment my pronunciation. He gets all atwitter over that. Says I've a twisted tongue."

"Father Dennis taught you?" She huffed and rolled her eyes. "In less than three months? You take me for a fool if you think I believe that, *Alan the True!*"

"Nay, he's not taught all by a long mark. A few phrases only. I but repeated aloud what he whispered to me on the battlement. That was where ye heard it, aye?"

"Your own father declared you could speak French, Alan. Not to mention the Latin and even a bit of Italian. Explain that, if you can," she demanded, crossing her arms over her chest.

Alan's mouth dropped open and his eyes darted back and forth as though he sought an answer from the room at large. When he spoke, he sounded as confused as he looked. "Why would Da lie about this?"

"Why, indeed!" she remarked. "So, you see why I find it so hard to repent to you! Adam said you could read, as well. And write. I know that's true. I saw you write at our marriage!"

"My name only. I learned that early on, before I left home. Wrote it in the dirt ever so often, that I might not forget how."

"Ha!"

"'Tis true, Honor!" He sighed and raked a hand through his hair. "I have learned my letters at Father Dennis's hand since I came to Byelough. I do read a bit now, though not as well as I would like. Not as well as I will."

Honor searched his face for the lie. It would be easy enough to ask the priest. Still, she did not want to believe Alan. Besides, what reason did Adam of Strode have to praise his son to the skies for skills he had never mastered? "We shall ask your father."

Alan sat up and slid his legs off the bed.

"Not now!" she exclaimed, grabbing his arm.

"Why not? The man has made ye think I betrayed Tavish, yerself, and all yer people. Should I not wake him and make him answer for it?" His brows furrowed even deeper. "Or mayhaps ye dinna wish him to recant? If I'm guilty, this lessens yer own guilt. Aye?"

"Yes," she admitted, determined to hold to her new vow of truth. "It would."

He turned and cupped her shoulders with his hands. "Listen to me, Honor. I swear by all that ye hold holy, I couldna read when I came here. I couldna write, but for my name. French, save for a few phrases not meant for a woman's ears, I could neither speak nor understand. As for Latin or—what was it, Italian?—I know naught of those. Where would I have learned? Why would I want to?"

Honor knew. In her heart, she knew, but still did not want to admit Alan was much the better person than she. But that vow she just made, never to lie to him again, prevented any further pretense of his guilt. She had misjudged him.

Honor sighed and toyed with the edge of the sheet as she spoke. "When you were a child, before you went away to the Highlands, did you study with your father?"

"Aye, I suppose. I recall little of it, other than how to make my name."

"Not surprising," she granted. "You were barely a weanling then. Most likely when you mimicked a few words, it spurred his fatherly pride. I suspect his memory embellished on that as the years passed. Were your letters easy to learn when you sat your lessons with Father Dennis?"

"Aye, not that difficult." He smiled as he ran a finger

over his lips. "I see what ye're saying. And here I thought myself very canny to grasp everything so quickly."

She pinched the bridge of her nose and blinked her eyes hard. Her head ached abominably. "So *you* did not lie, after all."

Alan lay back and pulled up the sheet to his chest. With his gaze on the fire, he said nothing for a while. When he did speak, it was a whisper. "I did. Once."

The admission surprised Honor. "How so?"

"When I allowed Tavish to believe I could read what he had written to you," he said softly. "I confessed it at our wedding, if you remember. A lie of omission."

Honor knew now that confession had cost him a great deal at the time. Alan had probably worried over it ever since it had happened.

He continued, "Tav was dying, Honor. Weak and almost past speaking. I couldna see making him read what he had put down on the parchment, yet he needed my opinion. I said 'twas braw advice he gave and I would see ye followed it."

"Now you regret it," she said in a flat voice.

"Nay, not so," he declared. "Could I have read every word, Honor, I would ha' done no differently. Do you regret it? Our marriage?"

"I believe I do."

He uttered a small, wry chuckle. "Well, I did ask ye for truth."

"So you did. And you shall have it, always," she promised.

"I suppose I am guilty of misleading now and again. Your father thought I meant to beat him and I did let him worry on it."

"Ha, worse! You held a knife to his throat and threatened to kill him that morn on the battlements."

"Oh, I meant that. I would have done, had his men not rode away!" Alan declared.

"Would nothing ever induce you to lie, Alan? To tell a blatant falsehood?"

"Absolutely not."

Honor nodded. He had answered exactly as she expected he would. "Then you will never understand why I did so."

"'Twas the fear," he acknowledged. "I do ken that much. But we must face our fears, Honor. We must face them armed with truth. That is the *only* way."

"Ah," she said, sighing. "I should have wed the comte, then. Let him do as he would, perhaps kill me as he had done to his other wives. I should have faced him squarely with no defense save the honest fact that I feared for my life."

Alan said nothing, which to Honor signified his agreement.

"You are a self-righteous idiot, Alan of Strode," she said softly. "There is a truth for you. Sleep well on it."

Honor turned away from him, drew up the covers to her chin and closed her eyes. She had said what she had to say, now she could sleep.

Chapter Sixteen

Adam of Strode had no qualms about killing an enemy. He had done so a number of times. He also had ordered the deaths of traitors and other criminals in his capacity as shire reeve and warden of the border. Some deserved death and he had provided it with the fair and perfunctory justice people praised him for.

But he did not believe Diarmid Hume deserved to die. Not for doing exactly what the man had been trained to do. Adam feared that Alan would eventually allow the love for his wife to sway him in that direction and would later regret the action. Adam knew he needed to prevent that happening.

Should he broach the subject now? Alan probably would not listen to any advice so close on the heels of their early morning argument. Adam thought he had fixed things between Alan and Honor, now he had explained the mix-up. That wise young daughter-in-law had figured it out all by herself anyway. It was Alan who raised such a fuss.

Imagine, the scamp making such a to-do about his own father's boasting about him! How was a man to know his son would forget everything learned at the knee of his sire? Damn old Angus for neglecting the lad's lessons.

Damn the rogue, too, for discarding all the letters Adam had sent to his son, and for replying that the angry young Alan wanted no more to do with his parents. Adam blamed himself as well. Instead of respecting the stripling's wishes, he should have risked a trip to the Highlands to see what was what. The poor lad must have felt himself deserted after months with no word from home. Then years.

Adam shook off his anger at Angus and his own bull-headed pride. He must put all that aside for now until he had solved this problem with Hume.

Alan said the priest was teaching him what he needed to know. Still, there were other things than reading, writing and French to be taught. Like prudence, for instance.

No one could have expected Angus to teach Alan that, of course. The fool didn't know the meaning of the word, let alone understand the concept. Alan was likely to lop off Hume's head on a whim. That's certainly what old Angus would have done.

He opened the topic carefully. "Alan, you have not said what you intend to do with your father by marriage."

"Nay, I've not. Still undecided." Alan munched on a slab of bread, his elbows resting on the table.

Adam thought the boy had gotten over his fit of pique now. At least he had stopped snapping out his words. "Why not talk to the man again? See what he intends if you set him free. No doubt his solitude has softened him a bit, eh?" Adam suggested.

"Oh, I know verra well what he'll do. Head straight home and round up another contingent to add to the one we sent packing. Likely drag his friend, that comte, into it as well. We'd suffer a muckle army at the gates—if not through the tunnel—inside a month. Ye're not proposing I release him, are ye?"

"No, but perhaps you could make peace, somehow reason with him to let your marriage stand and explain the matter to the comte de Trouville."

Alan snorted and threw down the crust of bread. "*You* reason with him! I would probably throttle the wretch." He leaned back in his chair as they watched Honor leave the solar, carrying her child to the Frenchwoman seated by the fire. "Honor wants me to kill him."

"Still?"

"Well, she's not mentioned it again, but her wishes were clear enough when we first took Hume," Alan said. "I mislike the idea, Da."

"As well you might, thank God! Bruce would have your head for it."

Alan laughed. "Aye, I know that. I'll wait at least until Hume reports to him what is happening at the French court. Then we'll see."

"Look, son," Adam said tentatively, "Hume's only done as he was taught to do, you know."

"To hurt his child? Sell her into marriage?" Alan scoffed.

Adam shook his head sadly. "Every man is taught by his father's example, Alan. Thanks be to God I have no daughters of my own, nor did my own sire. Though I escaped that lesson by chance, I've seen enough of this happen all around me to know it is the usual way of things. Fathers arrange matches for the children and enforce them however they may. 'Tis only that you were so far removed from regular family, you do not realize—"

"And whose fault is that, Da?" Alan snapped.

"I have apologized, son. How was I to know Angus would abuse the honor of fostering you? Your mother thought—"

"My mother left me. Knowing what her brother was, she left me there, Da. As did you."

"I know." Adam brushed a hand over his beard and then reached for his ale. "I wish I could make it up to you, all that you suffered. It is my fault. And hers. War was imminent, border skirmishes constant. She knew you would be safe that far north, but feared I would be killed."

Alan shook his head and blew out a breath between his teeth. "She loved her husband best. I suppose I cannot fault her for it."

"No, you should not. I know you love Honor's child as your own. Would you not put Christiana somewhere out of harm's way and rush to join your wife were she in danger of death?"

"Aye, I would." Alan replied in a clipped voice.

"And we would not have left you so long had Angus not told us you wished it. He wrote that you were well content there and so set against us, you'd not answer our letters."

"So, if I say I forgive ye both, may we let this subject lie? I weary of it."

"You will pardon me if I do not feel *absolved*," Adam said sarcastically, "But, yes, let's not dwell on it. I would speak more of Hume and his fate. Shall I talk with him?"

"As ye like," Alan said, rising from the table, "Just see he is well guarded when ye do. He's not to have run of the place, and keep his hands bound if ye bring him out of the storeroom."

Alan walked away a few steps and then turned. "And he is not to see or speak with Honor under any circumstance. I'll not have her disturbed by the old rogue."

Adam nodded. He thought long and hard about what he would say to Hume. How did one go about changing an ingrained attitude toward women? Especially one that most men adhered to with little thought. Best to see first just how tame the imprisonment had rendered the fellow.

Honor saw Alan quit the hall. The men lounging around the tables followed him out, groaning to each other good-naturedly. Time for weapons practice, she thought, thankful that Alan had not chosen to exercise himself in another way.

She marked well how he had laid that cedar rod close to hand in the solar last evening. Strange that he had not used it on her, given her behavior. She had pushed him further than anyone with right mind ought to have done.

Honor saw her father-in-law descend the stairs to the kitchens. Now what was he about? Moments later, the guard who usually minded her father's makeshift cell came up, stretching his arms above his head and yawning. Surely Alan had not set his own sire to guard duty. The man was a guest, for heaven's sake. Honor went down to apologize until Alan could set things right and assign someone else.

No one lingered in the open area around the huge fire hole or anywhere else in the kitchens, for that matter. Honor recalled that most of the folk were busy setting up the fires outside for candle making. There would be naught this day but cold meats for the midday meal.

Just then she noticed that the door to her father's cell stood open. Had Alan's father released him? Surely not. As Honor approached cautiously, she heard voices and stopped just out of sight. What was Lord Adam up to?

"No, I cannot grant you run of the place, Hume. My son forbids it," Adam said.

"Forbids it," her father mimicked, and then snorted inelegantly. "And you mind your whelp, do you?"

"'Tis his keep, after all. And you are his prisoner."

"And you have no say over your own get! Pathetic!"

Adam laughed. "Neither do you, it seems."

Her father's voice sounded deadly when he replied, "Nay, but I shall. She will pay for this travesty, you mark my words!"

Honor sank down onto the stool where the guard usually sat and buried her face in her hands. She should not listen to this, but could not bring herself to leave.

"Plan to beat her again, do you?" Adam asked as he might have inquired how Hume meant to spend the day.

"I should! The little wretch has given me naught but headaches since she sprouted! Out of the goodness of a father's heart, I did not force her to a match until she ran years past the age to marry! Then you'd have thought I'd consigned her to the gallows! Since she was but twelve, I had tried to deal with that stubbornness of hers, to make her tame."

Honor heard Adam grunt. She could not tell whether he agreed with her father or not. "Ah, but then you arranged a very profitable union for her, did you not?"

"Aye," her father said, sounding wounded. "The man's friend to the king, a distant cousin, in fact. Widowed, wealthy and right smitten with Honor, too. 'Twould have been a good union. Seeing as how he is a royal favorite, I could not have denied his suit in any case. But would she have him? Nay, thief that she is, she took the very documents binding her, likely bribed my priest to follow, and stole off into the night. Took me a good year to find her!"

"Hmm, resourceful child!" Adam exclaimed.

"Naught to take pride in, I can tell you! Not for a daughter," her father replied. "Spiteful wench!"

Adam chuckled. "Ah, but how many women do you know with such courage, Hume? Tell me, is her mum such a one?"

''Her *mum* is a dutiful wife, a good woman who knows her place. Shocked by it all, she was, poor Therese. Clung to me like a limpet these past months. Had she not needed me near for comfort, I'd have found our wicked offspring sooner than I did.''

Honor smiled into her palm. She knew well the purpose of her mother's clinging. No one could feign helplessness better than Lady Therese.

For years, Honor had hated her mother's subservient attitude, the toadying, the teary eyes and trembling smile. Even more than that, Honor had hated the fact that her mam received everything she ever asked for and suffered not so much as a slap.

Then, not long before her leaving, truth had dawned and Honor understood why. Her mother used her wiles to sway the man. Unfortunately, that awakening had come too late to help Honor. No matter how she wheedled and pled, or how prettily she wept, her father's mind remained set on her marriage to Trouville.

''She got it from you, then!'' Adam of Strode declared.

''What?'' her father asked, obviously still dwelling on her mother's docile nature.

''Her pluck, of course! That daring fortitude!'' Adam said. ''Why, I cannot begin to tell you, Hume, how fortunate I feel that we share such a daughter. God's word, what a backbone that lass has, eh? Make fine grandsons, will that one!''

Her father mumbled something Honor could not make out.

''Now, now, 'tis only your pride she pricked, man,'' Adam soothed. ''That Frenchman's seed might have weakened your line had Honor settled for that. Don't you see it, Hume? Fate took a hand in this! Sent Honor here to my son. Why, together they will make a whole keep full of braw lads and bonny maids!''

"No chance of it! The comte de Trouville will come for her now, I promise you that much. He'll not be pleased that Honor has flung his offer to the winds. I sought to save her his wrath by reaching her first. I wager he'll not be long in coming once he knows where I am and why,'' Hume said. "I don't like to think what he might do if retribution is left to him. He's not known for his leniency.''

"And you are?'' Adam asked calmly.

A long silence, then, "Once I was. 'Twas a disservice I did her then, Strode. A huge error in judgement. As a child, Honor had her way, and I let her. She grew into a willful woman, one who needs a firm hand. Honor has defied me in this matter of her marriage and that must not go unpunished.''

"Right, then. I shall tell my son. He's her husband and should be the one to chasten her. You may witness the beating.''

"Nay!'' her father exclaimed. "He cannot strike her! I'll not allow it!''

"And why not?'' Adam asked conversationally. "You'd rather have the pleasure yourself?''

"Pleasure? 'Tis no pleasure to lay rod to one's own child! Surely to God you know that!''

"Nay, I never beat mine,'' Adam said.

Her father laughed bitterly. "That's why he's such an unholy terror, that son of yours. Ill-mannered as a bothy-bred peasant. Sounds like one, too!''

Adam growled. "I bid you good day then, if you're to sit there and insult my son!''

Honor heard the rustle of rushes.

"Strode, wait!'' her father ordered Adam. "Could…''

could I see the babe?'' When Adam said nothing, her father added, ''Just the once?''

Still no audible answer, but there must have been a shake of the head for her father sounded infinitely sad when he spoke again. ''Does she have the look of my Honor? Is she beautiful?''

''Oh, aye, a faery babe,'' Adam declared with a smile in his voice. ''She will turn a few heads, that one!''

''Her name?'' Hume whispered.

''Christiana,'' Adam said. ''Alan calls her Wee Kit.''

Honor heard a sniff. After a small silence, her father demanded, ''He is kind to her, this Alan of yours?''

''In his heart, she is his daughter.''

''That does not answer my question!'' her father declared.

''He is kinder by far than you ever were to yours,'' Adam said. ''Think on that, Hume.''

''A moment more?'' her father asked, a reluctant plea. ''When the comte comes…?''

''Aye?''

''Hide Honor. And hide the child.'' Hume cleared his throat. ''Perhaps tell him they are dead?''

''He poses that much of a threat?'' Adam asked, his voice sounding worried.

''He is a vindictive bastard who will stop at nothing to get what he wants. Unless she bends to his will—which she will surely not—I fear he will kill her. Or else what she holds dearest.''

Strode scoffed. ''And you would have married your only child to such a man, Hume? How the devil could you even consider such a thing?''

''No choice,'' her father almost whispered the words. ''If I could not have made her willing, she would have gone to him unwilling. That might have meant her death.''

"Yet you would return her to him even now if you could, unwilling and in danger of losing her life?"

"No, of course not. I know a convent where he would never have found her. I meant to put her there once I got her home and tell the man she had died."

"Not that it would have changed the outcome, but why did you not say as much when you came?" Sir Adam asked.

"Because one of my men might later have carried the tale of my plans to Trouville. Look, I am only a Scot, with no power in France save my wits and wealth. He has the King's trust and kinship. You tell that son of yours, beware this man, for he *will* come for her with everything he has."

"Consider us warned," Adam said succinctly.

Honor rose and quickly ducked into the recess of another storeroom as Adam exited her father's cell, locked the door and shouted up the stair for the guard to return.

Memories of her growing years marched through her mind. She had adored her father once. Perhaps if she had never loved him and trusted him the way she had, the punishment he dealt her later would not have seemed so great a betrayal.

Now she knew why he had turned into such an ogre, demanding her compliance of a sudden when he had been so lax before. The very things he once admired in her abruptly engendered his fear for her—and thus his fury— once she reached womanhood.

Even then she admitted to herself that he had not unleashed his full power on her. Had he done so, she might have been crippled by his blows. She had supposed at the time he did not want her too damaged to sell in marriage.

Many times when she had railed against him, he did not beat her, but simply locked her in, much as Alan had done to him now. Only in a smaller, more uncomfortable place.

And without food. Cruel man, even if he did believe he had reason to be. Even if he thought treating her so might save her in the end.

Her father's words to Adam explained his behavior, but Honor could not forgive him yet for all she had suffered at his hand. To think he would have given her to the comte had she not run away. Had he been a braver man, a better parent, he would have rushed her off to Scotland himself to save her. His scheme to save her had come too late to count for anything.

Pray God, Alan would treat Christiana more gently once she became a woman. She believed he would. But it would not hurt to teach Christiana how to placate a man, rather than stoke his temper. She smirked at her thoughts. How could she teach that when she had never properly learned herself?

If only her own mother had not depended solely on example for Honor's lessons, things might have worked out for the better all around.

Tell a man what he wanted to hear, that was the way. Praise and exalt, flatter and applaud. Though she could never use those tricks on Alan now. She knew that much. Nothing but absolute honesty of word and deed would serve for that husband of hers. So be it, for she had promised.

She noticed that he had left off his former efforts to please her. He had given up his careful pronunciation in favor of his natural way of speaking. He dressed as he pleased now, usually favoring the highland garb. No longer did he toss her pretty compliments at table. Did he believe for a moment that she liked that proper, courtly fellow better? The thought made Honor shake her head.

Though his attempts to change himself had flattered her, Honor did not wish him changed at all. However, even though Alan abandoned the affectations, he was still not himself.

More than anything, Honor wanted him to be as he had first appeared to her. She missed the warm smiles and ready laughter, his tenderness and his boisterous sense of fun. Had she turned him into this dour knight he was now? And if so, could she mend the mistake?

A week later, Alan wished to heaven he had never belabored so the subject of honesty with Honor. Though relieved that she felt safe enough with him to attempt a gentle teasing, he did not want her making light of something so serious. "Enough is enough," he warned, struggling hard to sound gruff.

"But I am making amends," she said, wearing the face of innocence.

As though he did not ken what she was about, making such fun of him. She beat him about the head with every silly fact she could put to words, the more ridiculous, the better. The dark scowls he assumed did nothing to deter her. Nothing.

"Well, you do have ugly feet, Alan. I felt obliged to tell you that, because *in all truth,* you are a man vain about his looks. Did you not ask me if you appeared aright before we came to table?"

"Ye canna even *see* my feet now, Honor. I'm wearing my boots."

"Just as well," she declared with a knowing nod. "They put people off, those feet of yours."

"Hist! Close yer mouth and eat yer supper!" Alan fought the laughter that threatened to ruin his reprimand. Sly minx. She must know very well he had forgiven her everything. Otherwise, she would not be doing this.

Though they spoke no more about Honor's trip to Dunniegray, Alan did understand he had been the cause of her flight. He forgave her that. He also admitted to himself that Honor had done the only thing she could have in avoiding a marriage to the comte. It had taken courage to put both those plans into effect.

A woman could not fight injustice the same way as a man. Honor wielded the weapons she had with finesse. These past few days she plied humor like a broadsword, slapping him lightly with the flat of the blade, pricking him now and again with the sharp point. She wanted him laughing, with her and at himself.

All he really wanted to do was give in to it, then throw her over his shoulder, slap that pert wee rump of hers and haul her off to their bed. Of course, he'd had her in bed for well over a week of nights, for all the good it did.

He had not approached her as a husband in all that time. That would signal a total surrender on his part, an admission that he had overreacted and carried the retribution too far. Why he resisted, Alan couldn't say. Pride, he supposed. Mayhaps a wee bit of leftover anger.

"Just eat," he repeated, spearing a chunk of meat with his knife.

"Impossible. How should I eat with my mouth closed?" Her smile was so sweet.

He ignored that. She gave him a few moment's respite while she dipped her fingers, wiped them on a cloth and then tasted her food.

Then she frowned. "Ah, this venison is undercooked. And the beets taste quite earthy, do they not? I shall tell Cook," she said and started to rise.

Alan grabbed her elbow and jerked her back into her chair. "For pity's sake, woman, ye've already alienated nearly everyone in the keep by saying what ye think. *All* that ye think! Cook will be serving us weeds and half-baked rats if ye dinna mind yer tongue.''

"But—"

"But me no buts! Keep that mouth of yers closed or I'll be closing it for ye!'' he said.

Her sudden recoil told him the picture he had just put in her mind. Surely she knew what he meant! But she sat there wide-eyed, staring at his hand. Alan glanced down at it, fisted on the tabletop. Quickly, he opened it, grasped her neck and drew her to him for a hasty kiss.

Well, it began as hasty. Her lips, still opened in surprise, melted under his like spun sugar. And tasted so. What pure confection, he thought, his mind shifting from mild pleasure to dark imaginings. On and on he kissed, delving deeply as he could into the silken warmth and sweetness. Her tongue tested his own heat as he withdrew his.

Only when Janet's delighted giggles raked his ears did Alan recall that he and Honor were sitting at table, sharing a meal with a hall full of people. Reluctantly, he pulled away.

Honor's face had turned a shade not far removed from the beets she had mentioned. Alan laughed and again leaned close. "Very earthy,'' he whispered, nodding. "But let's not tell Cook.''

"You are a beast!'' she muttered.

"Guilty,'' he admitted, slicing off a small chunk of the roast and popping it into his mouth. He prepared another bite and offered it to her with a grin. She wrinkled her nose and turned away.

When she turned back, she looked prepared to speak again. "Ah, ah, ah!'' he said, brows raised in warning.

"I was only about to say that you have a strange method of discipline, sir. 'Tis not much of a deterrent, your threat.'' Her lips twitched as though she quelled a real smile. The urge to cover them with his again almost over-came his good sense.

He knew very well that he had aroused her. That silvery glint in her eyes told him so. Other than making jest of his stand on truthfulness, Alan was not yet certain what end she had in mind. Mayhaps he should make an end to it himself. "Flirting a bit, are we?" he accused.

"Yes," she said with a smile. "I am. Is it working?"

"Well enough to call a halt to supper with two courses yet to be served," he admitted boldly, intending to bring a blush. Devil him, would she? "Do ye wish to go to bed? Just say so."

"Yes," she answered, meeting his eyes directly. Smugly.

Truth or taunt? So she thought to make him sit here and suffer through the meal, did she?

"Verra well," he said, standing immediately and yanking her to her feet by her arm. She gave a small yelp as his voice rose over the murmurs and laughter along the tables. "Excuse us."

Conversation halted. Everyone gaped. Forty pairs of eyes followed as Alan swiftly conducted Honor toward the solar. Wherever this odd exchange of theirs led, he meant to get there in the privacy of their chamber. He turned at the portal and faced their audience. "Do continue the meal."

Chapter Seventeen

"How dare you embarrass me so!" Honor hissed the moment he closed the solar door. "I only meant to—"

"Tease me, I ken that! Jeer and taunt and then tempt," he said, abandoning his good humor. Now he believed he understood the game. "Do not think to lead me merrily along your way by my nether parts, Honor. It cannot be done. Believe me, stouter women than you have tried, so be warned!"

"Stouter, indeed!" she all but shouted. "Fat and frowsy women! Sinful sluts, no doubt!"

"No doubt," he agreed. "But charming as they were, I kept my wits. I do as *I* wish! So you see, no amount of eye batting or tongue kissing sways my will even a wee bit."

Honor leveled him with a gray-blue glare that in no way matched the lips she stretched into a smile. "Well, you are *here,* are you not?"

No answer for that one. He was definitely here, having left a perfectly good supper to dance to her spiteful little tune. "Why do you mock me thus, Honor?" he asked seriously. "To what purpose?"

She sighed and strolled to the window seat, looking out into the darkness. "You shame me," she said softly.

"Just now? Ye asked for it! I—"

"No, not that," she said, swinging her hand toward the closed solar door. "I told you true out there, I did want to go to bed," she replied, "with you."

He made some sound, not quite a word, of disbelief.

She faced him then, her gray eyes full of questions. "Making light of our troubles is not the answer, I see that now. So I must ask you outright. Why is it you keep yourself from me, Alan? You desire me, I know it. Yet you never turn to me in the night. You fight your feelings as though they are demons. Do you think my dishonor will taint you? Have I not promised, vowed on the soul of my child, that I will not repeat my transgressions?"

"And ye're angry because I asked it, are ye not? That is the reason for all this spewing of truths that serve nothing these past days. Ye make a jest of your promise to me."

"I did so only to show you how rigid is your thinking. How unforgiving you are. I lied. I admitted it, gave you my reasons and pledged not to do so again. Yet every word from your mouth challenges my honesty, questions my commitment and conveys your distrust. Now you tell me a truth, Alan. Can you never forgive me? Or love me?"

"Love?" he asked, tempted to scorn her, but unwilling to see more hurt in her eyes. And, unless he lied to her, he could not deny what he felt. "I do love ye, Honor. I think I did so even before we met. Through Tav's praise, I came to know ye—or so I thought—and believed ye without flaw. Then," he said, sighing, and pausing to seat himself on the cushions beside her, "I found ye played false. 'Tis devilish hard to trust a thing ye say."

"Or to bed me." she added, sounding a little petulant.

He shifted about so that he did not face her, lest he drag her into his arms and overwhelm her then and there. "Like as not, ye could twist me round yer finger, did I let ye rule me with that fair body of yers. Make me swear dark is light, steel is gold, down is up. Persuade me to do anything ye wished."

"I could do all that?" she asked with a small laugh.

"Aye, and more," he assured her angrily. "No man likes to be used in such a way, Honor. I would have ye love me for myself, not trade favors for all that I might yet do for ye."

"Ah, I see," she said. "And you will never accept that I do love you, no matter what I do or say?"

Alan shook his head, still not daring to look at her. Not daring to believe.

"Then you may leave this room with your pride intact, husband," she announced firmly as she put as much distance between them as the confines of the room allowed. She crossed her slender arms over her breasts. "Go, and do not trouble yourself further that I will try to seduce you to my bed or to my will. Do whatever you like, be it for me or against me. I shall never ask you for another thing so long as I live."

"Ah. I suppose now I am to yield and offer ye something grand for that generous statement. What is it you wish for me to do now?" Alan asked wearily.

She remained silent.

"Come now, 'tis a ploy I recognize. Ye promised truth," he reminded her.

"I pray you leave before I hit you with something hard," she said softly, giving him her back.

He strolled over to her, trailing one finger down the side of her arm. "Here I am, playing right into yer hand, Honor. Tell me the thing ye most want."

She whirled. "I want a real marriage! I want peace between us! I want you to cease treating me as some broken thing you cannot bear to touch!"

"Oh, I can bear to touch, I'm thinking," he said, and cupped her left breast.

She slapped his hand away. "But not *tonight!*"

"Well, hell!" He stepped back, furious. "How can ye say all that and then—"

"Honestly!" She spat the word. "Very honestly I say it! Get out of here and leave me alone!"

"Done and done!" he shouted and stalked to the door. "Ye'll let me know when ye decide on the *peace between us* part, aye?" He slammed the door hard, reveling in the satisfying bang.

A crash against it followed immediately. *The water urn?*

Then he looked up. The entire party of castle folk sat much as he had left them, mouths open and wide eyes trained on the solar. So much for privacy.

Alan resumed his seat and methodically ate every scrap served him. He met every questioning gaze with a warning glare and turned aside every attempt at conversation.

When he had finished, he wiped his eating knife and slid it back inside its sheath. "I bid ye good eve," he growled as he left his chair. No one said a word.

As he stalked off to the stables, he grumbled under his breath. "Silly woman. Thinks to make mock of me, does she? Already *has* done," he scoffed at himself. The embarrassment, he would get over. Not that he had ever cared much for what others thought of him anyway.

Hadn't he played the fool more times than he could count? Sometimes to lighten a deadly situation or to put an adversary off his guard. At other times, he made a jest of himself simply for the fun of it all. He'd done that the night of their wedding to take Honor's mind away from her grief over Tav's death. Still, for *her* to make him out a jester did not sit right at all.

She hated that he would not trust her, but trust must be earned, must it not? Honor had done nothing toward that end. Why should he give faith freely where it was so undeserved?

Honor had stirred him up apurpose, teased him unmercifully, and then turned him away. But for long moments there she herself had worn the look of a woman aroused. Let her stew in her own juices, then. Let her worry where he had gone this night, and to whom.

And he was sorely tempted to find someone to make her worries real.

If the stables were cold, Alan did not care. 'Twould serve her right if he caught the ague and she had to nurse him through it. He kicked the hay into a deeper pile and threw himself down. God's own truth, he did not deserve this! A shrew, she was, with a bloody fishwife's tongue. He flounced around trying to find a bit of comfort. Sleeping with the animals again. And there was Honor, snug in their soft bed. Nay, she'd not trammel herself thinking he had sought another. They both knew no woman at Byelough would betray the lady so by taking her husband to bed. She was probably lying there in that soft warm nest, still smirking.

Love, indeed. Peace? A jest. How had he landed himself in all this? "'Tis all your fault, Tavish Mac Ellerby!" he muttered toward the top of the barn. "Ye shoulda known I'd not be made of husbandly stuff!" He growled his frustration. "And she's no' the angel ye thought her to be, nor told me she was! If ye're hanging about up there laughin' yer ass off, damn ye for it!"

Did he imagine the chuckle? God's bones! He jerked upright.

"Ah, lad, you remind me of myself!"

His father.

"Jesu, I thought me Tav had answered," Alan muttered.

Adam's hearty laughter rang off the walls. Horses nickered and shuffled in their stalls. "Ripped you up, did she?"

"Aye."

"We heard. Ho, women thrive on such! She's in there feeling all righteous about now. But come morning, she'll have had her fit and be done with it all. Never a boring moment with a lass such as yours."

Alan groaned. "I could do with a boring moment or two. She wants peace between us, and then shouts at me! She wants love, she says, then orders me to leave her be. And throws things! What am I to believe of her, I ask you? The woman is a bale of contradictions."

"You can remedy that easily enough," his father said. "Give her back to her father and be rid of her."

"I don't want rid of her. I love her, for God's sake. You know that. Hell, *she* knows that!"

Adam nodded and dropped to the hay beside Alan, and assumed a half-reclining position as though he meant to stay a while. "Honor is not your enemy, son. She is but a woman afraid, and not without reason to be."

"Meaning?"

"You expect perfection of her, Alan, and no one is flawless. She cannot please you in that. From what I gathered by my conversation with him, she could not please her father, either. I expect she grew weary of the effort and sought to please herself. Small wonder." Adam sighed. "Even so, you should know Dairmid Hume is not your true enemy. Or hers. He loves his daughter."

"Of course he does," Alan said sarcastically. "I suppose that is why he pummeled her about and tried to sell her to that lecherous friend of his.''

Adam shook his head. ''He simply did not know what to do with a woman who spoke her mind and demanded choices. What seemed amusing and clever in the child no longer set well with him once she came of age. Hume, by his early indulgence of her, created a being not in step with her peers, an unbiddable daughter.''

Alan laughed with scorn. ''And now, an unbiddable wife!''

''A treasure. One which you will lose, if you do not have a care. Just as Hume did. Though he used a hateful approach, her father only tried to make Honor more submissive so that she would survive her marriage.''

''To a man who has buried two young wives! Did he believe her better off dead? I swear I cannot fathom a father such as he,'' Alan said.

''I repeat, he is not the foe to worry over. This count he promised Honor to will come, Alan. Hume warned as much. I think he fears it more than you, both for Honor and for himself. He realizes that her life might be in danger. The choice of husband for Honor was not his idea. I believe he was forced to the agreement. We need to prepare for another attack.''

''Honor is mine. I will hold her,'' Alan vowed.

''And I will help you if I can. But Byelough is not the strongest of keeps. Its best defense is that it is not easily located, but I do not doubt he will find it. After all, Hume did. What worked with Hume's men will not work with this Frenchman. He'll not care if you slit her father's throat on the battlements. Like as not, that would please him well, since Honor is Hume's heir. What will you do?''

''Prepare as best I can with what we have. The weather

grows colder and 'twill snow soon. I doubt he will attempt us until the spring.''

His father grasped his arm and looked at Alan, his steady gaze imploring. ''Son, you cannot depend on that. Bring Honor and come with Janet, Richard and me to Gloucester. She'll be safe there and so will you.''

''To England?'' Alan threw back his head and laughed with real merriment this time. ''Ye still dinna ken what ye've done, do ye? 'Tis a Scot ye've made of me, and a Scot I'll stay forever!''

''Oh, do stop with that thrice-damned burr, will you? Annoying me won't solve your problem,'' Adam muttered, his frown darkening. ''I think me Dairmid Hume's not the only father without an apt hand for the task!''

He rose from the hay and brushed off his clothes. ''If you mind nothing else I say, lad, at least make things right between you and your wife. Leave it too long and you will regret it. None of us knows the number of days left to us, and pride is a cold bedfellow.''

Alan did not answer. He already regretted every harsh word that had passed and every reason he had to distrust Honor. But he did distrust her still, and that was a fact he could not deny.

All that aside, whatever happened, he would protect her against any and all threats until he drew his final breath. He would never give her up.

As the days passed Honor realized that the man must have no inclination to forgive her. That last attempt at seduction had fallen so flat they could have made a hearth-stone out of it. Oh, he wanted her, she knew. But he staunchly refused to act on it, and far be it from her to approach him again. Let him play the martyr if he would. He still slept in the stable as though she had banished him to it. Would not even lay a pallet in the hall. He lived like a temporary guest at Byelough and not a very welcome one, at that. That thought gave her pause. Did Alan view himself that way?

She stared into the fire as she cradled Christiana in her arms. The child had grown fat and rosy, a winsome cherub who dimpled at everyone and everything now. At least the babe had carved a place in Alan's heart. He could not resist her, coming each evening for his hour of play and fatherly foolishness. The memories of those hours dragged a smile from Honor. She always watched them, hanging back, hungry for a small measure of what they shared. He threw her questioning gazes at times, almost as if he wondered why she did not join in. But she would not intrude. How could she risk his rejection in the event she had misread that look?

The hall stood nearly deserted now save for a few of the women preparing the tables for the evening meal. Alan would be nearly finished with the archery practice about now. His father would be there as well, adding suggestions, offering advice.

That old fellow might have the right idea. Adam simply ignored Alan's frequent displays of ill humor and marched right along, playing the loving parent as though nothing were wrong. As a result, Alan did occasionally ask his father's opinion. And she had even seen them laughing together now and again. Would that work for her as well? Should she offer smiles and sweetness to counter her husband's wretched grumbling? 'Twas a thought.

That grumbling grew worse each day. Honor longed for the happy, guileless knight who first came to Byelough. She feared she had disillusioned him completely where women were concerned, for he did not even seek another to replace her. He thought he had loved her, but he had only loved the false paragon she had presented to Tavish. Guilt ate at her, and self-directed anger took huge bites as well. Only fear of further scorn kept Honor silent on the matter of their marriage.

"Well, you are not perfect, either, my fine honest fellow," she murmured. "Not by a long mark. But I love you still." Nothing would ever make Alan believe that, of course, so she might as well not say it, even to herself.

She handed Christiana to Nan when prompted and rose to take her place at table.

"Good even, my lady," Alan said gruffly as he joined her at the board. His hair shone wet from its recent dunking and he smelled of strong soap and fresh air. "How went your day?"

"Much like any other, sir," she answered, determined to establish a pleasant conversation. "The men progress well?"

"Aye, they do that," he replied, still not meeting her eyes. He seldom did so these days. "Honor," he began, sounding reluctant to continue. After a small pause, he did so. "'Tis time we met privately. I would settle this unrest between us if you would have it so."

He cleared his throat and fastened his gaze on something across the hall. Honor knew the offer had cost him a great deal in terms of pride. The least she could do was to abandon some of hers.

"I would. Accompany me to the solar after we finish here."

He said no other thing, but busied himself with the food, offering her the choicest portions as a matter of course.

"Sir Alan? My lady? There are players without begging entrance. Three of them," David the Younger called out from the doorway.

"Melior?" Honor cried happily. "He has returned?"

"Nay, Lady, they be strangers. Mummers out of Edinburgh, they do say."

"Bid them leave," Alan ordered, cutting into a portion of jugged hare. "We need no strangers in this keep." He held a cube of it to Honor's lips.

"What can it hurt, Alan?" she asked, refusing his offering with a small shake of her head. "Look around you."

He glanced at the faces down the table wearing looks of disappointment. "Oh, very well, then. Let the jongleurs in, David, but mind you, only the three. If there are more concealed somewhere hoping to fill their bellies, make them wait without. We shall send food to them by their fellows when they've done here."

A cheer went up and everyone began speaking at once. Honor had not realized before now how glum Byelough had become these past days. Nay, weeks! "Thank you, husband!" she said happily and returned his grudging smile with one of delight.

"We shall still meet later? Alone?" he asked impatiently.

"Of course! Immediately after these three have lightened our hearts with a bit of music. La, I have missed it since our Melior remained with Ian Gray."

Alan's expression darkened at the mention of the two men. Honor knew he felt they had betrayed him by helping her escape, but he should have gotten over that by now. "Do not scowl so, for goodness' sake," she admonished playfully. "Where is that merry knight who once made me laugh?"

"I do wonder that myself," he admitted wryly, at last meeting her eyes. She saw desire flicker there for an instant and it gave her courage.

Honor placed her hand over his and gave it a squeeze.

"Be that fellow this night, Alan. I do vow you shall not regret it."

His smile reappeared, widened, and became very real. "Done."

Just then, a motley trio of tumblers cartwheeled across the hall and landed in unison on bended knee before the dais. Applause drowned out their words of greeting.

David rushed forward and handed the shorter of the three the gittern he had been minding for them. The player strummed it heartily and the other two burst into a rousing song familiar to everyone. Honor clapped with glee when Alan began to sing along. He had a deep, melodious voice which merged well with the others.

Never could she recall a finer evening. Late into the night they played songs new and old, performed acrobatics, and even a play ridiculing the recently defeated English king. The tallest of the three wielded an imaginary sword and smote the others down, proclaiming himself Alan the True, hero of Bannockburn, a rather blatant attempt to flatter their host. Alan took it none too seriously, fully enjoying the farce.

Next the newcomers sat cross-legged on the floor in front of Honor and blended their voices in a song of such sweetness it drew tears from her eyes. The chanson lauded a knight who had moved heaven and earth to win his lady love. A tribute to Honor followed, praise for her beauty and good nature ringing out most eloquently. Not even Melior could have done better. Honor felt charmed and thought Alan looked moved, as well.

When their song ended, he rewarded them generously with coin and a goodly measure of the food left from the meal.

"We entreat you, my lord, allow us space in your stables to sleep, for this night is a cold one." The smallest man shivered for effect. The other two also beseeched with hopeful nods and smiles. "Tomorrow we shall entertain again and then be off," the spokesman added. "What say you, sir?"

"Nay," Alan said. "There's no freeze upon us, you'll not suffer."

Honor thought his refusal might have to do with the fact that he slept in the stables himself and did not wish their company. She smiled, trying to appear provocative as she asked, "What harm can they do? The place will be *empty* tonight save for the animals, will it not?"

He took her meaning. She could see the sudden heat flood his eyes at her oblique invitation.

"'Tis clouding over, sir," David announced. "Most likely will rain."

Everyone chattered at once, adding their pleas to those of the newcomers. Alan blew out a breath, and with a rather promising look at Honor, relented. "Very well. One night."

Gaiety erupted again, everyone jubilant over the idea of the mummers remaining a while longer.

When the excitement had died away and all began seeking their beds, Honor strolled with Alan across the hall to the solar. Though she had instigated what she knew would happen shortly, her heart fluttered with trepidation. And eagerness, she had to admit. He would view her suggestiveness as a forward move, perhaps even wanton, but she wanted Alan to return to their bed. How else would she ever convince him that she loved him?

She could feel the tension in his arm right through his sleeve and sought to soothe him with small talk.

"Thank you for extending our hospitality to those three, Alan. They were very entertaining, were they not?"

"They do know a fair lady when they see one. Described you quite well," he remarked. "Though I do wonder where they heard of my exploits. A rough soldier, one of thousands? Not even a knight at that time."

She tilted her head, gazing up at him from under her lashes as she ran her palm along his forearm. "But you are legend, I am certain! Everyone twixt here and Stirling must be singing your praise. Alan the True—"

He clasped a large hand over her own as though to still its movement and looked away. "Do not let us dwell on *that*. Most of our mean speech to each other centered on my clinging to that distinction."

"As you say," she replied in a small voice, resenting the rebuff. She sighed heavily. "Why is it you wish to speak with me, then?"

He turned as they entered the room and carefully closed and bolted the door. When he faced her again, he approached quickly and took her by the shoulders. "Words have led us to this pass and I would have no more of them." With that, he lowered his mouth to hers and took it without compunction.

Honor struggled under his siege for only a moment until the softness of his lips registered in her mind. No anger. No punishment. Only sweet demand. She melted against him, offering up whatever he desired to take, perhaps more than he intended to exact. She opened beneath his gentle assault, welcomed the invasion, went out to greet the victor with velvet promises of treasure and comfort within the keep of her body.

When he finally abandoned her mouth and moved to her neck, Honor experienced the strongest need to tell him how she had missed his embrace, how she had missed him. "Oh Alan, I—"

"Hush," he ordered, and enforced that with another mind-rending kiss that left her no choice. Never once did he relent, and soon Honor could not form a coherent thought, much less a word. Sheer pleasure filled her senses to bursting, the harsh rasp of his breath against her face, the fresh-washed scent of his skin, the urgency with which he grasped her to him.

His growl of need reverberated against her chest, more potent than any plea, more persuasive than anything he could have voiced. Honor slid her fingers through his hair and held him to her while his own hands seemed intent on committing her body to memory all at once. She felt the links of her silver belt slide over her hips and heard them clunk on the floor. Before she could even think to assist, he had her surcoat unlaced and gathered up to her waist along with the supple gown she wore underneath. His lips left hers only long enough for him to tug both garments over her head.

Again, he drowned her in a kiss so deep and heartfelt, she nearly swooned with the force of it. Vaguely aware of the bed at her back, Honor held fast to his shoulders as he laid her down and followed, covering her completely.

For what seemed eternity, they kissed, parting only to gasp for breath and free him of his clothes. Impatient, Honor wished him clad in his breacan, which would require less time to shed. He yanked at the points of his hose and cast off his smallclothes. At last she felt the weight of his bared body press her down. She opened her mouth to tell him how glorious it was only to find her lips sealed again with his own.

"French," he rasped as he broke the kiss and his lips trailed down her neck. "If ye must speak."

"Tout à fait?" she gasped.

"Aye, entirely!" he growled, obviously intent on driving her mad.

"Pourquoi?"

''Because I want no words I ken,'' came his unsteady whisper. He nuzzled the underside of her left breast.

''But you do understand me anyway!'' Honor cried, pushing him away.

Alan gave his head a small shake and then sighed as he looked down at her. ''Nay. By chance, I recognize the few things you said, but I will never understand you.''

If he had not sounded so sad about the matter, Honor would have shoved him off the bed. ''You hate me still,'' she said.

''I never did so. Never! 'Tis just that I do not wish to hear you say…and not mean…'' Slowly he rolled off her and lay back. He threw one arm over his face. ''Ah hell, we are at it again.''

''Never mind,'' Honor said softly. ''I could try Latin.''

He raised himself up, propping on one elbow and leaning over her. ''Honor?'' he whispered, brushing her face with his hand. ''You see? Every time we talk, it mucks up matters somethin' fierce. All I want to do is hold you, love you.'' He leaned over her then and brushed his lips across her cheek. ''Instead I hurt you and I do not mean to.''

''Then be quiet,'' she advised him curtly. ''Just say no more or use your Gaelic.''

''I should have asked, before coming to your bed again,'' he said, ignoring her suggestions, ''but I feared you'd say me nay.''

Honor cocked one brow and smiled at him. ''Cold in the stable, was it?''

He did not return the smile, but bit his lips together for a moment before speaking. ''I could not keep from you any longer.''

''Nor did I want you to,'' she admitted, warming to that abject honesty of his, holding his face between her hands. She noted he must have shaved just after practice. She caressed the cool, taut smoothness of his skin. How she had missed touching him. "Now, will you cease conversing, or must I employ your own method of ensuring silence?"

"By all means," he said, lowering his mouth to hers. "Shut me up."

She complied. At the moment, Honor did not mind that he still mistrusted her. She did not care whether the chill of his bed in the stables or his grudging love of her brought him here. All she knew was that Alan's body rested firmly against her own and would soon belong to her again.

His hands surrounded her breasts, gently, almost reverently, as though they belonged to some person other than the one whose lower body seemed all eagerness. She shifted her hips and opened herself to him with a wordless plea.

With unerring accuracy, he entered, measuring out the pleasure so slowly, she felt fit to scream with impatience. Once inside her, he stilled and sighed with such satisfaction, she shivered at sharing it. All the way to her soul he possessed her with that one inexorable thrust. Her body undulated of its own accord, encouraging him to seek an even greater depth, a greater oneness. He withdrew just as lingeringly and offered more sweet torture. Honor's head swam, her heart leapt and her entire being seemed wrapped in such euphoria, she could not bear it.

Suddenly, he plunged again, far more quickly, and she had no cause to plead for surcease. A soft wail escaped her as he moved with no attempt at pace or rhythm, only a frantic reaching she echoed without thought. Abruptly and without warning, her world fractured into starbursts of light and color the likes of which she had never seen. His roar reverberated in her own chest as though it had come from her. Once more he drove deeply and she felt the sweet liquid rush of his warmth fill her completely.

How could she not love him? How could she not tell him so? But she dared not darken this wondrous moment by reminding him of his doubts. So she held him fast, her arms locked around him, her fingers dug into the muscles of his back, as they both struggled to capture a steady breath.

All too soon, he eased his weight away from her and moved to her side. He brushed a kiss over her breast, her neck, and then his lips touched hers, softly as the flick of a butterfly's wing. The candle had burned down to nothing, so she only felt the smile she could not see.

Alan drew her head to his shoulder, his arm surrounding her and his free hand grasping one of hers. "Sleep now, sweeting," he whispered. "All is well."

All certainly was not well and she knew it, but hopefully time would make it so. She would convince him, by deeds rather than words, most likely. But soon he would know without a doubt that she loved him beyond all reason. Somehow. For tonight, this wonderful, longed-for night, she would give all that he asked and more. Surely he would at least begin to believe a little.

With that thought in mind, Honor waited until his chest rose and fell with the even breaths of contented sleep. And then, satisfied to remain silent, she began to touch.

Chapter Eighteen

Hours later, a thunderous pounding on the door awakened Honor. Alan already had on his hosen and was reaching for his sword. "What? What's amiss?" she asked, still sleep grogged and weary from their loving.

"I dinna ken," he answered absently, tossing her the bedrobe. "Put this on." He strode for the door, shouting, "Cease th' damned racket!"

Honor arose and had just fastened the robe when Alan lifted the bolt. The door shot inward so swiftly, he stumbled backward toward the bed and fell against her. Before he could right himself, a scuffle ensued. His sword clanged to the floor, and they were surrounded by men in mail shirts and helms.

The tallest intruder clasped her arms behind her and held a knife to her throat. Alan shook off his captor and started to rush forward when another cracked him over the head with a sword hilt. He dropped to the floor at her feet.

Struggling, ignoring the blade at her neck, Honor screamed, "Nay! Do not hurt him more!"

As though oblivious to her demands, the men grabbed Alan beneath his arms and dragged him into the hall.

Honor followed, and would have done so even had the brute holding her not forced her to it.

They had been invaded. Some force had taken Byelough in the dead of night. Who were these people and what did they want here?

She could not tear her worried gaze from Alan who drooped lifelessly between the two who had hauled him from the solar. She had never seen him vulnerable before and it frightened her witless. He wore no shirt or shoes, only his loincloth and the dark hosen he had donned to open their door. Blood dripped from the gash on his head, leaving a crimson trail upon the flagstones. Honor felt the warm stickiness of it wet the soles of her bare feet. A horrified moan broke from her throat.

The men dropped Alan on the floor directly before the dais.

Honor gasped when she looked up and saw the man responsible for this outrage. He sat in the lord's chair, the loathsome beast, firmly ensconced there by means of treachery.

He smiled. "Ah, so here is my betrothed at last! Pray how is your health, my lady?"

Honor could not summon breath to answer. She looked again to Alan, who lay unconscious at her feet. His chest rose and fell softly so she knew he lived. The wound on his head still wept red, but did not look fatal as she had feared it would.

"Bring him around!" the comte ordered. One of the men snatched up the flagon that sat before his master and dashed the contents directly into Alan's face.

Alan started at the shock of it, then lifted a hand to clear his eyes. When he raised himself to his elbows, the waiting soldier placed a foot on his chest. Alan surrendered and lay still, but his gaze darted immediately toward the one who had issued the order. Honor suspected then that Alan had not been senseless all along, but merely feigning unconsciousness and assessing the situation.

"Comte de Trouville, I presume?" he said calmly, as though he were standing proud and meeting a new acquaintance. Honor could not help admire his aplomb, though it seemed rather pointless.

"Yes, I am come. Surprised you, did I?" Trouville asked, switching languages without hesitation. More for convenience than courtesy, Honor was certain.

"Well, guests usually do announce their arrival in a more congenial manner." Alan glanced around the hall, deserted but for the comte's men. "And at a more reasonable hour. Your entrance required the assistance of the jongleurs you employed, of course."

"But of course," the comte confirmed, a grin hovering about the sardonic set of his lips. Honor admitted the scornful expression did little to hamper his looks, however. Trouville was not ill-favored in his appearance. Straight, dark hair, impeccably cut and combed, enhanced the strong, square face with its slender nose and slightly tilted eyes. Piercing eyes that suddenly fastened on a person with deadly intent.

Most women at court had thought him handsome and would have been happy to marry him. Two women had died for their mistake, though Honor supposed not many knew that. Did they do so, they wisely kept it to themselves. If Honor had not befriended one of the women who had attended his last wife, she would never have known herself.

"Where is Hume?" the comte asked conversationally, toying with one of Honor's silver goblets which someone had procured for him. "I understand he enjoys your hospitality here."

"Aye," Alan admitted with a polite smile. "Shall we fetch him from his rest to attend you?"

"By all means! Let us make a party of it," the comte said.

His tone changed abruptly as he addressed his men, ordering them to locate Hume and bring everyone into the hall.

Then he reverted to English, his voice again smooth as cream. "I have found my beloved and it is time to share my joy."

Alan laughed. "If the only way ye can procure a woman is with a knife at her neck, I say ye have damned little to rejoice about."

At a nod from the comte, the soldier whose foot rested on Alan's chest gave him a stout kick in the chin. Alan grunted.

Honor bit off a scream. Instinctively, she knew that any further defense of him would incur worse treatment. Perhaps she could placate the man and at least give Alan time to recover. "My lord, allow me to summon the cooks to prepare you a meal. You must be tired and hungry. We could settle all of this after you have eaten and rested."

He displayed a mirthless smile and inclined his dark head in admonishment. "Ah, sweet lady, do you seek to gain my favor? There are better ways than food, though the thought of a bed to lie on does stir my...imagination. Later, perhaps?" He turned from her to regard the folk his men were herding into the hall.

"I do not have to ask who *you* are!" Adam of Strode boomed, shaking off the hands that guided him forward.

"Well, well, the good baron!" Trouville said by way of greeting. "The good, *English* baron. Ho, here is a find indeed!"

Honor did not miss the fact that Trouville only feigned

surprise at Lord Adam's presence. He had known very well Alan's father was here well before he saw him. With sinking heart, she realized someone of her people had already answered all of the comte's questions, probably under duress.

Trouville continued taunting. "Bruce will like to see you, I think. What a nice gift for the good King Robert to promote relations between France and Scotland. Delighted to meet you, Lord Adam. Your son does share your looks, if not your loyalties."

"My son is a Scot, Bruce's man, and wed to this lady by his king's direction. Do not think my pledge to the English crown will affect that in any way."

The comte fingered his chin as though considering that. Then he shrugged and glanced around the room. "Hume?"

"Here, my lord."

Honor saw her father then. She had expected him to look wasted and ill-kempt after his weeks of confinement. He did appear paler than usual, but otherwise quite well. "Papa!" she exclaimed. "Please—"

"Hold your tongue, girl!" he ordered. But his eyes held a warning, not a reprimand. Honor, for once, obeyed.

The comte de Trouville stood, looking at each person in turn before settling his gaze on Honor. "I would know more of what transpired to bring us to this point, my lady. Hume's captain came to me immediately on his return to France. He wished me to effect his lord's release from this place. Until that time, I believed you laid low with some illness that delayed our wedding. I must say, you do look remarkably fit for one so direly afflicted."

He glared at her father and then returned his evil gaze to her. "A lie, obviously. It was only when that man reported that I learned of your unsanctioned marriage to Lord

Tavish. That was a false union, as any court will tell you, for you were contracted to me.''

Alan's father stepped forward, impatiently moving the sword that guarded him. ''The Bruce himself ordered this one, however. If you still feel wronged, set the fine and my son shall pay it.''

The comte laughed without humor. ''Oh, assuredly, he will pay.''

Honor jumped as a loud wail interrupted the harangue. *Christiana!* Did the comte know of her?

''Halt that confounded noise!'' Trouville ordered curtly.

Honor bit her lips together, wanting desperately to rush to her child and give comfort. Draw comfort, as well, she admitted. Instead, she remained helpless, the soldier's knife resting against her skin.

She watched Nan and Janet exchange whispers and then children. Janet opened her heavy bedgown and gently tucked Christiana beneath the folds to suckle.

Honor squeezed her eyes shut and sighed with relief. What would the comte do when he found she had not only wed, but had a child? Had the captain of her father's guard told him of that, as well? No, he could not have known. But anyone here could have told him after he arrived.

''My lord,'' Alan said, his voice calm as ever, ''Could we dispense with all this until morning? I feel somewhat at a disadvantage here.''

Trouville laughed aloud as he regarded Alan sprawled on the floor, half-naked, and streaked with blood. ''I daresay you do.'' He ran a hand over his own face and wiped away all trace of mirth. ''However, I wish to settle this now, tonight.''

He strolled around the table and stood above Alan, looking down at him. ''I never come into a situation completely uninformed. Word has it you are a brave and honorable man. Tales of your feats in battle are becoming legend. Even in your present state, you show me no fear. I do wonder, could you be as deceived by all this as I have been? People call you Alan the True, do they not?''

"Aye, so they do," Alan admitted without humility.

"You were but a younger son, a mercenary, when you fought last. Bruce must have knighted you soon after Bannockburn."

"Aye, he did so."

The comte lapsed into French again. "Take him to the chamber there," he ordered the man who had kicked Alan so viciously, "and allow him to clothe himself properly. Sans weapons, of course. I would see his dignity restored, even if he must carry it with him to the grave. Late as he has come to the honor, a fellow knight deserves that much."

The men allowed Alan to rise as Trouville returned to his chair behind the high table.

Honor closed her eyes and prayed. Once the comte knew the full truth of what she had done, he would punish her severely. Whatever happened to her now, she had to accept. But if he would listen, she must convince Trouville that Alan had no hand in the deception. Only the truth might save both Alan and her father.

Heaven only knew what might save Christiana, for Trouville's retribution would most probably extend to what he would consider her ill-begotten child.

God give me guidance, she prayed, and give it quickly.

Father Dennis appeared at her side as though summoned by her prayer. "Have courage, my lady," he said in his most resonant voice.

He was the only one of her people within the hall left unguarded to wander at will. Since her captor now had lowered the knife from her throat, Honor ventured speak-

ing to the priest. "Good Father, would you be so kind as
to check the storage room? See whether we have enough
victuals available to provide this company with the welcome they deserve?"

He looked at her as though she had lost her wits, re-
quiring such a task of him.

"Those *gray* grain sacks, Father Dennis. See they're
brought to the kitchens, if you will."

She watched the light dawn. *Finally*. Honor watched the
priest saunter slowly and unquestioned toward the stairway
leading to the kitchens. She only hoped he would increase
his speed once he reached the bolt-hole. It was a long way
to Ian Gray's keep. Help might be too long in coming no
matter how much he hurried.

She dared a glance at Alan, who walked a bit unsteadily
between two burly guardsmen toward the solar. What a
brave knight and good man, her Alan. And to think she
had brought him to such a pass.

For every soul he had worked so hard to train to weap-
onry here, the comte de Trouville had brought several
well-armed and seasoned warriors. Even did the women
and children count, Byelough's people were still outnumbered. If Ian Gray came to their aid as she hoped, like as
not his men and most here would be slain. Pity she had
not thought of that sooner.

Trouville seemed content while he waited for Alan to
garb himself appropriately. He sipped at his ale as though
he had nothing better to do. Now and again, he regarded
her with faint amusement. Finally, he spoke. "You might
have saved the good father the trouble, my lady."

Her eyes flew to the stairway where Father Dennis reappeared, moving with a bit more haste now since he was
prodded by yet another of the comte's men. Honor sighed
with defeat.

"No one enters, no one leaves," Trouville declared quietly, "until this matter is resolved."

Honor's heart thudded in her chest. She could see it in his dark, pitiless eyes. Someone would die this night. "Mercy, my lord," she whispered.

"For whom?" the comte asked idly. "Yourself or him?" He gestured toward the solar door.

Alan stood strong and unbowed, attired in captured English clothing. He wore a brown sark and leggings underneath a forest green woolen tunic which bore no design. Though the garments were plain and unornamented, girded only with a simple belt of gold links, her husband appeared a noble prince of a man.

Though he looked solemn, dignified and above defeat just as he was, a part of Honor wished he had chosen to wear his breacan. Once more, before she was taken away or worse, Honor wished to see the heart-stirring sight her husband made as a ferocious highlandman.

"Bring the accused forward," the comte demanded. "Sir Alan of Strode, Lord Dairmid Hume and the lady Honor."

Each was flanked by two of Trouville's guards and led to stand several ells apart in a semicircle before the dais.

Their erstwhile judge sat back in the lord's chair and regarded them in turn.

"Understand this. If I find Lord Hume has done me this ill turn and deprived me of the person and properties due me as Lady Honor's husband, he will answer for it with his life.

"Should Alan of Strode insist on the legality of this underhanded match, I shall be forced to make the lady a widow so that I may wed her."

The comte raked the people of Byelough with a menacing glance. "And if the lady alone has played me for a fool, then both men shall be spared." He paused, then resumed quietly, "However, *she* will die where she stands."

Honor heard a collective gasp and then silence swept through the hall.

The comte himself broke it. "Lord Hume shall speak first. Tell us how this treachery commenced."

Honor watched her father's lips tighten with what looked to be desperation. His eyes sought hers and she detected an apology in them. "My lord, my daughter had naught to do with this offense to you. I learned that she feared marriage to so high a personage as yourself. The marriage documents were altered. I replaced your name with another, Lord Tavish Ellerby, a young man who once visited our court. He seemed gentle and unassuming. I—I felt Honor would be happier here. So I made her come."

The comte nodded, tongue-in-cheek. "And chastised her soundly for her reluctance to do so, I would reckon."

"Aye, my lord," Hume admitted softly. "But she had no say. I forced her to it. All of this is my doing. All my fault."

"Well now," Trouville said, turning to Alan. "What have you to say to all of this, *Alan the True?*"

Honor watched Alan take a deep breath, bow his head for a second and then face the comte directly, looking straight into his eyes. "I demanded the marriage, Trouville. Her father sent her here to wed Ellerby, who was my friend. When her husband died from his wound after the battle near Stirling, I thought to gain this unprotected keep and the lady for my own."

Alan's chin, darkened from the guardsman's kick, raised a trifle as he continued without pause. "With Bruce's sanction, I rode into this place fully armed and compelled the lady to surrender all. She had no other recourse. Anyone," he said in a voice that would brook no disagreement, "*Everyone* who was present at the time will swear to this."

Alan swept the hall with a glare, halting at each face, daring them to gainsay him. "The lady is blameless."

"Will you set her aside?"

"I will not."

"Not even to save your life?"

Alan shook his head. "All know we have lived as man and wife. To set aside our marriage as false would besmirch her good name, my lord. I know you would not wed her then, but only have her as your mistress. Kill me if you must, but know you Honor has only done her duty as a daughter to Lord Hume, as faithful wife to Tavish Ellerby and then to myself. I repeat, she is blameless and without fault."

Trouville inclined his head as though accepting Alan's words as fact.

Honor could not let this stand. She wanted to scream at Alan to renounce these lies of his, to speak truly as he had ever done. The comte would kill him, surely, and her father as well. She surged forward to set matters straight.

"Hold your tongue, woman, I am not ready for your version of this!"

Then he steepled his long fingers under his chin and resumed his questioning of Alan. "Since you never lie, tell me about this child she bore," the comte ordered.

"'Twas a sickly daughter," Alan replied in a steady voice. "Surely that's of no consequence to yourself." He held out his hands, palms up, and shrugged. "'Tis a pity, but seldom do the wee ones survive their first months hereabouts. Lady Honor is presently unencumbered."

"Except with a husband," the comte commented dryly. "But no matter for long." He turned to her father. "And you, Hume, what say you of this child I heard mentioned?''

"In all the time I have been here I have seen no child named as my daughter's get, my lord," he said truthfully. "I swear to it."

Honor knew her turn had come. The comte swiveled his body in the chair and sat forward to regard her with his keen, narrow eyes. "Very well, my lady, now you may speak."

"My lord," Honor said softly. "I beg you to forgive these men. Their untruths are spoken out of love for me and I am properly humbled by their stout defense. But I must tell you all so that you will spare them."

"Careful, lady," the comte warned, "for I have little patience and even less mercy with a guileful woman."

"Then you will know I speak no lies here," Honor said, her voice stronger than before. "I have no reason to say this other than it is what I must confess. 'Twas I who changed the documents and wrote in Tavish Ellerby's name. My father beat me many times to make me willing to wed you, but I refused. I promised him that if he forced me to it, I would make such a scene as the French court has yet to see. That caused the delay in your plans to wed.

"Then I stole the contracts, altered them and lied to my first husband, saying that my father had relented toward his suit."

The comte held up a hand to halt her words. "May I ask why you set yourself against me?"

"You may, my lord," she said quite frankly. What did she have to lose here? "I had it in confidence that you had killed your first two wives, and chose not to suffer their fate."

Harsh cries rippled through the crowd, but the comte silenced them. "Do continue."

"I wed Lord Tavish Ellerby. He went to war with the English and did not survive. When Sir Alan of Strode brought home the body of my husband, he carried orders from my Lord Ellerby and from Robert the Bruce for me to wed with him. I did so and right gladly, for I feared for my future and that of Byelough and its people."

"He did not compel you, then?" Trouville asked.

Honor hesitated for a moment. "In a way. He called on my duty to my husband and to King Robert of Scotland, but he knew nothing of my former betrothal at that time. Once I confessed all, he…threatened to punish me."

"And has he done so?" the comte asked.

Honor met his curious gaze. "Not as yet."

"You do know what your confession of these deeds forces me to consider. I have said you will die where you stand."

Alan rushed toward her, but the guards restrained him. Honor noted it took four to hold him and prayed he would cease struggling before they cut him down.

"I understood you at the outset, my lord," Honor said boldly. "Have done with it if you will, for I do not wish to survive my husband. And, God help me, I would not marry you if you slew every other man available!"

The comte rose and leapt across the table to land in front of her. The guards grabbed her arms. Alan's roar rattled the very stones of Byelough as the guards wrestled him to the floor.

"Cease!" Trouville thundered. Everyone stilled.

Honor knew the end had come. She braced herself to face it as bravely as she knew Alan would have done. Might still have to do. At least Christiana would live. Thank God Trouville had not asked her about her babe. Honor did not feel she could have lied as well as Alan, despite all her experience. Chin up and tears in check, she stood straight and waited.

The comte stared long and hard into her eyes. "Then God help—"

"Trouville!" Alan thundered. "If yer so certain *God* is listening to ye and thinks ye right in this, then I demand a trial by battle! I stand for the lady."

"Unarmed?" the comte asked, amused.

Alan pursed his lips as if to think on it, and then grinned menacingly at the comte. "Well, aye, if that's the only way ye believe ye can win."

"Bring his sword," the comte ordered abruptly.

He looked down past the men sitting on top of Alan and those pinning his limbs to the flagstones. "Men will no longer call you Alan the True after this day, Strode. You have foregone your reputation with these lies of yours. Would you now forfeit your life for this woman?"

"I would forfeit my *soul* for this woman," Alan stated.

Trouville raised his brows, nodded, puffed his cheeks and blew out a breath. "So you love her."

Alan simply looked at him and did not answer, probably because it had not been a question.

"As do I, unfortunately," the comte declared with a sudden grimace.

Chapter Nineteen

Did she not stand in fear of Alan's life and her own, Honor would have laughed at the absurdity. Oh, of course Trouville loved her. Just as he must have loved the other two women who were given to him like sweets on a plate. Now he planned to take her as well. How would he love *her* to death, she wondered.

Trouville motioned the men to allow Alan to rise, and then turned to Honor. "If I engage in a fair battle with this fellow, Lady Honor," he said, nodding toward Alan, "and if I best him, will you wed me as you should have done?"

"I have told you, I will not," Honor said calmly and resolutely.

"If he should win, my men will leave you in peace to live out your life here in this pile of rock. You have my word, which is worth a great deal more than yours or his. If I prevail, then you must promise to marry me willingly within the hour and return with me to France."

Alan interrupted her next refusal. "Aye, she will."

Honor stared at him, suddenly furious that he would agree to anything Trouville proposed. She would not allow Alan to risk his life when she had just done all within her power to save it. The comte's reputation with a sword made him one of the most feared men in France. "I will *not!*"

"Dinna be daft, woman! Refuse and one of us is goin' to die. Most likely *you,* since ye seem so bloody well set on it!" Alan declared. He quirked his lips and raised his brows at the comte. "You will forgive her, my lord, she is a wee bit—"

"Overwrought?" the comte supplied.

"Aye. Not always contentious, though. Ye need not think that of her," Alan confided dryly. "She can be sharp-tongued, but spirit in a lass is to be admired, wouldn't ye say?"

"An overabundance of that quality does not sit so well at times," the comte argued.

"But ye will make allowance for it, aye? Have I yer hand on that?"

Trouville extended his arm and they shook hands together. Like old friends.

The sight rendered Honor speechless, and knew she had better stay that way. If she voiced the thoughts she was thinking at present, neither man would wish her to live. She looked down at the blade resting beside the comte's left leg, imagined it slicing into Alan's flesh, and her anger quickly shifted back to fear.

"Honor?" Alan said gently. "Do this for me. Agree."

She looked deeply into the eyes that held such love for her and knew she had no choice at all. After what Trouville had just said, Honor did not feel he would kill her. Later, mayhaps, but at least not where she stood, as he had threatened. But he would kill Alan just to clear his way to have her and the lands her father had promised him.

"Very well," she muttered, almost choking on the words. "I will."

Trouville nodded and turned to the man holding Alan's sword. "Give the man his blade. *À outrance?*"

"Aye, to the death." Alan stretched his arms above his head, to the side, and back, muscles flexing beneath the rich green wool. Honor watched as Alan accepted his sword, kissed the hilt and stood ready.

The guardsmen cleared a ring around the two combatants. "If I fall," Trouville shouted, "every man in my employ is to quit this keep on the instant. My brother will see to you when you return. And, mark me well," he said, eyeing every one of the hardened soldiers. "If one of you interferes, I shall kill you myself. Any last words, Strode?"

Alan looked strangely at ease as he spoke. "Aye, to you, my lord. Should you by some off chance be the victor, I would you treat my lady well. Your word on it?"

"My solemn oath. She will fare far better in my bed than yours, my friend." He jumped back with a harsh oath as Alan's blade nicked his tabard.

Neither uttered anything further save grunts and curses as they swung the heavy swords. The clanging of steel echoed off the stones in the cavernous hall, punctuated with yelps and cries of encouragement from those watching. Honor could not make a sound. Eyes round with fear and throat closed in terror, she followed every move, unable to look away.

Trouville drew first blood when the tip of his blade nicked the top of Alan's wrist. With a redoubled effort, Alan attacked driving the comte back against the table on the dais. Swords locked at the hilt.

Honor marked the distended veins in Trouville's neck and the redness of his face. Alan seemed unaffected except for the thinning of his lips and the green fire in his eyes. He sprang away and held his sword before him with both hands until the comte regained his footing.

Again they clashed, sparks flying off the blades. On and on they fought, neither able to find a weak defense to plunder. Sweat soaked their hair, poured off their faces and ran into their eyes.

Suddenly, Trouville sneezed.

"Bless you," Alan muttered.

"Merci," said the comte with a loud sniff. He blinked. *Clang!* Honor jumped.

As though Alan had been resting up for it, he suddenly pushed forward, swinging madly. Trouville's defense turned wild and frantic. Desperate. Honor clasped her hands beneath her chin and prayed.

With one mighty thrust and twist, Alan sent Trouville's blade flying. It tumbled into the circle of knights, nearly severing one man's foot.

A cheer rose above the shouts of outrage as Alan pinned the comte to the floor, sharp steel at his neck just above the silver gorget. "Yield!" Alan demanded.

"To the death. We agreed," Trouville taunted.

"I'd not like to kill a mon for an untimely sneeze," Alan said, smiling. "But if ye say ye canna live without the lady, then I guess I must. Could ye find another to *love,* d'ye think?"

"Possibly," the comte admitted, eyeing Alan's blade with wary eyes. He swallowed hard as the point drew a few drops of blood and quickly added, "Probably."

Still, Alan did not remove his blade from its position. "Honor is mine. I'll keep the lady one way or the other. Give me your vow as a brother knight that you will leave us be," Alan demanded. "'Tis no disgrace on yer head, Trouville. I ask yer solemn word as ransom for yer life. A fair request."

The comte lay there considering, his brow furrowed. After a long, tense moment, he replied, "Well, if you must beg, Strode, then I suppose I shall have to agree. Let me up.''

"Say it," Alan ordered and raised his head to insure attention. "Witness all, this vow!"

"She is yours! I *vow* to leave you be!"

Alan released him and offered his arm. When they were both upright, Trouville turned to his men. "Form up and march out. Hume, come with me."

Alan moved to Honor's side and slid his arm around her. She hugged him, relishing the feel of his heat against her. Bless God, he lived. *All* had lived.

"My lord," her father said to Trouville, "I would stay and make amends to my daughter."

Trouville marched over and angrily snatched him up by the front of his padded jack. "Do not think I'm unaware of how you once treated her, Hume! And I know it was not solely on my account. I do not hold with beating and starvation of the weaker sex. There is no way to amend it!"

"You *killed* two of them! Is that better in your eye?" her father shouted. He quailed and shrank away, belatedly realizing what he had said.

Trouville, obviously still shaken by his fight with Alan, abandoned his calm reserve and answered heatedly, "My first died in childbed and the other in a brangle with her lover! That bastard I did kill, and rightly so!"

"My apologies, my lord. But rumor—"

Trouville cursed roundly and shoved her father away. He looked at Alan. "What say you, Strode? Would you have him here?"

"I believe Honor wishes retribution," Alan said, cocking one brow as he looked down at her.

Honor leaned into Alan's side as her father approached

and dropped to one knee. "Daughter, I have wronged you."

She understood him better now. Perhaps he had tried to save her from herself by forcing obedience, but there were better ways to do it than with the rod. "Go back to France, Papa," she said in a whisper.

"Honor, I truly do regret—" He buried his face in his hands and wept, his final words unintelligible. The sight of so mighty a man undone stirred her pity. And he had lied for her this night to try to save her life. She looked to Alan, not knowing what to do.

He hugged her to him, reassuring her without words that she would always be safe now. Then he nodded toward her father as though she should do something. Honor dropped to her knees beside her sire and put her arms around him. He only wept harder. "'Tis done, *Papa*. Naught can undo it, but I will forgive you."

He twisted around and caught her to him, a tight embrace that frightened her just a little. "Will I never see you again? Your mother—"

"Go home, *Papa*. See to *Maman*. Give what you promised to the comte de Trouville for his troubles. Perhaps we may visit again some day. 'Tis too soon to know."

He got up, moving wearily as an old man might. Words seemed beyond him as he traced the side of her face with one finger. Then he nodded once and let her go, hurrying past the comte and heading for the door to the hall.

"A moment, Hume," Trouville called out. "Come here."

Her father obliged reluctantly, tears streaming down his face unheeded.

Honor sucked in a horrified breath as the comte approached Janet, who was holding Christiana in a death grip. Alan's hand clutched his sword and held it ready.

"We would see this babe of yours, madam," Trouville said to Janet. "Uncover it if you please. Come, Hume, and see how spindly these Scots grow their infants. Look at this one."

Both men stared down into the blanket Janet had moved aside. "Lovely for a dead thing, eh?" He shot Alan a smirk. "Strode? If you cannot find a man to brave wedding this poor little ghost, come and see me when she grows. My devilish son is ten and likely game for things other-worldly."

Alan shrugged and slipped his free hand over Honor's mouth. She watched as Trouville dragged her weeping father away from the granddaughter he had just seen for the first time.

The comte had known all along, Honor thought. Either someone had told him or he had guessed from her frightened looks in Janet's direction.

Trouville's spurs rang on the stones as he marched Hume out and slammed the door behind them.

Honor felt her legs give way. Alan caught her close to keep her from sinking to the floor. Weak with relief and exhaustion, she pressed her face to the front of his tunic.

"'Tis done and done, sweeting." He had bowed his head low, near her ear as he whispered the words. "Dig deep and find some more courage for me, eh? Our folk need yer assurance now, and I need to make certain Trouville goes."

Honor locked her knees and pushed away from him. She inhaled deeply and raised her chin. Her fingers plucked at his sleeve. The sword cut the comte had given Alan looked wicked, but the bleeding had nearly stopped. "Hurry then and see them off. You will need sewing."

"Honor?" he said softly, looking at her so intently as he brushed her tangled hair back from her cheek.

"Aye?" she answered, suddenly breathless again for different reasons.

"I want ye to know this, lass. Ye faced death wi' the truth just now. Th' bravest thing I ever saw a woman do." He grinned down at her and raised one ruddy brow. "However, 'twas a mite overdone. A body can take honesty to extremes, y'know."

Honor punched him in the gut. "Not *your* body, you lying knave! What the devil were you about spouting all those lies at Trouville? Trying to die?" She paced away angrily and then stalked back again, throwing up her hands. "Lord, deliver me from martyrs! If you ever—"

He kissed her. He grabbed her arms and held her while his mouth ravaged hers. All anger, along with all her other thoughts melted away like summer snow as his lips grew softer, enticing her to return what he gave. Suddenly Alan released her and turned her sharply around. He slapped her lightly on her backside and gave her a little push. "Go and find yer needle, hinny. When I come in again, ye can stitch yer lesson in my hide."

She would, too, Honor promised herself as she watched him go. His happy laughter as he left the hall wrung a reluctant smile from her heart.

What more could she wish for now? All the enemies were vanquished, all her fears dismissed. But at what cost to Alan? Oh, he seemed joyous enough at the moment. He had just defeated one of France's most dreaded knights. What would he feel, however, when he finished crowing about that and realized fully what he had done this night? Would Alan be able to forgive himself for what he had sacrificed trying to save her life?

Trouville had been right. Tonight's witnesses were numerous and certain to spread word of these doings. No man would remark on Alan of Strode's honesty again when they spoke of his feats. The one thing he had put above all others, he had thrown to the winds in her defense. How would he live with that?

Honor cursed her runaway tongue. She should never have railed at him for the lies. Fright for him had simply stolen her wits.

With a dispirited sigh, Honor put aside that worry and set about calming the women and children of Byelough who remained in the hall. The men had followed Alan out to watch the invaders leave. It must be nearing dawn and all would be ready to break fast when they returned. In any event, she could not imagine anyone returning to bed and sleeping after this night's occurrence.

Chapter Twenty

Alan had a final word at the gates with Trouville and Honor's father. As he hoped, they parted from Byelough on more or less amicable terms.

For all of Trouville's prating about his love for Honor, he seemed remarkably sanguine about his inability to wed her. Or mayhaps he was simply relieved to be alive. Alan smiled at that. He had very nearly killed the man. Would have done had he not promised to leave Honor be. Now Alan felt glad it had not been necessary to administer that *coup de grâce*.

Hume begged again to be allowed to stay a while. Neither Alan or the comte hesitated in denying him that right. In that they agreed. Hume should go home, and that home did not lie in Scotland. In a few years it might be possible for Honor to put all the bitterness behind her. If so, and if she wanted to, Alan knew he would take her to visit her parents.

For now, however, Honor needed a long spell of peace and contentment. He meant to see she found it. He ran a hand through his sweaty hair and then wiped it on his tunic. Truth told, he needed the same as Honor. This past year had taken its toll on him.

He had dispatched all of Honor's dragons—Ian, her father and Trouville—without slaying a single one. Most knights would take little pride in that fact, but Alan felt immense relief that no one had suffered death at his hand. All life seemed infinitely precious at the moment.

More than he'd ever wished for, he had now. Alan felt humbled by that and enormously thankful.

The first pale rays of morning sun crept over Byelough as Alan walked alone back to the keep, exhausted more by the profound fear he had endured than by the sword fight.

He could honestly say he had never known such terror as he had experienced since meeting that wife of his. Even now his mind's eye reconstructed those imaginings. Honor in the throes of childbirth, bleeding out her life. Honor buried in a bog, clutching Kit, expelling her last breath of air. Honor lying decapitated on the floor beside him tonight. He shuddered and shook off these horrors which had plagued him in turn with their near reality.

"No more," he muttered to himself. "All's well. All over and done." His steps quickened with the urgent need to see her, hold her and assure her he would keep her safe.

Everyone had gathered in the hall by the time he arrived. Honor darted here and there, speaking to this one and that, issuing orders and pointing. Several of the men busily assembled the tables as for a meal and maids stood waiting with the usual linens to spread. They might think it a new day, but he was not finished with the night's business yet. Not by a long mark.

Short of hauling her off to their bed and ignoring the daylight, Alan wondered how he would manage to get her alone. The lord of this keep could order it so, he supposed. She would comply as was her duty. But where lay the fun in that? He hid a smile behind his hand.

He moved closer to her, staggered and grabbed his injured wrist. The piteous groan he issued drew her immediate attention. Honor whirled and threw her arms around him as though she could support his full weight. "Alan!" she cried. "Oh, you are worse than I thought! Come, sit!"

"Nay," he moaned. "I need to lie flat. My head spins so."

She guided him toward the solar, taking great care to go slowly. Alan dragged one foot in front of the other. Off to one side, he saw his father scowl with concern. Alan turned and winked broadly at him just before Honor closed the door. There, mayhaps his father would insure their privacy, Alan thought.

Honor guided him to the bed and helped him to sit down. Then she lifted his legs to the mattress and pulled off his boots. Alan groaned again, just for good measure.

"Just rest you there. I'll gather my things." She worried her bottom lip and wrung her hands together. "I should get you wine first to dull the pain."

"Nay," Alan said, restlessly moving his head from side to side. "I'll endure. Just get it over. Do what you must."

He watched her from beneath his lashes as she dutifully cleaned and sewed up the small gash on top of his wrist. At each prick of the needle, he issued a pained grunt. No feigning there, he thought. It hurt like hell.

When she tied the last knot, he turned to his side facing her. "Now, my leg," he gasped. "Could you help me with my hose?"

"You are hurt elsewhere? Oh, let me see!" She untied the points fastened to his waistband and hurriedly tugged off his hose, examining his limbs as she did so. "I see nothing that—"

He sat up so abruptly she gasped.

"Behold!" he said with a huge grin. "I am healed! Ah, lady, I am blessed among men!"

"And cursed among women!" she cried, hands on hips now. Furious with him for his trickery. "You are not hurt at all, you deceitful—"

"Knave. I know." Alan laughed and grabbed her by the waist, lifting her to the bed. "But I love it when ye coddle me. I love it when ye care. I love *ye!*"

Honor rolled her eyes and shook her head. "What am I to do with you?"

"What a question!" he said with an exaggerated leer. "Believe me or not, I do have an answer!"

A giggle escaped her, right through the frown she was wearing. "I would wager you do!"

After a long and mind-rending kiss, she drew away from him and looked deeply into his eyes. "Alan, I do thank you for all you did today. I know what it has cost you and I am so sorry for that."

He leaned back on one elbow and played his fingers over her serious little face. "The lies, you mean," he said, not even pretending to misunderstand.

"Yes," she affirmed, catching his hand in hers and kissing his palm. "Alan, I wish I could undo many things I have done. Some I would not change, for they were necessary evils. But I cannot bear that you deserted your most strongly held belief because of me. It was to no good, after all."

"Oh, but it told the comte that I loved ye more than anything. Yer own bold truth that followed convinced him ye cared for me as well. 'Twas why he gave us a fighting chance, I'm thinking. He knew then he could never win yer heart for himself."

Honor smiled sadly. "Win my heart? He would have killed me."

"Nay," Alan answered with a chuckle. "The mon's merely bluster under all that polish of his." He rolled his right shoulder to ease the ache. "Got a damned good sword arm, though."

"He was right on one thing," Honor said with a weary sigh. "You'll never be known as *Alan the True* again. I do regret that for you."

He sighed and shook his head. "Dinna fash yerself over it." Could he possibly tell her all he had realized in those few moments when her life hung in the balance? He ought to try, he decided. Otherwise, she would probably always hold herself responsible for the sudden collapse of his integrity.

"All these years," he began, speaking in a low and earnest voice, "I spoke only truth. But I did so for the wrong reason, Honor. Ye see, 'twas not for the right or the wrong of it all, but for sheer vainglory. I did it only for the pride I took in what others said about me."

"Then this has destroyed that pride," she said, still forlorn.

He laughed softly. "Well, I do hold pride in other things," he said. "Honesty is a good thing, a very important thing." Alan searched for the words to make her understand. "But hearing myself lauded as *Alan the True* by everyone in the known world would have meant nothing at all to me had I lost ye, Honor."

"Still, I rue that loss for your sake," she said, casting down her liquid gaze.

Alan feared she might weep and would have done anything to prevent that. He tapped her lower lip with his finger. "Why don't we think me up a new sobriquet, eh? Something highly deserved and ever constant."

He pretended to think on it as he trailed his hand over her arm and shoulder. "Well then, what d'ye think of *Alan the Eager?''* Grinning wickedly, he slid one finger into the front of her gown and tugged her closer. ''Or *Alan the Ready?''*

Honor placed a hand over his heart and started to smile. Lifting her shiny gray gaze to his, she mimicked his lilt, ''Weel, highlandman, what d'ye think of *Alan the Beloved? For ye are that, like it or no.''*

''Oh, lass,'' he whispered, his eyes near as full as his heart. ''That has a bonny sound to it. A verra bonny sound, indeed.''

Epilogue

Midsummer 1318

Honor watched contentedly from a small distance as Alan spoke to Christiana.

"Pick it up," he said to her, pointing to a small stone nearby. Chubby fingers closed around the rock. The four-year-old marked Alan's every move as he located another for himself.

"Place it just so, sweeting," he instructed as he laid his offering on the pile covering Tavish's grave. "Now, close yer eyes and give yer father a wee prayer on his name day."

"Pray for you?" his Kit asked earnestly.

Alan squatted down to her level, his arm surrounding the small shoulders. "Not for me, hinny. Ye know verra well that I'm yer da. But yer *father* lies here, under the cairn." He sighed, and Honor could see him gathering up his patience. "Say yer prayer for him."

Christiana folded her hands, closed her eyes and muttered the hasty grace she always said at table.

Then she looked up at Alan, her forefinger resting on

the crude wolf's head device Alan had once carved on the boulder. "Father cannot, so I said thanks for him. For this apple," she explained and scampered away to play.

Honor approached, laughing. "Tavish would have loved her, would he not?"

"Aye, he would." Alan agreed. "Will she never understand?"

Honor linked her arm with his as they strolled beside the bubbling stream. "Of course she will. When she grows older."

"We have so much to teach her, Honor. Where will we find all the words?"

Though he could read and write well now, Alan continued his studies. Honor knew he still felt sorely his lack of proper education.

"Most things she will learn by our own doing of them. Thank heavens you have taught me to look for the good in people. I would she learned that first of all. And to seek the truth in her heart, of course."

Alan chuckled wryly. "Should I also teach her the use of a judicious untruth?"

"I expect she will learn that as well. You set a fine example there this morn when you complimented me. *Lovely*, indeed! Dark moons beneath my eyes from lack of sleep, a belly the size of a feast day haggis." Honor fondly rubbed the small mound.

Alan's hand joined hers. "Ye're always beautiful to me. Never more so than today."

"Well done, o ye of the silver tongue," Honor quipped. "See what you say four months from now when I grow large as a cow. Then your pretty words may leap from judicious untruths to outright lies!" She sneaked a sidewise, flirting glance. "But do not leave off telling them on my account."

He laughed aloud and tweaked her nose. "Tonight I'll be showing ye how lovely I think ye are. We'll plead fatigue and sup in the solar, what say?"

"It is Friday. I fear we'll have a guest."

Alan groaned dramatically. "Not Gray *again!* The rogue's here once a fortnight, I swear. Takes his godfathering task too seriously, if ye ask me. Bringing Kit so many gifts will spoil her, mark my word."

"Are you jealous, Alan? You must know she loves you more than anything in the world."

"Exceptin' her cat," he grumbled with increasing good humor.

"Well, yes, there is the cat," Honor agreed with a smile.

For a while, quiet reigned on the sunlit bank, the stillness broken only by the sound of childish laughter and the rushing water of the nearby burn. Honor wanted to freeze the moment and keep it forever.

"Yer parents should arrive come Michaelmas. Will they make it for the birth, ye reckon?" Alan asked softly. He drew her back against him and surrounded her with his arms.

"I hope so," Honor replied. "I wish our whole family could be with us then. We must send Da Adam and Janet word of the new child when a chance arrives." At Alan's nod against her hair, she continued, "Forgiving your father was a very wise thing to do ere he left for England. Given the state of things between our countries, there may be no further visits."

"Aye, and I shall miss little Dickon most of all." Alan admitted. "I did once promise him that, unlike Nigel and myself, we would know one another in the years to come."

Honor lay her head back and looked up at him. "Your brother has two who love him dearly and will find another when he's grown, just as you have done. And there are always letters. Richard will know you.''

Alan released her and sat down, drawing her with him. He stretched out on the grass, head turned to one side so he could watch Christiana chase a butterfly. When he spoke, his voice was thick with feeling. ''I owe so much to Tavish for his trust in me.''

Honor leaned over to kiss his sun-warmed cheek. Together they welcomed their daughter as she skipped over and wriggled out a cozy place between them. ''I love him dearly for sending you to me. I wish I could tell him so, Alan. I wish he could see Christiana and know what a very fine legacy he left to her. And to us.''

A sudden breeze ruffled the graceful leaves of the rowan tree under which they lay.

''He knows,'' Alan whispered. ''He knows.''

* * * * *

My Secret Admirer

**Savor the magic of love
with three new romances
from top-selling authors
Anne Stuart,
Vicki Lewis Thompson and
Marisa Carroll.**

My Secret Admirer is a unique collection
of three brand-new stories featuring passionate
secret admirers. Celebrate Valentine's Day with
these wonderfully romantic tales that are
ideally suited for this special time!

Available in February 1999 at your favorite retail outlet.

HARLEQUIN®
Makes any time special ™

MEN at WORK

All work and no play?
Not these men!

January 1999
SOMETHING WORTH KEEPING by Kathleen Eagle
He worked with iron and steel, and was as wild as the mustangs that were his passion. She was a high-class horse trainer from the East. Was her gentle touch enough to tame his unruly heart?

February 1999
HANDSOME DEVIL by Joan Hohl
His roguish good looks and intelligence drew women like magnets, but Luke Branson was having too much fun to marry again. Then Selena McInnes strolled before him and turned his life upside down!

March 1999
STARK LIGHTNING by Elaine Barbieri
The boss's daughter was ornery, stubborn and off-limits for cowboy Branch Walker! But Valentine was also nearly impossible to resist. Could they negotiate a truce...or a surrender?

Available at your favorite retail outlet!

MEN AT WORK™

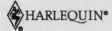 

COMING NEXT MONTH FROM

HARLEQUIN HISTORICALS